I0747543

THUGS IN SKIRTS

RAYCHELLE MEYERS

Thugs In Skirts

Printed in the United States of America

First Printing, 2023

ISBN-13: 978-17357901-8-3 (Paperback)

ISBN-13: 978-1-7357901-9-0 (E-book)

The first edition of this book was printed in 2023.

Published by Eat My Lyrics Publishing Company, LLC

https://eatmylyrics.com

TABLE OF CONTENTS

ACKNOWLEDGEMENTS

This book is dedicated in memory of my two sisters, Patricia Parker & Kathy Winston. Within 9 years, cancer ripped them both from my grasp.

Kathy passed away on December 1st, 2007, of bone cancer. My oldest sister, Patricia (Pat) passed away December 4th, 2016, of breast cancer. I was devastated to lose both of my beautiful sisters, but I promised myself that I'd keep their memories alive through my work & business ventures.

They both witnessed their baby sister breaking the cycle of poverty in our family. They were my biggest supporters & were always very proud of me. They will forever be alive in my heart with cherished memories.

The experience of encountering their deaths altered how I viewed my own life, which drew me closer to God. So, thank you Pat & Kathy for being my loving, hilarious, & crazy sisters, & for giving me your love, laughs, & wild moments to hold onto. We definitely had our ups & downs, like sisters do, but best believe, no one could ever take our places.

This book represents unbreakable bonds, which is extremely important to me.

Thank you to my husband, Cadillac Meyers, for allowing me to be me. For giving me space & me-time when needed. You've supported all my crazy ventures, whether I succeeded or not. So, thank you, Lac, for your undying support. It means the world to me. I'm extremely blessed to have a husband like you. You're absolutely everything.

MEET RAYCHELLE MEYERS

Raychelle Meyers was born & raised in an impoverished neighborhood in Fort Worth, TX. Growing up, she & her family lived in a rundown home built by her great-grandfather.

Raychelle watched her older sisters leave the nest as she & her brother remained with their stay-at-home mother & their entrepreneur father. Their father started several businesses, however, many of them failed; therefore, Raychelle's family struggled, often.

When business was slow, they went without lights & water. Eventually, Raychelle's father started a successful carpentry business. Sadly, he soon became ill & passed away from Lung Cancer in the year of 1987; when he died, his business did too. Worst of all, he left his wife a widow & his children, fatherless.

Soon after being dealt one of the worst hands known to mankind, Raychelle & her family were forced to move out of their home due to tax issues. This home which her great-grandfather crafted was later demolished.

Seven years thereafter, Raychelle decided to break the chain of poverty in her family by starting her first business. She knew it'd be a challenge, but as a daddy's girl who was inspired by her father's hard work & dedication, she had the gall to impact change.

Raychelle launched her own private childcare business at the age of 23. This business was designed to care for children of busy corporate moms. Unfortunately, it was closed due to landlord property issues, but it ran successfully for 4 amazing years.

Raychelle then began working as a Teacher's Assistant at a Head Start Program. A few months later, she was promoted from Childcare Teacher to the Corporate Office as USDA

Nutrition Monitor. After dedicating 5 years to the company, she resigned in 2008 & started a youth nonprofit organization called Apples & Oranges Corp. At Apples & Oranges Corp, youth are empowered by developing good eating habits through food & nutrition, as well as leadership, & entrepreneurial skills.

All in all, Raychelle has accumulated 20 years of experience in business. Today, she oversees an operating budget of $9 million while managing over 75 poverty-fighting programs in Texas. Besides overseeing Apples & Oranges Corp, she owns & manages 7 different companies.

In 2016, Raychelle became a Film Producer & worked with Maximum Achievement DNA Films, a 5-time Emmy Award-Winning film company. Her first film as a Producer was The Soul of Success: The Jack Canfield Story. She's currently working on her first independent documentary film called Secure the Legacy, a documentary film about the life of her extraordinary mother, Mary Parker.

Raychelle is not only the Author of Thugs In Skirts; she's also the Author of two innovative books- Confined Minds: Break Free from Imprisoned Thoughts & Boss Girls in the Boardroom.

Raychelle's been featured on a variety of radio shows across the globe; she's also been featured in major magazines & publications like Forbes, USA Today, Huffington Post, Voyage Dallas Magazine, & an International Magazine in China, BridgeAfrique Magazine.

Raychelle has been a guest speaker at The University of Texas at Arlington (UTA). She was featured in the University's Shorthorn Newspaper where she shared her expertise on local child hunger & how her organization fights hunger in communities across Texas.

She was spotlighted on the Television Show "Times Square Today" in the heart of New York Times Square, which was later aired on NBC, ABC, CBS, & FOX News.

Currently, Raychelle is a Real Estate Investor & Realtor who lives with her husband, Ulysses, in the DFW area of Texas. Together they have two adult children & two grandchildren. In October 2017, they adopted their two grandchildren, Julian & Legend. Despite her busy schedule, Raychelle takes time to enjoy her family because life is a gift. She thanks God every day for His gift by doing what caters to her soul- teaching, traveling, reading, writing, photography, camping, singing & praising the Lord.

To learn more, visit: https://www.eatmylyrics.com, https://www.raychellemeyers.com, & http://www.brick-stonerealty.com .

THUGS IN SKIRTS

~~Chapter 1:~~

How They Met

Bailey Brooks & Trinity Woods were always tight. They gracefully met at Red Velvet Elementary, when life was good. Bailey was fawned over because she was biracial; her mother-Black, & father- White. She was a product of *The American Dream*. She lived with her mother & father for many years until he went to prison for a business deal gone bad. Her father: Todd was a Real Estate Investor. Her mother: Sara works from home, thriving in an e-commerce company she owns & operates. She also had a younger brother named Brent; they got along quite nicely.

Trinity, on the other hand, is a shy Black girl who lives with her mother: Reece, & older brother, Trey. Trey works for a local diner & her mother is employed as a Clerk for Billy's Youth Program. Trinity's dad lives in New Jersey because he & her mother divorced early on. Things are amicable between the two, however, Trinity still missed what family felt like- Bailey's friendship filled that void for her; it was then that they became best friends until the end, literally.

Life seemed pretty blissful until the harsh realities of the world sat in. The two made it throughout elementary & junior high- always close- not so much as ever keeping one secret from one another, until they entered hell's halls of Ulysses Academy- where princesses turned into pit bulls, & their lives were forever changed.

Bailey & Trinity approached the massive doors of what appeared to be such a nice school to attend. Little did they know, the Devil's minions were waiting for them, all over again.

Bailey stepped fresh in her neon jacket, blue jean skirt, white tank, & high-top neon boots. She had a wicked sense of fashion- anything vibrant & unique, she owned it. Bailey believed in expressing herself through colors because she was such a quiet individual. Her internal personality screamed, *"This is me, & I'm owning it!"* Her hair swayed to & fro, catching the eyes of any boy who adored a nice blonde. She rocked a brand-new pair of glasses she couldn't wait to wear, all to see a new world she'd soon live to regret.

Trinity arrived, dressed to impress in her beautiful skirt ensemble, all black. She wore her kinky curly hair in two ponytails- she was giving rock star vibes!

The girls were so excited. As they observed the school, they quickly noticed they were in rare & uncharted territory, but they hadn't been conditioned to be afraid of what was different, so they shrugged it off & carried along.

The UA was great at opening its doors & arms, but its students- not so much.

Bailey & Trinity went to the office, gathered their schedules, & headed to their classes. As the girls walked the main hall amongst their peers, they heard someone behind them who didn't sound so welcoming.

"Oh my God, what the fish is she wearing?" a snide Allison shrilled amongst her friends, Maci & Kaylee.

Bailey & Trinity both looked at each other in unison but decided to keep walking. They were very familiar with this bully & her trolls.

"I know you heard me, highlighter! What the hell are you wearing?!" Allison snapped as she moved closer to Bailey.

Trinity turned around, mid-walking, & stopped in the center of the hallway, which made Allison & her girls stop too.

"What's the problem, short stuff?" Allison asked Trinity.

"If we can go to class in peace, there won't be a problem." Trinity exclaimed with the biggest smile on her face.

"Trinity. Let's just go. It's okay." Bailey pleaded while tugging at Trinity's hand.

"Oh. I see. You do what she says? Is it the blonde ponytail?" Maci questioned in laughter.

"Yea, is she like your Massa or something?" Allison seconded with a devilish grin.

Trinity stepped to Allison's face & stared her down for several seconds. Allison ceased her laughter & backed away from Trinity. She used to try her luck when they were in middle school, but she never went above your average shit talking & poking around.

"Gather your feelings, Freshman. It's truly not that serious." Kaylee exclaimed as they walked around Bailey & Trinity to get to the other side of the hall.

As the Academy's student body introduced them to its "bad bitches," the girls stood in a trance, trying to find the courage to move their feet. They thought they escaped the devil once & for all, but there she lied in the halls of the UA.

Bailey & Trinity stared one another in the eyes for what felt like hours until the bell rang.

"I'll see you in third period." Trinity said as she grabbed Bailey by the shoulders.

"Okay, sorry I left you hanging back there." Bailey admitted.

"We are best friends. I'd fight the entire school for you." Trinity reassured.

"But what about-" Bailey started.

"The whole school!" Trinity yelled in laughter, which shattered the awkwardness.

"Should we be worried?" Bailey asked Trinity.

"Oh, I think not. I could totally take them on." Trinity said with balls bigger than a bull.

"But you've never had a fight before." Bailey whispered under her breath to Trinity.

"I could totally hack their accounts & give them bad credit before they're even old enough to use it." Trinity whispered back with a shrug.

"Ha, ha, ha." The girls cackled as they split to go to class.

See, Trinity was clever. She knew in this modern world; the greatest revenge was via computer. She could hack anything & anyone. For instance, she hacked her father's bank account when he began missing child support payments. She also utilized her skills to help her mother pay rent when she fell behind, crazy what a little phishing email can do.

For just a moment, their first day of school had gotten better, the teachers were nice, & some students were pleasant, & well- the boys were cuuuute! Not that these girls worried about boys at all. They loved being top of their class- so where there was focus, there were no boys.

The day grew long but they made it to the end. The girls met up after school & recounted what their morning was like. They vowed to continue their paths to New York, with no fret about what the school year could possibly bring. Needless to say, they weren't prepared at all.

Allison, Maci, & Kaylee continued to make Bailey & Trinity's lives a living hell. Their year became unbearable, but they stuck together, at least that's what Trinity thought.

Allison had it out for Bailey more than she did Trinity; sometimes- she & her girls followed Bailey to most of her classes & waited for her to exit so that they could give her something to holler about.

Bailey had undergone sessions of serious torment. Allison & her minions always snatched her by her long, blonde ponytail. They'd shut it in their lockers & instruct her to walk away- so they could watch the locker snatch her body back into it.

Allison made it a tradition to hold Bailey's face into the toilet & flush until she screamed for help. Maci eventfully smeared feces on every neon-colored skirt Bailey owned. Often, she'd walked into the halls smelling exactly how they made her feel... shit. Bailey wondered why they didn't like her, but between pretending to be happy & maintaining all A's- her plate was full.

They hated that she dressed so freely & fun. They always badgered into her head that she only dressed that way because she couldn't afford anything name-brand. Bailey didn't know how to handle such incidents because she had never been bullied to this magnitude before. In jr. high, she & Trinity dealt with Allison & her mean girls, but it was nothing like this. Apparently, they were taking things up a notch.

They most certainly went for Trinity as well, but Trinity had thicker skin. Allison kept those racial slurs coming. She also learned that speaking ill of Trinity's father or messing with her hair was the quickest way to put her on mute, so she went for the jugular- a lot. Trinity confided in Bailey about being bullied when they were apart, but Bailey didn't utter a word about what they were doing to her. She even tried to downplay Allison's behavior at times, by saying, *"Oh, yea- you know how she is."* Trinity would've known that her best friend was lying & hurting if she weren't so damn good at smiling. No one ever knew because Bailey's personality was just as bright as the clothes she wore. After being tormented, she'd go to the nearest girls' restroom, & cry for what felt like days at a time, & then re-enter the halls smiling as though nothing ever happened.

Bailey continued this front until the school year was over. By then, she had her routine of coping with Allison, Maci, & Kaylee down. She knew which hallways to avoid, which teachers to walk out behind, & which restrooms to steer clear of, but they always found her.

It was now Sophomore Year. Although Bailey & Trinity faced an obscene number of encounters with Allison & her girls, they still managed to make it to the top of their class, wrestling close in grade point averages. They didn't have other friends at all, only their books & each other.

The teachers would've been great alliances if only they had the time. They were too busy being bribed & blackmailed by the parents of every rich kid in the building. Talk about privilege.

Luckily, as time moved along, the girls met a Korean Doll named Naree Gem. Naree lived at home with her mother: Sena, who worked as a head nurse for the most prestigious hospital in the county- Philadelphia Patients & Associates. Her father: Jun, worked as a computer Programmer at a company called IT & Logistics. Naree's sister: Ari & brother: Jin attended Waterfall High in another county due to their programs of interest. Naree's family had quite the background, which aided her in the ability to possess such qualitative communication skills.

It was an encounter of unfortunate events that led these girls to become a triple threat.

"So, tell me. Do you speak English, or will I have to translate for you?" Allison snickered as she breezed by Naree in the basement on her way to class.

Naree picked her head up. Students froze in anticipation of her response. Her cold black hair fell over her eyes as she looked up at Allison. Her gut told her not to mouth a word, but per usual, she went for it. Naree was just as well at reading people as she was at communicating with them. She knew that with girls like Allison, there was absolutely no talking, but if her mouth could save her from having a bad day, it was worth a shot.

"I get it. I'm the new girl. But, hey, let's just talk about this." Naree suggested as she looked toward the doors that led her to freedom.

Allison rushed Naree & shoved her to the ground. Naree stayed on her knees & decided to place herself in fetal position.

"Okay- so, maybe we got off to a bad start. Hi, my name is Naree, & I transferred from-"

"CHINA, YEAH, WE KNOW!" Allison yelled.

"What the peasant is she even doing?" Allison asked her audience.

"Well, don't just lay there!" Maci commanded as she walked over to take part in the mean girl festivities.

"Oh, darling. This one must be a little slow." Kaylee joked as she took her place next to both Allison & Maci.

They stood there like they owned the place. When they were together, they were invincible, everyone knew it.

"Listen girls, we can truly get along. I rank pretty high in the friend department." Naree continued.

Bailey & Trinity watched from afar, afraid of what may happen next. They held hands & clenched tightly, hoping the trolls wouldn't sniff them out today too.

Allison grabbed Naree by the hair & pulled her up from the ground. Naree stood to her feet & began to whimper lowly as she followed the grip of Allison's hand right into the locker.

Back to the floor, she went. The impact was so loud, it sounded like cars crashing into one another. Each student gasped as it was official that Allison had gone too far this time.

Blood spilled from Naree's nose like secrets in a confessional. Bailey & Trinity stepped forward at Naree's defense. They knew they were now susceptible to receiving the same treatment, but they couldn't witness this any longer.

"Oh, well if it isn't the fucktarded." Allison laughed.

"Let's go, I think Principal Ritton is coming." Kaylee said.

"We pay for him to be here. We're not going anywhere." Maci said as she walked up to Naree & smushed her own blood across her face.

More students gasped, and the rest walked away because what was intended to be funny was now cruel & unkind.

Bailey moved closer to Naree & went to help her up, but Maci slapped her hand.

"Wanna be twins?" Allison asked, insinuating that she too would have a bloody nose if she didn't back off.

"Maybe you all should just stop." Trinity said as she got closer to Bailey.

Maci grabbed Naree by the back of her head & shoved her face onto Bailey's light green skirt. She rubbed her nose into the center of it, & then dropped Naree back to the floor.

"Oh no! Appears you've started your period." Allison shrilled, as she snapped pictures of Bailey, rallying up echoes of laughter from her remaining peers.

Trinity walked up & shoved Maci into Allison. Surprised at herself, she stood behind what she did.

"You're gonna pay for that." Allison said as she motioned for the girls to follow her out the back door.

"I'll be seeing you." Maci seconded as she followed the leader.

Naree sat on the floor & continued to whimper like a wounded animal. The halls grew silent, as the remaining students withered away. Bailey looked at her skirt & shook her head.

"It's okay that you ruined my favorite skirt, no need to cry."

Naree chuckled lightly as she smiled through her tears.

"My kind of girl." Trinity said as she helped Naree from the floor.

Naree used her hand to cuff her nose as she looked up with an even wider smile at the girls.

"Thank you." she said.

"The closest restroom is behind this wall." Bailey pointed.

"After all this time, I didn't even know there was one down here." Trinity said in surprise.

Bailey looked away from Trinity, she didn't want to confirm stories untold.

There lied in the coldest restroom of Ulysses Academy, Bailey Brooks, Trinity Woods, & Naree Gem. The mirrors showcased these girls cleaning their faces, their clothing, & their souls.

Each of them discovered they had their final class together, Forensic Science. They vowed to sit together, so they could survive the semester as best they could.

As the tardy bell rang, the girls hurried around the corner & into the classroom doors of Mrs. Albright.

"Have a seat, ladies, so that we can get started."

"Yes maim." They all responded in unison.

As the girls took their seats, they were greeted by not one, but two smiling faces- Emma Banks & Scarlett Perez.

Emma's White & lives with her mother & father. Her father: Ethan is a former Realtor, currently disabled, & her mother: Laura works at an amazing art gallery, Seen & Unseen. She also has a younger sister named Karra; she completely adores her.

Scarlett is Hispanic & Italian. She's currently being raised by her mother: Marcella, who is a Paralegal for a firm located in downtown Philly, Justice 4 U 2. Unfortunately, Scarlett hadn't laid eyes on her father since she was 2 years old. She doesn't have any siblings, but she considers Emma family; their mothers have been best friends since before they were born. It was through their friendship that they grew to become inseparable too.

Mrs. Albright went over the Syllabus for the semester & informed the class that a project would take place involving the cores of forensic science. She gave them all leeway to choose their partners as this was going to impact 60% of their grades. Bailey, Trinity, Naree, Emma, & Scarlett all joined forces.

Instructions for the project were passed down each row & signatures were collected to solidify the formation of all groups.

"Now, I know that everyone utilizes social media in this day & age, but in this class- we will do things old school. You are to work face-to-face concerning any group projects, no Facetime or voice memos. Participation from every student is required, I will know who's been present in every aspect." Mrs. Albright announced as she continued to go over her expectations for the semester. All students were encouraged to follow up accordingly if need be.

Everyone took a few minutes to swap numbers. The girls quickly noticed they all had one thing in common- coffee. They created a group chat & planned to meet at the nearby coffee shop, Wake-Up Philly, as often as possible. Bailey & Trinity smiled from ear to ear, as they had just made 3 friends today.

On their way home, they discussed how things were finally looking up. As the year moved forward, Bailey, Trinity, Naree, Emma, & Scarlett all became best friends.

Nearly every day since the first week of class, the girls hung out at Wake-Up Philly. Emma & Scarlett knew not to be friendly with Allison & her crew because Bailey, Trinity, & Naree alerted them to their bullshit.

Bailey & her girls were nowhere near popular, but they racked up quite the attention because they always wore funky colorful clothes to school- particularly, they always rocked skirts, never pants. It's almost as though, they were crafted only to find each other.

Bailey was more outrageous with her style though; she stood out like spiked hair from a mohawk! Allison & her girls could not STAND it! Generation Z has quite the rep for being toxic as hell, but one thing Gen Z loves is authenticity. They love when people embrace who they are & simply be themselves, proudly & loudly- Allison didn't have one leg to stand on in that department. She wasn't authentic, she was the Grim Reaper in designer clothing.

Allison panicked that she & her girls were losing their touch, so she decided to put her evil to bad use. Into the Counselor's office, she went.

"Hi Allison, I see you're doing well in your studies. Is there something more I can do for you today?"

"Actually, now that you say that. I need to be transferred to a class that Bailey Brooks has."

"I'm not sure I understand. You'd like to be placed in a class with Bailey Brooks? I don't recall the two of you being friends, & it's been confirmed via transcript that you've taken the proper courses leading to current."

"I think you should verify that again." Allison stated as she crossed her legs.

Counselor Strickland took a moment to confirm that Allison's request did not constitute a change. She then looked at Bailey's courses & saw that all her classes were AP, Allison's were not.

"I'm sorry Allison, but as I stated before, your request does not constitute a change in your current schedule."

"Your findings do not move me, Strickland."

"Allison Parker."

"I recall my father ensuring your father never saw the doors of Windham Gates' Prison for embezzlement of funds from this very school. Good times, right?" Allison reminded as she smiled, staring through the glass doors that displayed Bailey in her view.

"That is a brief of-"

"Confidentiality. Keep up, Strickland. I need a class with Bailey Brooks. If you don't want me to leak those files, switch a class. Also, don't forget to add Maci & Kaylee- you know their last names." Allison threatened as she stood from her seat. She dusted her dress off & took her place in the halls of the UA.

Several minutes later, she received a notification that read: "Please delete this email after confirmation of your new schedule. You are now enrolled in AP English with Bailey Brooks. I have no idea what this is about, but please keep my father out of it."

Allison smiled as she met up with Maci & Kaylee in the lobby.

"So, did she do it?" Kaylee asked.

"You know she did. What are you, on crack?" Maci questioned.

Allison laughed.

"I'm not the only one who has a new class, ladies. Looks like Bailey will have some new friends in AP English."

"What's the big deal with her, anyway?" Kaylee questioned.

"Does it matter?" Maci asked.

"Uhm no, I was just-"

"It's either you're with us, or you're against us, Kaylee. Stop being so weak all the time. It's giving peasant vibes." Allison snapped.

Allison & Maci laughed hysterically. Kaylee chuckled through her discomfort as they made their way to 1st period.

1st period quickly became a thing of the past when lunch arose & Bailey was spotted with her crew. Allison walked into the lunchroom & thought it was the perfect moment to flop Trinity's tray from her hand.

"Oops, didn't see you there, Felicia."

"Allison, what the f-" Trinity started.

"What the hell is your problem?" Emma asked.

"Oh baby, now I know you don't want to eat your lunch from a toilet seat." Allison responded.

"Let's just go you guys." Bailey pleaded in the most convincing tone.

"Aww, *let's just go you guys*. Listen to the baby. She's a good wittle doggy, yes, she is." Allison mocked while clapping her hands together.

Bailey, Trinity, Naree, Emma, & Scarlett all left the lunchroom & headed outside to eat on the steps. They were pissed but they didn't want any trouble.

"This is much better." Scarlett exclaimed while taking deep breaths. Allison & her girls gave this one terrible anxiety.

As the girls found their peace in the pockets of sunshine dancing around the school, they failed to notice there was mischief stirring behind them.

"Aghhhhh!" Emma yelled as she turned to grab her hand. Allison stood above her on the steps, smashing her hand into the pavement with her brand-new heels.

"If you ever try to come for me in front of our student body again, I will destroy you." She said as she stepped down even harder.

"Do you understand?"

"YESS!" Emma screamed.

Bailey, Trinity, Naree, & Scarlett rose from their steps & went to remove Allison's foot, but she snatched it away.

"Don't you ever fucking touch me! Peasants!" Allison said as she returned to the lunchroom with Maci & Kaylee trailing behind her.

Emma clutched her newly released hand & choked back tears as Allison walked away.

"Are you okay?" Scarlett asked with anger in her eyes.

"I'm okay, bitch almost broke my hand."

The girls all laughed. Emma had a way with words for sure. No matter how serious the moment, she was bound to say something humorous.

The girls all did their group handshake with Emma's good hand, hugged, & then continued to their classes.

"See you all in 7th-p." Trinity said as she danced away from the group.

"Right, it's the only place that makes sense around here." Emma seconded.

"It's because we're all together." Naree added in.

"Awww you guys." Bailey said melting in their pool of sisterly love.

Time shot by like a gun as the girls waited to reunite. Bailey made it to AP English, which was her 6th-period class. She went in & completed her routine, which involved speaking to everyone, getting supplies on her desk just right, & then opening her book to begin reading aloud.

Everyone loved when Bailey read aloud because she was passionate about the stories, & she made quite the transition with playing characters. Mr. Sutton closed the door & then motioned for Bailey to begin reading the novel for the month, *Oh Hear Me*, which captured the tale of how a teen overcame depression.

Bailey was quickly cut short when the door opened.

Mr. Sutton confirmed the schedules that were handed to him & then announced, "Everyone please welcome Allison Parker, Maci Karr, & Kaylee Lopez."

Instantly, Bailey's book dropped to the floor. A piece of her walked straight through them, & right out the classroom door- too bad her body didn't actually move.

"How the hell are they here?" She pondered.

"Ms. Brooks, go ahead & get us started while the girls take their places."

"Uhm, okay." She began to read but felt Allison's eyes piercing the side of her face, she had the nerve to sit directly next to her.

"Someone else can read today." She said abruptly after.

"But you always read." Mr. Sutton responded.

"It's okay. I'll read tomorrow." She insisted, hanging her head low.

Tomorrow never came again. Bailey withdrew from reading day after day. Mr. Sutton recognized the shift in her spunky attitude, but he chose to ignore his instincts. Allison requested the task of reading in Bailey's place, Mr. Sutton permitted.

Students noticed that Allison picked on Bailey during class; Monday through Friday, anytime Mr. Sutton stepped away, Allison & her girls were right there, destroying her notes, homework, & playing catch with her backpack. On days when Allison felt her best, she'd toss Bailey's backpack right into the trashcan & spit on it. Bailey would be so terrified to get it out, she'd just leave it in there until the next class started. She grew weary. She often wondered how much more of Allison's antics she could take.

During PE, she found herself trapped in the girls' locker room, buried underneath Allison & her minions. They'd paint her face like a clown, dip her blonde hair into the ugliest of colors, & taunt her with names like broke whore & weak bitch. When they were certain she was at her lowest point, they'd force her to walk into the boys' locker room upon completion of their sick game. Some took pictures & recorded her, others shook their heads, but even they did nothing. One boy in particular hated when they tortured her but because he belonged to Allison, he knew he had to fall in line.

The semester was winding down. Bailey's mother noticed that her smile was fading but because she still carried such a glow, she chose not to read into it. Bailey was also unhappy at home, she struggled in ways that only her mother was privy to. Her light derived from the love of her friends & the fact that she'd *make it home.* Often, she honestly never thought she would.

Allison & her followers eventually blackmailed their way into Bailey's 7th-period class, Forensic Science. Ending school with Trinity, Naree, Emma, & Scarlett made her days of strife worth it all. She'd rush to class super early to avoid being found by Allison, but also to discuss hanging out at

Wake-Up Philly with her girls, the only highlight of her day. Now, that was all about to change.

The bell rang, so everyone grabbed their books & turned to the appropriate chapter: Life after Death in *Forensics R Us*. Everyone truly enjoyed this class; they were currently learning how blood tells a story even when the victim stops breathing. Bailey & the girls were crafting their project to embody some pretty amazing aspects from each chapter, they couldn't wait to see it all come together. They had no idea their project would soon feature *Life after Bailey Nicole Brooks*.

Allison, Maci, & Kaylee came waltzing into the classroom, handing their schedules to Mrs. Albright.

"Class, we have a few new students. Please welcome Allison Parker, Maci Karr, & Kylee Lopez."

"But- the semester is almost over." Scarlett said aloud, not realizing the classroom could hear her.

Allison scowled at Scarlett from across the room.

"Ms. Perez." Mrs. Albright said in a firm tone.

"Yes maim." She responded apologetically.

Bailey was shaken to the bottom of her foundation, what foundation she must've had.

"Since it's so late in the school year, you girls will partner together in the project required for this class. Please grab a syllabus from the first tray & get seated."

Suddenly, the energy in the room shifted. Allison, Maci, & Kaylee found open seats near Bailey, Trinity, Naree, Emma, & Scarlett.

"Funny seeing you here." Allison said slyly as she glanced over at Bailey.

Class was unsettling, & uncomfortable, but Bailey & her girls fought to maintain the normalcy of their comradery.

Mrs. Albright took a moment & caught Allison & her girls up to speed with the project & informed them they'd be held just as accountable as everyone else.

"If only life held them accountable too." Bailey thought.

Mrs. Albright stepped out of the class after instructing the students to read today's chapter. She went to get Allison, Maci, & Kaylee's textbooks from their school library.

Allison stood from her seat; Bailey immediately became intimidated. She flinched, lightly.

"It's okay." Trinity whispered.

Allison headed to the front of the class & got their attention.

"Hey guys, wanna see something?"

"What are you doing?" Kaylee questioned.

"Shut up Kaylee. Allison, do it."

"Like I need your permission." She laughed.

Allison plugged her phone into Mrs. Albright's projector. There lied a picture of Bailey plastered across the main wall of the classroom.

The classroom became a sea of whispers.

Bailey put her head down as tears ran like fathers from their children. She had finally been broken.

"Bailey, why didn't you tell me she did this to you? TAKE THAT DOWN!" Trinity yelled as she cried angrily.

Mrs. Albright's students were shocked more than anything. Maci & Kaylee stood to the floor demanding the room as well.

"I mean this is Forensic Science, right? Doesn't she look dead already?" Allison asked, maliciously.

Bailey looked up at Allison & was fed up. Trinity, Naree, Emma, & Scarlett stood up & began walking to the front of the classroom.

"Don't even try it, peasants. You touch my phone &
your face will match your best friend's." Allison threatened.

The girls came to a halt in the center of the classroom.
They stared with aches in their hearts at this picture of
Bailey. She was half naked. Her face was smeared in various
colors, & her hair had been braided around her throat. She
was drenched in what appeared to be light yellow paint, but
it was urine. Allison & Maci were the culprits. Her body had
bruises on it, each one marked a moment with them.

As Bailey's head hung low, she replayed that day in
her mind, it was one of many. She remembered screaming for
her life, but no one came. Not only were they not coming
because Allison ran the school, the locker room was in such
a secluded area of the building, they'd never even hear her-
might as well have been soundproof. Bailey screamed from
her soul, regardless, because she held hope in her heart. She
remembered kicking, fighting, & shoving each of those rich
little shits but they overpowered her. She was so
embarrassed that she chose not to report a thing. She felt
they could kill her & get away with it. Why bother, ya know?

"Everyone please follow @BrokeBailey on all social
media platforms." Maci petitioned.

"Yeah, & don't forget to go BrokeBailey.com, we are
taking donations so that she can buy better clothes." Kaylee
added on.

"Yea, so she can like- dress better." Maci laughed.

Allison unplugged her phone & began walking back to her seat. Maci & Kaylee followed.

Bailey's Girls still stood in the walkway- frozen. There were merely no words.

"Let's go." Trinity said to Bailey.

"You leave, I follow." Allison threatened.

"So, follow. There's 5 of us, & 3 of you." Emma snapped.

"True, but all of you are weak bitches & let's just face it. I always win."

"Exactly." Maci & Kaylee added in unison.

Mrs. Albright walked back into the room.

"Is everything okay, girls? You all should be reading. Your class projects require every bit of this time."

The girls' eyes spoke but their mouths didn't.

"Oh, yes maim, everything's fine. Just providing feedback on life after death."

"Oh, great. What did you all come up with?"

"Emptiness." Bailey responded.

Suddenly, the room grew cold. The girls went back to their seats & sulked in anger & sadness.

The bell rang but this time its presence represented something different. Bailey confirmed she was no longer keeping quiet. She let her friends know she'd be telling her mom & promised to catch up with them later. She went home & bared her soul to her mother.

"Mom. I've been keeping something from you."

"Well, what is it care bear?"

She fiddled with her thumbs.

"For years, I've been bullied by a group of girls at school."

"The ones who come to our house?!" her mother asked, enraged.

"No! Mom, those girls are my best friends, my sisters. I literally mean girls at school. Rich ones. They hate me. They targeted me in jr. high & have been on me ever since."

"Years? Bails how could you not tell me this?" Sara questioned, feeling betrayed & confused.

Bailey shot her mother a look.

"Okay, you're right. I won't make this about me. Go on."

Bailey stared into the distance.

"Well. Their names are Allison Parker, Maci Karr, & Kaylee Lopez. They have tormented me in ways I wish I could forget. I've been peed on, spat on, & jumped on various times. They've spent the past several weeks painting my face like a clown, abusing my hair, & calling me broke whores & weak bitches. Today, they embarrassed me in front of my peers. They plastered a picture onto the projector, displaying one of my worst days of torment from them. I was nearly naked because they ripped the clothes from my body, & they braided my hair around my throat. Come to think of it, I thought that I would die that day. I could barely breathe, it was as though I were slipping away, but it didn't hurt. I actually imagined death to be quite peaceful after this encounter. They've magically appeared in two of my classes, which is strange because it's near the end of the school year- usually in-house transfers don't occur in this manner. They talk about my clothes, & even have a page accepting donations for me to buy new clothes, they announced it today, *BrokeBailey.com*. All this to say... mom, I want it to stop. Please make this stop."

Bailey's mother gripped her hands & stood to her feet.

"This will not stand." She said, pissed. They messed with the wrong damn kid.

Bailey stood too. She stood even though her knees felt weak. She stood even though her heart was hurting. She stood even though she was on borrowed time. She stood.

"I'm so sorry you've been going through this alone. I know you've been suffering emotionally, but I thought it was due to recent events. I'm also very sorry about that as well. I feel I cannot say it enough." Sara began.

"Mom." Bailey said, trying to shrug her off.

"No, I should've told you that Todd isn't your biological father." Sara admitted.

"That doesn't pain me, mother. What pains me is that had I not needed a bone marrow transplant; you never would've uttered a word." Bailey explained.

"You don't understand." Sara responded, shaking her head.

"Oh okay, but I'm supposed to understand being placed in a room, at a doctor's office with you & Dad- no Todd, & be told he couldn't be tested because he wouldn't be a match? That he's not my real father. After all these years? That makes me feel like the literal shit those girls smear on me sometimes." Bailey cried.

Sara took in her daughter's last words, they stung.

"You were so sick, Bails; you were a child. I just didn't want to break you in that way." Sara shared.

"No Mom! You didn't want to break YOU. You waited until I nearly died to come clean!" Bailey yelled.

Bailey & her mother both began to cry. She was 13 years old when she had to undergo bone marrow surgery. Unbeknownst to Sara, both parents had to be tested to save

Bailey's life. In hindsight, Todd was Bailey's father; he raised Bailey & sacrificed like any parent would to give her the life she deserved. On December 27th, Sara realized her perception of Todd would in no way help Bailey, so in the final hour, she contacted Bailey's biological father to brief him on the matter & arrange for testing. This truth contributed to Bailey's depression. When she blacked out, standing at her bedside was a man she never knew. After the surgery, she never saw him again. It's been 3 years; she still hadn't managed to work past her mother's betrayal.

"I can fix this; I will work to repair our relationship. Let me start by making sure I handle each of those bullies for you. Do you want to change schools? I'll enroll you anywhere you want to go." Her mother pleaded in desperation.

"I cannot leave my friends." Bailey responded as she reflected to herself. She flashed back to every dark moment in her life & thought about how her best friends didn't know the biggest gag of it all- that she was just some sick dunce who didn't even know her father.

The next morning, Sara contacted Philly P.D. & every board member from the UA's Independent School District. She reported Allison, Maci, & Kaylee for all the damage they'd done. She relayed to everyone the trauma inflicted on her daughter, & expressed how important it is they follow up, or that she'd be forced to take legal action. All parties informed Sara of their protocols in place for situations such as this & assured her that it'd be handled accordingly.

Time went by, the only thing handled was Bailey. Allison & her gang were ruthless & untouchable, they knew it.

One week later, Sara took out a lawsuit against them all. She obtained not one ounce of justice for Bailey because Allison's father: Frankie utilized his authority as an attorney to shut everything down before it even gained enough coverage to take flight. Allison & her girls didn't so much as receive suspension from school for bullying Bailey. As Frankie so eloquently put it, there was no evidence. Bailey referred to social media & the website they announced but it all disappeared. Little did they know, she did too.

Bailey's friends were so upset. They tried their best to weigh in on the situation by providing statements & offering themselves as witnesses, but none of it helped one bit. It just made matters for Bailey much worse.

It was now 1 month until the school year was over. Bailey & her girls just wanted to see it through. They met at Wake-Up Philly to go over their project but were compelled to discuss how they wanted to help Bailey fight back.

"I know that she messes with you all too, but some days, I just wonder why me. Like, it feels so personal." Bailey expressed in a trance.

"It's not personal, Bailey. Allison is just a nasty person. Her minions are even worse. How bout we take our minds off them by preparing for the pep rally tomorrow? You

know, matching skirts, neon-colored socks, & all the fixings."
Naree encouraged with a smile.

Bailey smiled too.

"I just... wish-" Bailey started.

"Oh my GOD!" Scarlett shouted.

"What is it?!" Bailey asked.

"It's you. Pictures, videos, & postings. All you. She just made it all public!" Trinity shrieked.

Bailey was fair skinned, but after this news, she became pale & thin as air.

"Let me see." She said a notch above a whisper.

Bailey held Trinity's phone in her hands. There were posts that led back to jr. high with captions that read "What a weirdo #BrokeBailey, #BrokeBailey wore dirty clothes to school today, #BrokeBailey likes being friends with poor, fat, geeky girls, fuck your ugly skirts, #BrokeBailey is a clown, #BrokeBailey is a bad friend," & so much more. She saw videos of them spitting on her, pouring paint on her, & shoving her to the ground. She also saw another set of viral posts called the Locker Chronicles – which is where she got to relive placing her ponytail in the locker & shutting it for the last time. That's when she decided it *would be* the last time.

Bailey dropped Trinity's phone. She jumped from her chair & left the coffee shop.

The girls chased after her, but she begged them to leave her be. Bailey made it home & told her mom, again. Sara contacted Philly P.D., they informed her that unless the girls were physically harming Bailey currently, there was nothing they could do. Sara contacted several law firms. After confirming her claim was concerning Allison Parker, they refused to move forward & encouraged Bailey's mother to send her to another school.

Bailey met defeat. She was now French kissing the Grim Reaper. She went to sleep, numb & empty. Morning came; her mother begged her to stay home, but she said she promised the girls she'd be there. Her mom encouraged her to leave if things got too tough, she confirmed she would.

Bailey made it to school, met up with her friends, & took pictures with them in their funky colored skirts for today's pep rally. They asked Bailey if she was okay, she told them she'd be lying if she said she was. She informed them that she stayed up all night, trying to report each picture and video posted of her, & then confirmed as of this morning, everything's still there. They all hugged it out & did their handshake in melancholy. Mrs. Kipper saw the girls & motioned for them to enter the auditorium, as they were due to be announced for their GPAs. The girls all went in & took their places in the front row. Bailey hopped up & informed them she'd be right back. She developed some anxiety, so she went to the bathroom & then headed backstage. She paced & spoke life into herself but she felt as though she'd just been passing through all along. Immediately, she dug through theatre props & grabbed a rope from the back.

"Settle down everyone, we're about to get started." Mrs. Kipper announced.

Just as Bailey promised her mother, *she was leaving.*

The curtains opened like a pair of legs. Something horrific was about to happen, it'd soon stun the entire audience & school officials in attendance today.

Bailey's body came shooting down from the 2nd floor. There was a rope laced around her neck. Her head dropped & tilted to the left side as her eyes rolled to the back of her skull. She grasped for air, all the while, her legs abruptly jerking until her body suddenly fell silent. She was a girl of very many words, who knew she'd never speak again.

Teachers & students rushed to the stage & began tugging the curtains closed- the curtains would not budge. They tried to rescue, no- cut down the 16-year-old body dangling, exposed for everyone to see, but it was too late.

Bailey's best friends stood in shock, sadness, & fury. Trinity darted towards Bailey's lifeless body, but as she got close, Mrs. Kipper held her off. Right behind her were Naree, Emma, & Scarlett. Trinity gave Mrs. Kipper a look as she cornered her to the edge of the stage.

"BAILEY!" She yelled, reaching for her body. The girls were able to get her down, but as they stared beyond the crowd, there stood Bailey's mother. She was at the school demanding disciplinary action for Allison, Maci, & Kaylee. She knew Bailey & her friends were being honored during the pep rally, so she decided to pop in. Her eyes were not prepared. Neither was her heart.

"Remember Forensics, she's not dead. Let's roll her to the side, blood could be keeping her from breathing." Scarlett sobbed.

"Baillleeeyyyy!" Her mother yelled as she shoved through each student & teacher in her way. She ran until her legs gave out. She kneeled below the stage & prayed harder than any sinner she ever knew.

The girls tried many ways to revive Bailey, but she wouldn't come back. They all laid beside her until the ambulance arrived. Bailey was pronounced dead at the scene. Ulysses Academy had teenage blood on their hands. Bailey's Girls were physically there, but they too died inside.

"I thought we were enough." Trinity said as she sat center-stage, sulking in her best friend's blood.

"Me too." The remaining girls admitted in unison.

~~Chapter 2:~~

<u>Fatal Impact</u>

Grief lingered in the hallways of Ulysses Academy. Since Bailey's suicide, the sun had gone down & come up again- seven times, which felt like the devil smiling during the worst days of their lives.

Bailey's mother was currently being held on the Psych floor at Philadelphia Patients & Associates' Hospital, - she was not okay. As any mother would've, she lost her shit.

Sara hunted down Allison, Maci, & Kaylee & harassed them every day because all she could imagine was her baby hanging from the ceiling of a place she sent her to for freedom, inclusion, & stimulation. She recounted every level of torment her daughter informed her of, & began to reenact it all, except this time- she was the bully.

Sara caught Allison & her minions after school, during break periods, & at their favorite hangout, The Social Bar. She spent days yelling at them & letting them know she knew they were behind this tragedy, that they killed her daughter. Well, on one particular evening, Sara got tired of yelling. She caught Allison in the restroom at the Social Bar.

"What the demented shit are you doing here, Lady?" Allison questioned as she stared Bailey's mother up & down.

"I could ask you the same thing, with this being a bar & all, but let's not waste our time today." Sara answered.

"What do you want? You want to tell me how you know I killed your-?"

Sara locked the restroom door & snatched Allison by the back of her head.

"You little bitch!" She said as she guided her right into the most disgusting stall there.

"Get the fuck off me, you wrinkled peasant! What do you think you're doing?!"

"Teaching you a lesson since your mother didn't."

Down went Allison. Gurgling toilet water & yelling for her girls- all she could see was Bailey's face as her eyes opened & closed.

"Tell me! How do you like it?!" Sara screamed as she flushed the toilet repeatedly. Some of Allison's hair began going down with the waste, as her head twisted to its current, her arms went flailing everywhere.

"PLEASE!" She screamed as she struggled to overpower Sara.

"How many girls have you done this to?" Sara asked as she jerked her away from the toilet.

Allison sat in a pool of defeat & toilet water, sobbing.

"You've ruined my entire outfit. You crazy old bitch!"

"That's all you care about. You killed my daughter, you rich little cunt! Stand up!"

Allison slowly stood to her feet. Maci & Kaylee began knocking on the restroom door.

"Hey, why is the door locked? Let us in." Maci directed.

"Yea, like are you hooking up with someone or what? Open the door." Kaylee added.

Allison said nothing.

At that moment, she recalled a time when Bailey said nothing. A time when Naree said nothing. A time when even she... said nothing.

Sara stared her in the eyes & told her, "I'll be seeing you." She unlocked the door. As Maci & Kaylee stepped in, she made her way out. Kaylee became a shell of herself after witnessing the anger brewing in Sara's eyes.

"Oh my God! What did she do to you?!" Maci asked as she moved closer to Allison.

"Don't touch me." Allison said, making her way to the sink to clean herself up as much as possible. Ironic, isn't it?

Maci fixated on Allison in the mirror, she hadn't seen her this mute since last witnessing her meltdown after gaining 5 pounds.

"You know what you need to do." Maci said as she stood beside her.

Allison looked up from the mirror & made eye contact with Maci.

"Oh, it's already done." Allison said after snatching her makeup bag & exiting the restroom.

Kaylee stayed behind for a moment, choking back sobs of regret. She felt they were worthy of being exposed, after all, they did push Bailey to her death. She braced herself & reunited with her crew.

"Time to put mommy to bed." Allison said as they all made their way to her car.

"What are you gonna do?" Kaylee asked.

"You mean, what are WE going to do, right?" Whose side are you on anyway?" Allison asked.

"You know she's not built like us. I don't even know why we bother." Maci acknowledged, throwing shade.

"Fuck you Maci." Kaylee snapped.

"I have stood beside you both in every antic but the moment I ask a question, I'm not down enough? I'm not built like you? You're absolutely right. Ustedes putas lo pueden tener! (You bitches can have it!)." Kaylee yelled as she walked away.

"Kaylee, get in the car." Maci instructed.

"It's fine, let her walk." Allison said as she sped off.

Kaylee walked & walked until she found herself sitting in front of Wake-Up Philly. She stared through the glass at Trinity, Naree, Emma, & Scarlett from afar. She attested to the light that died inside them all, as they continued to grieve their best friend.

"Will Maci & Allison even miss me when I'm gone?" She wondered. She kept walking until she found herself at home. She had several missed messages from Maci & Allison, she left them on read as she greeted la familia (the family) & sustained the strength to make it to her room. It's a wonder she even associated with Allison & Maci because Maci was right about one thing, *she wasn't built like them.*

Kaylee is Hispanic & resides with her mother: Rebecca Lopez, who owns a boutique store near the Social Bar called Fab Lives Matter. Joined by her brother: West, & sister: Audrey, they have quite the amazing family. Rebecca raised Kaylee & West to be responsible, noble, & to honor God in all they do. Upon reflection of her behavior all year, Kaylee began to feel she was letting both her mother & God down. After winding down for the night, she decided to see what Maci & Allison had to say.

Maci:

6:52 pm: "I'm sorry.

6:53 pm: "I hope you made it home safely."

7:00 pm: "It's still us against the world."

Allison:

7:32 pm: "Did you make it home?"

7:55 pm: "Wanna come over? We can drink Tequila & curse the ground Sara Brooks walks on."

8:47 pm: "Are you in or what?"

9:02 pm: "You know it's still us against the world."

Conflicted on how to respond, Kaylee slapped her phone down & went to bed. Meanwhile, Maci was over at Allison's penthouse, conjuring up a way to put Bailey's mother in her place.

Allison is the typical rich White girl; her parents were born into money & are successful themselves. Unbeknownst to her, she was adopted as an infant. Her father: Frankie is a powerful attorney & her mother: Louise is a U.S. Senator. She also has an older sister who lives in Cali, Ava Parker. Ava is the Head Coach of Cali's infamous Women's Basketball team at UCLA. Allison became a menace the moment she grew teeth. She always felt out of place in her family, but she never shared those feelings. Maci has been a rock & a punching bag in every aspect of her life, but this tea wasn't up for grabs. Maci met Allison at Buckingham Elementary, a place for the rich & elite children, only.

Maci's also White. She dwells in a mansion with the CEO of Bell Enterprises, Jim Bell- who is her father. Her mother suffered from various blood clots when she was born & died shortly after giving birth to her. Eventually, her father moved on & married the third love of his life, Paula Bell, who is a stay-at-home mother at this time. In their broken home, Maci's also entrapped with her younger stepbrother: Daniel Tatum.

"So, couldn't Frankie just get this old bag off our hands?" Maci asked as she knocked back a shot of tequila.

"Gross, don't call my dad Frankie." Allison responded while quivering in disgust.

"Of course, he can get rid of her. She's been harassing us all. I can let a lot of things slide but bringing pictures of Bailey from the morgue to us during lunchtime was bat shit crazy. She's got to go!" Allison elaborated.

"Well, I mean- he's not going to like kill her or anything, is he?" Maci asked with a side-eye.

"What. No! Ha, my dad would never kill anyone."

"Oh." Maci laughed, nervously.

"Uhm, yea. So, I'll talk to my dad. I even have access to some of his files, I could probably handle this myself." Allison insisted.

"But maybe you shouldn't this time. She really keeps stepping it up a notch every time she sees us. She put your face in a toilet- what is she going to do next? Run you over?" Maci pointed out.

"Don't let yourself off the hook. We're in this together." Allison reminded.

"I'm just saying." Maci laughed.

"Yeah, so am I." Allison reiterated.

"Did Kaylee text you back?" Maci asked.

"No, you?" Allison asked.

"No." Maci confirmed.

"You think I was too hard on her? Maci questioned.

"I'm the one that drove away." Allison stated as the room fell silent. Both girls spat out a belly-aching laughter that caused a knock at the door.

"Everything okay in here?" Frankie inquired as he began to take cheer in seeing his daughter enjoying herself.

"Yea Dad, everything's great." Allison responded as she cut her laugh short.

"Alright, ha, I guess I'll get back to work."

"Actually, Mr. Parker." Maci began while nudging at Allison.

Allison snapped out of her tequila impairment & hopped into *"baby girl."*

"Uhm, yea, Daddy. You know that lady who tried to like, sue us before?"

"Which one?" Frankie questioned, cocky & unbothered.

"Bailey Brooks' mother."

"Oh." He said as he stirred in silence.

"What about her?" He continued.

"Well, she's been like coming to our school, & taking out the loss of her daughter on us. Like it's our fault or something or the sort." Allison explained.

"Well, Allison, you know as cliché as it is- *hurt people do in fact … hurt people.* Sometimes we must overlook even the deepest of pains because it's not always about us."

"Yea, but today she took your daughter's face for a dive in a toilet seat at The Social Bar." Maci added.

"Oh, did she now?" Frankie questioned, struggling to find the audacity.

"Yea, Daddy, & she like totally ruined the new outfit you just bought for me. I guess she doesn't know $8,000 when she sees it."

"Well, don't you worry about it at all, I know what to do."

"Okay, Daddy. I knew you would." Allison smiled.

"I'm your father first. Remember that, always." Frankie said as he shut the door with a focused expression.

At this point, Sara was the only thing Allison was afraid of. She & Maci called it a night as they fell asleep, stewing in their drunken victory.

The next morning, Frankie spoke with Louise & informed her of the latest with Allison.

"She has no idea who she's messing with." Louise said as she topped off her mimosa with the finest champagne.

It was decided they'd act against Bailey's mother. They woke up Allison to get more details & then headed into the higher courts of Philly to make their move.

Meanwhile, in the homes of Trinity, Naree, Emma, & Scarlett, turmoil had been cast down. They were preparing to say their final goodbyes to someone who changed their lives, forever- *Bailey Nicole Brooks*.

With heavy hearts & strained thoughts, each girl managed to make it to the doors of Heaven's Gates' Funeral Home.

Friends & family greeted one another as they filled the pews & passed along copies of the program. Everyone began to take in Bailey's casket, ombre pink & yellow- bright & beautiful just as she was. Bailey's mother walked in with her son, Brent. He too was struggling to keep it together. As they took their places in the front row, the doors closed & the most beautiful music began to fill the room. There wasn't a dry eye in the building.

When the music ended, Sara stood & made her way next to the Pastor onstage.

"Thank you all for being here today." She began as she choked back the cry her body wanted to let out so badly. Pastor Hues took the liberty of holding her steady.

"It means more than I could ever say to know that you all truly loved Bails. She was special. She knew what joy was & that's all she brought. She-" Sara fell to her knees, right above Bailey's casket. She rubbed it back & forth as her body let out every cry it fought to keep in.

"They killed my baby." She said sobbing in every way she never knew was possible.

Pastor Hues began to pray over Sara. Everyone stood & bowed their heads. She cried like a mother who would never see her child again.

Trinity left her seat. Naree followed. Emma stood & walked behind Naree. Scarlett joined them all. Together, they hovered over Bailey's casket & held onto Sara.

"Father God, we ask that you cover this family today, & that you lift them up. Father, God we know that you are the Alpha & the Omega, & that you will bring justice for this family if it's the last thing you do. Father, God we pray that you keep them, & that you let them feel you in their weakest moments. Amen."

"Amen." A man approaching Bailey's casket in disbelief said. Sara looked up & right into the eyes of Bailey's biological father, Riley. She knew not to cause a scene, but boy did he have some explaining to do. Sara put her head back down & continued to sob. The girls looked at Riley but didn't think twice about it. Pastor Hues continued the program. Sara stayed right there next to Bailey's casket. She invited the girls to stay as well. Bailey's father sat next to Brent in the front pew. Brent continued to mourn his big sister.

To the stage, Pastor called Trinity. She walked up & took the mic from him so that she could recite her poem.

"They said hashtag Broke Bailey (#BrokeBailey), but in turn- they BROKE BAILEY & now we sit here in a space she no longer belongs to.

An Academy for the rich, a building where they bend the rules.

Bailey was special. She was my best friend.

She was the greatest soul of all, she was connected.

I haven't slept in 7 days.

I couldn't save her on November 9th, but right now if I could just find a way – to keep her alive.

I've heard bullies will be bullies, but why did my sister have to die?" Trinity recited as she walked down the stage & back down to Bailey's casket.

Pastor Hues continued the program & began to preach his sermon about eternal life. Even though every girl had been raised with different religious backgrounds, they all believed they'd see Bailey again. It was time to open Bailey's casket. Staff from the Funeral Home began to orchestrate this task so that it could be done, properly. There lied Bailey- fair skin, beautiful blonde hair in the ponytail she loved wearing, & a neon skirt she would've loved, had she been here to see it. Her top was sheer & had lace that complimented the colors in her skirt. The mortician did an amazing job with her makeup. No one could see the rope print that was tattooed across her throat. Nor could they see the pain in Bailey's eyes, she was finally at peace. Staff directed everyone to view Bailey, one row at a time. Everyone stopped & stared. Bailey's grandparents were torn to pieces. They sat with Brent who couldn't even make it to the casket to see her. Bailey's Girls were the last ones standing. They all stood in formation over Bailey & turned to one another to do their secret handshake while holding onto her, for the last time. Sara's mother broke down again. This time, Riley was there to catch her. She was such a wreck, she didn't even recoil. She just laid there in his arms like a newborn baby, she cried like one too.

As the program ended, everyone prepared to travel to the burial grounds. Sara invited Riley to ride in the family limo with her, along with Trinity & the girls. The ride there was long & quiet, but the arrival was heavy. Family & friends gathered at Bailey's plot. Pastor Hues said his final words.

"For his anger endureth but a moment, in His favor is life: weeping may endure for a night, but joy cometh in the morning." Psalms 30:5

Friends & family laid roses on Bailey's casket. Riley walked up & placed the hospital band from his first & only visit with Bailey onto the casket. Sara stepped forward with Brent so that he could say his final words.

"Bailey, it's Brent. I heard what those girls did to you. I didn't know it hurt you until now. I'm going to miss you so much. You're the greatest big sister ever, my only sister... I never told you that. I don't know how I'm supposed to let you go." He managed to say while laying a stuffed bear onto her casket.

"I'm so sorry, Bailey. Mama is sorry. GOD TAKE ME WITH HER!" she begged as loudly as she could while attempting to open Bailey's casket. She cried loud enough to wake the dead. Her pain sent chills through every breathing body there. Brent ran to his grandparents & cried aloud as well. They comforted him.

Riley stepped up & gently peeled Sara's hands from the casket. He motioned for the undertakers to do their job & consoled Sara until she calmed down. Sara canceled the repast & informed everyone she needed some time alone. Every broken heart gathered to say their goodbyes. Sara's parents decided to take Brent with them so that Sara could have time to grieve alone. Sara got in the family limo & rode back to the funeral home before parting ways with Riley, Trinity, Naree, Emma, & Scarlett. The girls' families shared their condolences with her & offered their support. Standing in the parking lot was now Riley & Sara.

"How did you find out?" Sara questioned.

"News travels quickly to the parent of a child, ya know." Riley answered.

"You may have assisted with her coming into this world, but you are not her father!" Sara informed him.

"Let's not do this today, please. I know I shouldn't have just surprised you in this way, but now, I have no chance to repair what's been broken. We both lost." Riley rationalized.

"No. You couldn't have possibly lost someone you never had." Sara cried while opening the doors of her car.

"I know Todd has been in prison." Riley began.

"How dare you?!" she yelled.

"Listen- I didn't mean it that way." He tried to explain.

"Bailey is HIS daughter. You have no right to beat your chest, not TODAY! NOT EVER!" She yelled while getting into her car & driving away. Riley called after Sara but gave up after she made it further up the road.

As Sara drove home, she reflected on how today, Bailey should've been at school. She imagined her daughter doing what she did best, learning. Instantly, she hit a U-turn & headed to Ulysses Academy. She sped like a mad woman.

When she approached the doors of the UA, her stomach began to turn & boil with anger. She walked in & headed into the auditorium. It was empty, caution tape was the only décor in that space.

Sara walked up to the stage & immediately began to relive November 9th. She imagined Bailey, hanging there.

She knew the only hope remaining in her daughter's heart bled onto the stage that day. She envisioned her daughter lying where she fell when her friends got her down. She rested beside her, unhinged. Since this space was unoccupied, Sara hadn't been disturbed or found upon entering the building. Hours passed, & before she knew it, the bell was ringing to send everyone home. She sat upright & braced herself to go home as well. She rolled from the stage & onto the floor, hungover from grief. She got up & headed back to the main entrance.

"OH MY GOD! What is she doing here?" a student whispered as she walked the hall.

"Someone! Notify Counselor Strickland!" Mrs. Albright responded.

Sara's mind was beyond her, she didn't hear a thing. She kept walking until she made it to the foyer, where Allison, Maci, & Kaylee stood, making amends.

"AGHHHHH, you killed my daughter!" She yelled running full force into their circle.

Every student there began recording her rant.

"Call your dad!?" Maci yelled.

Allison called him quickly, but she had no time to talk. Her phone fell to the ground as she panicked.

"YOU KILLED MY DAUGHTER. IT WAS YOU, YOU, &
YOU." She yelled again & again, pointing.

"Oh, woe is me, Old Lady. Shouldn't you be at a
funeral or something?!" Allison snarled.

"Allison!" Kaylee snapped.

"Bailey told me everything you three did to her.
Doesn't matter if Frankie Parker gets you off, you're not off
with me!" Sara yelled.

"They tortured my baby. Aren't you listening? Did
you see them do it? She said it happened every day. She said
they spit on her! Smeared shit on HER! THEY PAINTED HER
FACE LIKE A CLOWN & STRIPPED HER OF HER CLOTHES
FOR YOU ALL TO SEE!" She cried as she turned to students
who were gathering around.

"Will somebody say something?!" she yelled.
Reaching for any ounce of validation.

Students began to whisper amongst themselves.
Teachers rushed down the halls to the foyer. Counselor
Strickland approached Bailey's mother & rubbed her back.

"Mrs. Brooks, please let me walk to your car."
Counselor Strickland pleaded.

"NO. I'm not leaving until they admit what they did.
Do you hear me?! Did you know?!" She asked.

"I'm not sure what you're referring to but if you just let me walk you to-" Counselor Strickland began again.

"I said I am NOT leaving until they admit what they did. Allison Parker, Maci Karr, & Kaylee Lopez bullied my daughter every day! They drove my baby to feel absolutely nothing. You were here! She said they ended up in classes with her late in the semester. Didn't you notice anything at all?" Sara informed & asked again.

"Did you?" Maci asked Sara.

Sara leaped forward & nearly snatched the soul from Maci's body. She hit the floor.

"You're going to jail! You just wait!" Allison said as she went for her phone on the ground. Mr. Parker heard everything.

Sara then grabbed Allison & dragged her to the ground. She shook her & begged for her to admit that she bullied her daughter.

"Say you did it! You rich little shit! Say you did it. Broke whore, weak bitch- remember?! She slapped the taste from Allison's mouth. Strickland went to grab her & was punched in the face.

Kaylee helped Maci from the floor. Allison yelled for help, but everyone was so enveloped in obtaining the footage, that they didn't think to offer a hand.

"I know what'll do it." Sara said as she began lifting her dress up. She snatched her underwear down in a frenzy of rage & squatted on top of Allison. Allison's eyes grew wide, she yelled for help.

"Oh shit!" A student yelled.

"She's pissing on Allison! Mama gone mad y'all!" Another student yelled as they moved in for a closeup.

Deputies from Philly PD charged the doors & began going for Mrs. Brooks. They demanded everyone to make way as they slammed her to the ground & slapped her in handcuffs.

"She just needs some rest, okay; you don't have to do this. Her daughter attended this school. She committed suicide in our auditorium. Her funeral was today." Strickland explained as she began to shed tears herself. Guilt was settling in because she played a hand in Bailey's death.

"Maim, I'm sorry, but we have a mental health warrant for this arrest." Officer Bolin responded as they read Sara her rights.

"Those bitches killed my baby! Maci you're next! Allison Parker pissed on my daughter, so I pissed on her! You bullied the wrong kid! You hear me?! YOU BULLIED THE WRONG FUCKING KID!" Sara shouted as they hauled her away.

Allison stood to her feet more embarrassed than ever before.

"I hope you all don't believe that peasant." She exclaimed as she hurriedly darted to the entrance doors. Maci & Kaylee took off behind her.

Bailey's Girls hadn't been to school since her suicide, but after the funeral, their parents convinced them to go for the remaining half of the day. They stayed behind to collect all their missing assignments, so they weren't aware of the commotion. As Trinity, Naree, Emma, & Scarlett began to exit the building, they noticed the gathering of their peers & the Authorities driving away. Indistinct chatter poured into the room.

"I wonder what happened?" Scarlett conveyed to the girls.

"I don't really care." Trinity said.

"Right. They should be celebrating Bailey's life today, like we did." Naree sadly agreed.

"I was just-" Scarlett began.

"Yea. I know. I'm sorry." Trinity expressed.

"Did y'all see? Bailey's mom went bonkers again, but this time she peed on Allison!" Joshua reported.

"Again? What do you mean?" Emma asked.

"Oh. Yea. You all have been out since..." He began.

"Yea." Trinity finished.

"Bailey's mother comes up here every day & she calls out Allison Parker, Maci Karr, & Kaylee Lopez. She says they killed Bailey Brooks. I personally believe it. Those girls are going to hell in first class." He continued.

"Yea, look. I've got videos." Jessica added in, making herself relevant.

The girls took some time & looked at the footage on Jessica's phone. They even watched the theatrics from today, it was a lot to take in.

"Guess we missed a lot." Trinity said.

"Uh, yea we did." Emma added.

"We've got to help Bailey's mom. She doesn't deserve to be in jail." Trinity plotted as her foot hit Allison's phone.

"What can we do?" Scarlett asked.

"Trin, let's take your car to the police station. We can start there. Naree orchestrated.

Jessica & Joshua found their way back to the crowd. Trinity noticed the phone next to her foot & decided to pick it up. She touched the screen, & vain as day, there she was- the wicked witch of Ulysses Academy. She powered it off & slipped it into her pocket before anyone could notice.

Trinity transported everyone to the Philadelphia Police Department. They contacted their parents & informed them of their whereabouts & then continued with their mission. Naree did the talking when they made it in. The officer on duty informed her that the deputies took Sara to the Psych unit at Philadelphia Patients & Associates' Hospital, under a mental health warrant issued from the higher courts. Naree requested a copy, but the officer refused- until he couldn't get her to leave.

"Allison's father initiated this warrant!" Naree shared.

"The lengths these people will go to!" Scarlett yelled.

"Hey, your mother works there, right?" Trinity inquired.

"Yea. We've got this in the bag!" Naree confirmed as she dialed her mother back.

Bailey's Girls made it to Philadelphia Patients & Associates.

"Hi, could we please visit Sara Brooks?" Emma requested.

"I'm sorry. No visitors at this time." Nurse Patricia informed.

"But she's all alone." Emma added.

"I'm sorry but-" Nurse Patricia began.

"Come on Pattie. Mrs. Brooks needs us right now." Naree stated as she began to take over.

"Naree. Baby, what are you doing here?"

"Let me handle this, guys- I saved her from losing her job with this mouth of mine." Naree whispered to them as she stepped up.

"What?!" Trinity shouted as the girls giggled.

"Not like that." Naree laughed. It was the first time any of them laughed since Bailey's suicide.

"Pattie, remember you said you owe me one."

"I know but the same Doctor who had my ass that day is here & I don't want to give her something else to gripe about. Please understand."

Naree folded her arms across the counter.

"Oh Ms. Pattie, I understand. I'm sure you'd also understand if I decided to clear my conscience & tell Dr. Landry that you were sleeping with her husband in the operating room after all."

"She's on the Psych floor, being held for observation. Please go to unit 13, she's in room 5."

"Thanks, Pattie." Naree smiled & winked as she motioned for the girls to follow along.

"She was sleeping with the Doctor's husband?" Trinity asked.

"I walked in on her & Mr. Landry going to pound town when I was trying to find a hideout to study in. They didn't even try to stop until I literally turned the light on. He won't even look my way now." Naree laughed.

"That is hilarious!" Scarlett shrilled.

"Yep." Shortly after, Dr. Landry entered the hall to locate Pattie because her med cart had been sitting for too long. She was on the verge of being reported to the Board of Nursing for shift abandonment." Ree further explained.

The girls gasped.

"Yikes!" Emma exclaimed.

"Yea & Dr. Landry was ironically heading right to that room, as I was running out. I stopped her & just started blabbing per usual & told her Patty was upstairs, having a hard time after the death of a patient."

"Oh God. Why would you say that?" Emma asked.

"Because it was true. She just so happened to be grieving with Mr. Landry."

The girls laughed again.

"Okay, guys we're here. We've got to be tough for Mrs. Brooks." Trinity instructed.

"Okay, got it. Tighten up girls." Naree encouraged.

They paced themselves & exited the elevator. Room 5 was to the right, so they walked slowly & together.

"Look, there she is." Scarlett pointed.

Mrs. Brooks was given a sedative to calm down. She sat in her room, staring at the wall.

The girls knocked & slowly opened the door.

"Mrs. Brooks!" Trinity yelled as she ran to hug Bailey's mother.

"Girls! What are you all doing here?" Sara asked as tears fell.

"We came as soon as we saw those videos." Naree said as she went in for a hug. Emma & Scarlett joined.

"Oh great. More videos." Sara facepalmed. "I'm sorry you all had to see me that way. I just cannot believe that Bails is gone. She was my only daughter."

"Well thanks to her, you've gained 4 more." Emma said, clutching her hand. Mrs. Brooks smiled.

They sat on the bed with Mrs. Brooks & relayed their deepest condolences. Everyone shared their most favorite memories of Bailey Nicole. Mrs. Brooks explained to them that due to her state of mind, she must be held for at least 72 hours or until she shows improvement. Naree handed Mrs.

Brooks the mental health warrant that landed her there. She became triggered all over again when she saw Mr. Parker's name, but she knew there was nothing she could do from a Psych unit.

Instead, she encouraged the girls to finish out their school year & to commit to their studies so that they could get out & make great lives for themselves, far away from bullies & bitches who want to be top dogs but can't handle being pissed on. Time was winding down, Naree's mother, Sena knocked on the door.

"I figured I'd find you all here." She said with the warmest smile.

"Hi, Mom." Naree greeted, squeezing her tight.

"Hi, Mrs. Gem." Trinity, Emma, & Scarlett greeted as well. Sena rushed over to embrace Sara. She informed her she petitioned to work her unit tonight. Sara expressed her appreciation & began to cry again. "You girls go ahead & get home. I've got it from here."

"Before we go. Mrs. Brooks, there's something we should tell you." Trinity said as she stood up.

"What's wrong girls? Did someone hurt you?" Sara asked.

"No. Those girls hurt Bailey, & we think there may be something more to all of it." Trinity explained.

"I'm lost & hurt too Trin, but I honestly believe those girls are just rich & entitled. Not used to being penalized for their actions. There couldn't possibly be-" Sara explained.

"Bailey said it." Naree admitted. Silence struck the room like lightning, as Bailey's mother grabbed her chest & stood up.

"Yea, she did." Emma confirmed.

"She told us that Allison's bullying felt personal." Scarlett added.

"What else did she say? I've got to get out of here." Sara said grabbing her things. Sena grabbed her by the arms & led her back to her bed.

"Girls. Mrs. Brooks must get some rest. We can figure this out when she's feeling better." Sena said tapping into her role.

"Okay, but Mrs. Brooks, I promise, we'll get to the bottom of this. We owe it to Bailey. We owe it to you. Could we please just go by Bailey's room? I think she may have left something behind, something we can use." Trinity pleaded.

Sara scrambled through her bag, digging for her keys. She handed Trinity a spare & encouraged her & the girls to do what was necessary to put Bailey at peace. The girls took the keys & pocketed them as they said their goodbyes to Sara & Sena. They headed out & went straight to Bailey's home.

When they arrived, the house was cold. The rush wore off as they began to remember hanging with their best friend in *this* home. They held hands as they made their way to Bailey's room. Before they began to search, they promised to keep everything the way she had it. The death of Bailey motivated them to take revenge against each bully responsible for her tragic ending.

"So that none of us are confused here. The plan is to make Allison Parker, Maci Karr, & Kaylee Lopez *pay* for the death of Bailey Nicole Brooks." Trinity announced.

"Yea & to end bullying for every victim whose life is impacted by this shit daily!" Naree added.

"There we have it, ladies. Our revenge pact shall be named: hashtag Game on For Bailey (#GameOnForBailey), we will utilize this to honor her forevermore." Trinity orchestrated.

"I'm all here for it. Those bitches want to make social media pages; we'll make em' too! We will start a movement like they've never seen before! #GameOnForBailey will be etched into the brain of every skull operating on any social media platform!" Emma shouted.

"I can see it now. We will end bullying, depression, & social suicides- one ambush at a time." Scarlett proudly confirmed.

The girls executed their secret handshake & split to cover different areas of Bailey's room. They found school photos & gifts they had given to her over time. They reminisced about how much they missed their dear friend. Melancholy filled the room, as they could tell Bailey's mother had been sleeping in her bed; there were empty bottles of wine & stacks of family photo albums surrounding the area. Once it reached midnight, they agreed to stop digging, & vowed to return another day.

Chapter 3

<u>Wrong Place, Wrong Time</u>

The girls continued to plan operation #GameOnForBailey, but they also decided to create a company that would ultimately change the game, *We Bitchin Fashion*!

Wake-Up Philly became their home away from home. They spent endless hours discussing their tactics & how they'd utilize everything they had to offer to take down Allison, Maci, & Kaylee for good. They valued the importance of education, so they promised to use their intelligence rather than violence. Despite them all coming from poor & dysfunctional families, you could bet your bottom dollar that each girl had something grand to offer.

Trinity's a clever Computer Hacker; she possesses quite the brilliance for any computer or gadget with a smart chip & has a GPA of 4.2. Naree's an eloquent & excellent Speaker & Communicator; negotiates like a pro with a GPA of 4.3. Emma's gifted when it comes to numbers, a Mathematician if you will. She's also a Fashion Designer & works diligently to uphold her 4.1 GPA. Scarlett's got a knack for the outdoors- camping & hunting is her bread & butter. Her grandfather ensured throughout their ventures that she was skilled in target shooting; she could literally take out a deer or a human with one kill shot. To no surprise, she conquered a formidable GPA of 4.5 after gunning for it!

As the girls put their heads together, they figured the best way to get vengeance on those snobby bitches was by hitting them where it hurt the most, their pockets. It was evident to them that *they* should become millionaires, in the name of Bailey. While doing so, they'd tarnish the reputations of each bully by exposing them to parts of their worlds that mattered.

"I am so sick of spoiled rich girls looking down on us & people like us because we're less fortunate." Trinity began.

"& less pretty." Emma added.

"Don't say that." Scarlett spilled in shock.

"Well, she's right. We don't *glow* like *they* do." Naree confirmed.

"More the reason we take our turn & show them what it feels like to be without." Trinity stated with an umph.

"What are we gonna do?" Naree questioned.

"Everything. But let's start with We Bitchin Fashion." Trinity answered.

"Would you all like the usual?" The Barista asked.

"Actually, Samantha, we were just talking about shaking shit up a bit." Trinity responded on behalf of them all.

The girls gave each other the eye, ordered a round of lattés & iced coffees they hadn't tried before, & told Samantha to spruce it up with Bailey's favorite thing, extra caramel. This moment solidified a turn of events for them. Samantha delivered their drinks & added one in dedication to Bailey.

Shits about to get real." Naree said as she held her latté in the air. One single tear crept down the right side of her face.

"In the name of Bailey, we will become millionaires by Senior year." Trinity joined, choking back sobs of her own.

"Millionaires by Senior year? I can dig it." Emma agreed while raising her iced mocha.

"Like a grave, like a grave." Scarlett committed with the raise of her iced mocha as well.

Bailey's latté sat in the center of the table, wafting steam into the air.

"We Bitchin Bitches!" The girls toasted in unison.

Bailey's mother was released from Philadelphia Patients & Associates' & life did what it did best, it went on.

Bailey's Girls dove full force into their mission, but after 6 months of presenting their business plan to local companies, they were burnt out & ready to give up. Turned out, gaining capital for We Bitchin Fashion was much harder than they imagined. At this point, they went everywhere they could, no one took them seriously.

"We're just a bunch of kids." Naree said as she & the girls sat in their favorite booth at Wake-Up Philly. Tonight's special was disappointment, with a side of doubt.

"Yea, millionaires where? By Senior year? Emma huffed, sipping & sulking in pity.

"We can't do this. It was a great idea, but we cannot do this. We must honor her another way. Maybe we could just-" Scarlett confessed.

"No. Trinity firmly responded. A mysterious man entered the coffee spot & sat at a booth next to Bailey's Girls. It was about 15 minutes to closing, so it was just him & them in the building, along with the Barista, Ryan Sanders.

"We have our plan & we're sticking to it. We can't give up on Bailey. I can hack Mr. Parker's account to obtain the capital we need to begin our company & stay afloat until we acquire our revenue." Trinity began.

"I'm with that. We said we'd hit them where it hurts." Naree stated, picking herself back up.

"Yea, like we literally have everything it takes to do this. Between your hacking skills, Naree's negotiation tactics, Scarlett's precision with target shooting & the outdoors, & my flair with numbers- we've got this! I can even manage the accounts & draw up estimates for how we can utilize the funds wisely. Scarlett can be on the lookout outside of Parker's residence while you find their weak spot on the inside." Emma continued.

"I'm sorry girls, but I do not feel comfortable with hunting Mr. Parker & his family, nor do I feel at ease with Trinity using her skills to take money that's not ours. We need to keep this clean so that our plans don't go corrupt. We could get into major trouble & lose every single scholarship we have lined up for college. Is that what you all want?" Scarlett questioned.

"Scar, chill. Let me unpack this for you. It's no big deal. My mother gets behind on rent sometimes, which means I don't have money for school clothes, supplies, or shoes. Hell, Trey sneaks food home from the diner, they get tired of him doing that- even though they'd have him trash it all anyway. I can't just sit back & do nothing, especially when it's all because my father decided he'd like to skip out on child support for a few months. We're left to fend for ourselves, so, when necessary, I hack my father's account to take the money he owes, so that life can be just a little easier for my mom. I make the swipe reflect as a garnishment, he's none the wiser." Trinity explained.

"Wow. You're a BOSS! What else have you done?" Naree inquired with cheer as Scarlett sat speechless.

"I've also gone into the portal of our rental office's platform & sent a bug to the owner's email which allowed me to access their systems, my mom didn't have to worry about rent for a while. She was informed of anonymous payments from a charitable organization, she never knew it was me. I don't use my hacking for bad. I use it to ... *level the playing field.*" Trinity unfolded.

"We all have GPAs ranging above 4.0, we're no fools. We can do this. How bout you just see for yourself?" Naree explained in attempt to comfort Scarlett.

"Hi there. My name is Ray." The mysterious guy began as he spoke from his booth.

The girls sat in silence.

"I know you don't know me, but I can really help you girls."

"We don't talk to strangers, Sir." Emma responded. The girls were terrified. He was a grown-ass man. What did he mean he could *help* a group of teenage girls?

"Wait a minute. Maybe we should hear him out. What's the worst that could happen?" Scarlett said with relief.

"I have the answer to your problems. If you'd just allow me a moment of your time, I can make things happen for all of you."

Desperation leaked from their pores, so they decided to discuss their plan more in-depth with this Ray character. After all, he was a well-dressed gentleman. They invited him over to their booth, & Naree took it away. Out of the girls, she was more vocal & aggressive, so she handled him accordingly. She expressed their problems & their mission, in great detail; from Bailey's suicide to their encounters with these bullies, & how revenge is due to hold Parker, Karr, & Lopez accountable for all they've done.

It was apparent that he was uninterested in anything relayed to him, he was 100% laser-focused on Trinity. He felt he could use her hacking skills to his advantage. Naree sensed he had an ulterior motive, however, she still felt through his confidence, his vibes were good enough to propose another meeting. Naree asked Ray to think about their business offer & to meet with them the following day for confirmation.

Ray envisioned Trinity as an asset to his boss' crime organization; they were lacking, her talent would catapult them to head of the cartel game.

As they sat & continued to converse with Ray, another mysterious man entered Wake-Up Philly looking for him. Things immediately began to take a horrible turn, as the guy approached him & began to scream about a deal gone bad.

"It's all your fault. Frost is dead because of the intel you gave us! You set us up!" Nichola yelled.

Ray stood ten toes in front of Nichola & pulled out his gun with no response. He shot him several times. The girls took a run for it to the back of the coffee shop. They watched Ray empty his clip into the chest of a man who seemed to have gotten the shit end of the stick. They proceeded to run for their lives. They barely escaped & were terrified beyond belief of the horrific murder they just witnessed.

"Well, there goes redemption." Naree stated.

At this point, they knew they were in grave danger because there was no way to leave the coffee shop without crossing paths with him. Ray called an associate to assist with locating Bailey's Girls. They were found in a hidden storage closet at the back of the coffee shop. Ray & his associate escorted the four friends to their crime boss. During the transition, everyone was crying & sobbing, except Naree.

"Listen. We're smart girls. We've got ideas that will completely elevate your organization. I know you need help because I sensed your lust for a come-up at the booth. You need something from us or at least one of us. We've all got something to offer."

"Stop talking." Ray instructed.

"Yea, Ree. This is not the time." Scarlett agreed.

"No! This IS the perfect time. Tell him who we are." Trinity pleaded with hopes that Naree's mouth could save them.

"We can assist with hacking; Trinity's got a mean streak for getting what she wants. Ha, & I know you've heard of a kill shot! If Scarlett gets her hands on your man's gun over there, she could take y'all out right now, she never misses a shot."

Ray stopped in his tracks. "I said stop talking."

"I would but Emma can do anything with numbers. She's like crazy special or something, you wouldn't believe it."

"Oh yea, & what can you do?" Ray asked, chuckling aloud.

"Well, let's do business & you'll see. Seems like the corpse in front of our booth had a problem with the way you orchestrate things, I can handle any business deal, nice & easy."

Ray was intrigued but he knew they had to die.

"We have skills that will enhance your transactions & increase your profits. We can even pose undercover for your business. Who would suspect a group of grieving, teenage girls?" Naree went on.

Trinity, Emma, & Scarlett feared Naree's proposition to spare their lives, but if it worked- they had no choice.

As Ray approached the boss' office, he pushed Bailey's Girls in because they were eyewitnesses. The boss was furious that Ray brought 4 young teen girls to him.

"Why are they alive & breathing? They should've been taken care of already." He asked.

Ray's boss, Bennie, went for his gun & aimed it at Ray's head for exposing his secret location to four young, teenage girls. Just before the crime boss blew Ray's head off, he froze in disbelief.

He lowered his gun while the girls continued to cry & beg for their lives. Naree desperately vocalized the importance of keeping them around. Ray snatched her by the throat & prepared to snap her neck. Her feet dangled from off the floor, she was so scared- she finally stopped speaking. Bailey's Girls cried harder.

The boss took a long look at Scarlett & stared at her as if he entered another world. Finally, he asked her to step forward. She stepped forward with tears in her eyes.

"This is it; I'm going to die. I love you Trin, Em, & Ree." Scarlett shut her eyes & flinched at the thought of dying.

He walked toward her & extended his hand out to touch her face. Scarlett opened her eyes & trembled in confusion. She wasn't sure why he was touching her face. He walked back to his desk, opened a drawer, & took out a photo. He walked back over to Scarlett & lifted the photo in the air.

"Is this you & your mother?" he asked.

Scarlett was stunned for a hot second, but she slowly responded.

"Yes. It is. But why do you have a picture of me & my mom?" She said as she began to relax.

Ray unhanded Naree, she fell to the floor & fought for air. Bruises stained her neck, tracing the hands of a man gone mad.

Everyone stood in silence, awaiting his answer. He responded in shock, "Because you are my daughter, & your mother is my wife."

It was at that moment that the girls' lives changed drastically, instantly, & forever. After witnessing the murder at Wake-Up Philly, it was official, - they'd be entering the business world, just not the way they planned. Bennie decided not to kill them, instead, he proposed an offer- their skillsets in wager of their lives.

Bailey's Girls were now embarking on a dangerous path. In hindsight, they felt it could bring them much closer to revenge on Allison, Maci, & Kaylee. Grief & crime go hand in hand after all. Wouldn't you agree?

~~Chapter 4:~~

Family Secrets

12 hours later, Bailey's Girls were alive & well, sifting through their thoughts, gathering how they'd fit in a world of criminal activity. As they sat in Naree's basement, emotions began to brew.

"This is all your fault. You just had to engage in conversation with that man!" Emma fired.

"Are you kidding me? I was trying to be GAME ON FOR BAILEY & y'all were being a bunch of pussy cats!" Scarlett fired back.

"Pussy cats? Oh, please- come a little bit harder than that, Scar. You had an issue with me hacking Mr. Parker's accounts to get OUR business off the ground- when it's HIS daughter that drove Bailey to hang herself in front of every student at Ulysses Academy!" Trinity spat right back.

"Trin, STOP!" Emma began.

"No! We wouldn't have even needed to grovel to some weirdo named Ray had you truly been GAME ON FOR BAILEY! We're supposed to do whatever it takes! Look at how quickly you forgot about that! Now, we must conform to becoming miscreants because apparently, your father wants to *use* a bunch of teenage girls, including his own fucking daughter!"

"Trinity, that's too far. We don't speak to one another that way. Last night was out of everyone's control." Emma stated, attempting to de-escalate.

"Yea, it's giving mean girl, Trin." Naree agreed.

"Nah, it's giving pedophile, if you ask me." Trinity blatantly responded.

The room fell silent. Scarlett's head hung low. She was just as taken aback as the rest of the girls, if not more. Trinity began to feel bad for her outburst, but she stood behind every word.

"Girls. We can't do this. Not today. We've got to get our stories together, our heads together, our alibi together. You know how the game goes; Wake-Up Philly is *our* spot. Cops might suss us out to take note of our whereabouts; we have to say we left before anything went down. The barista works for those horrible people- no offense Scarlett, so he won't say anything. We left 15 minutes to closing after discussing our school project. That's the story. Afterwards, we came to my house because my mother wasn't home from work yet." Naree suggested.

"She's right. We've got bigger fish to fry right now. We cannot waste time on petty things." Emma added.

"We went from becoming our own boss to being somebody's bitch in less than 15 minutes. I don't find that petty. I find it sad, so bite me, Emma. After all, you started this backlash. '*This is all your fault,*' remember?" Trinity mocked.

"Trinity. We get it. You're BIG mad. You were in charge, & now you're not." Emma snarled.

"Wrong. It's not that *I* was in charge, WE were in charge. How do we get our revenge if we're playing on a team that doesn't give a damn about Bailey? It's not fair to us. It's for damn sure not fair to Bailey." Trinity admitted as she choked back silent tears.

"That's true." Emma admitted.

"It's all good." Trinity chuckled, lightly. The ice had been broken.

"I'm sorry. I'm very sorry, I get it Trin, I do, but maybe we're looking at this the wrong way." Scarlett began.

"Yea. This could actually work to our advantage. We didn't die. Don't you all realize that? We were within an inch of our lives & we did not DIE! But Bailey did. We've got to snap out of this fear & go harder so that we can truly avenge her death. Her suicide will not be in vain. It doesn't matter if we don't get to start the way we planned, all that matters is we finish what we've started!" Naree explained.

Every eye in the room connected. Boy did Naree know how to set the record straight. The tension broke between the girls & they began to remember their purpose.

"I have to meet with him today." Scarlett began.

"Him who? That criminal who calls himself your father?" Trinity questioned, nonchalantly.

"Trinity?!" Emma shrieked.

"I didn't mean it that way, Scar. I'm sorry. It's just weird that suddenly he wants to meet you after Naree told him what you're capable of. What we're all capable of." Trinity expressed.

"I haven't seen him since I was 2 years old, yet he knew I was his daughter. Did you see the way he looked at me? He must love me. If he's as bad as we think he is, then maybe that's why he left, to protect la Familia (the Family). I say we use it to our advantage though. I'll confirm exactly what he wants from us & then I'll tell him what we need in return." Scarlett established.

"Now we're talking. We could truly be the baddest bitches in Philly! Parker, Karr, & Lopez won't even know what hit 'em! We'll have one thing we never even imagined...." Naree rallied.

"POWER!" They all cheered in unison.

Bailey's Girls shared a long hug & headed back to Wake-Up Philly so that Scarlett could meet her father without feeling uncomfortable. They avoided sitting at their favorite booth, all they could imagine was the murder that happened not even 24 hours prior. Ryan closed the doors & escorted Scarlett to the back of the shop. Trinity, Naree, & Emma gave her a nod of reassurance. Scarlett continued to the back but was taken into a different room than before. She spotted the barista's gun & prepared herself for the worst. If he tried anything, she was going to kill him- lucky enough, she didn't have to.

"Mí amor (My love), right this way. Bennie Perez instructed, seating Scarlett at his desk. Scarlett analyzed the room & quickly began to see that Wake-Up Philly had been a front all along; there was an entire operation being run right under the noses of cops who faithfully came in for a fresh cup of coffee, every day. "*Who the hell is this man?*" She wondered.

"It's been so long, mi hija (my daughter). I-"
"No. You don't get to do that with me. I want to know who you are & what you want from me & my friends." She interrupted.

"I understand this is a lot for you. I never imagined we'd meet under these circumstances, mi hija (my daughter). I am your father. I am also the head of a drug cartel & have been for a long time. Believe it or not, your mother was once part of this life too. When we found out she was pregnant with you, I vowed to care for you both, but your mother escaped me & my men. I was under the impression that we'd be a family, I guess she didn't like the idea of remaining low-key, but it had to be that way. I searched for you for many years, & then auge (boom), you found me." He thoroughly explained.

"I understand this bonding thing you're trying to do, but there's something seriously wrong with this story. You left us & never came back. There was no laying low, & my mother would never be part of any drug cartel, ha- estas muy loco (you are very crazy)." She giggled, nervously.

Bennie stood from his desk & walked over to his file cabinet. He pulled out a set of folders & handed them to her. She took the time to review them & saw that Papà was not lying. Between the crevice of each folder laid photos of her mother from the cartel, jobs that had been done by her, & evidence of an investigator, Taylor Hawkins, tracing the edges of the earth to find her. Scarlett threw the folders & deflected.

"It's all fabricated. Trinity could put together the same shit & make it pop just like this! It's not true. You didn't try hard enough! Do you know how important it is for a chica (girl) to have her Padre (Father)?" I looked for you, no fue justo para mí (it wasn't fair to me)!" She yelled.

Bennie walked closer to Scarlett & grabbed her tightly, she recoiled again & again. She didn't want to believe a word he said, but the proof was in the mocha-colored folders. She finally allowed him to console her, she cried like the 2-year-old she was when she saw him last. Bennie's men turned & faced the wall out of respect. On duty was Ryan, the Barista, Jase Marino, Carlos Reyes, & Nest Boswell. Bennie's right hand, Harvey Ross, was present but he exited the room to dismember Nichola's body, he was good at making people disappear- which is why he was Bennie's favorite.

"Padre (Father), I don't know what to say, how to feel. It's been years. You were just about to kill me & my friends but now we're supposed to kumbayá? Let's not forget to mention you want us to work for you now, in exchange for sparing our lives. Is my being your daughter not enough? You say you've been looking for me all these years, is this how you think fathers do things when they finally find their kid? You do understand that right? I'm a kid. A smart one. I've got offers from prestigious universities, & I have always been top of my class. I-" She ranted on.

"Te entiendo (I understand you), mi hija (my daughter), crees que no te conozco (you think I don't know you). I may not know your nickname or your favorite color, but I know that you're a killer. You're my daughter. You've been an assassin in the making, you just didn't know it. Your grandfather's blood runs just as cold as mine. You must trust me, mí amor (my love). I run a very tight ship, every man you see here works for me, they're my best guys but I must bring something new to the table, undetected- that's where you & your friends come in. This is Jase, he is going to take you home tonight. I'd like to meet again, but this time at another location. What do you say, mi hija (my daughter)?"

"You made your point last night. We have no choice but to work for you. We will comply under one condition." She began.

"I'm listening." Bennie confirmed, preparing to rebuttal."

"I had a friend named Bailey Brooks. She was one of the nicest girls I've ever met." She continued. Bennie's men all resumed their positions.

"She need help or something?" Bennie questioned.

"No. I do. Bailey hung herself in front of our entire school due to cruel & unusual punishment from girls named Allison Parker, Maci Karr, & Kaci Lopez. They bullied her to death, literally."

Bennie & Jase locked eyes.

"You know them?" Scarlett asked, scoping the energy around her.

"Not necessarily. However, the Parker name does hold some weight." Bennie confirmed.

"Well. My friends & I have chosen to bring the reckoning to each girl responsible for her suicide. We want revenge." Scarlet finished.

"Done." Bennie responded.

"You don't want to hear how?" she asked, confused.

"We're in two different worlds, mi hija (my daughter). I'm sure my men & I can handle a little high school revenge." He laughed.

"We also need to legitimately run our own business. Our goal is to become millionaires by Senior Year." Scarlett added.

"You drive a hard bargain, mi hija (my daughter)." Bennie acknowledged.

"Before Ray nearly snapped Naree's throat, you heard her say what we're all capable of. Do we have a deal?" She propositioned in a firm tone.

"You girls come by my office in uptown Philly. Jase will transport. Let's discuss what I need & if you all agree, then we're good here. If your friends don't comply, then I'm sorry, my men can't leave them breathing, mi hija (my daughter)."

Scarlett rose from her chair & nodded to confirm she was aware of the threat at hand. Jase escorted Scarlett back to the front of the store. The girls were happy to see she came back in one piece. Scarlett informed them Jase would be taking her home & also made them aware of the meeting scheduled with Bennie for tomorrow.

Scarlett's mind was consumed with betrayal from her mother, but she couldn't help but feel some sort of vibe between her & Jase. Just the smell of his cologne was enough to make her heart skip a beat. She input her address on his GPS & fell back. For all she knew, he killed people, she didn't wish to consort with anyone like that, but baby he was fine af (as fuck) to her. Had her on hush mode the entire car ride home.

"I'm sorry about the news Mr. Perez broke to you." Jase managed to say.

"Thanks." She responded while trying to avoid eye contact. She flashed a half smile & exited his vehicle. If she were a promiscuous girl, he would've gotten what she wanted to give, that's for sure.

Scarlett entered the doors of a home that felt like a lie. She decided that since her mother hid vital intel from her, she'd do the same. She was going into the family business & it'd be her little secret.

"Whose car was that?" Marcella asked.

Scarlett shrugged & headed to her room.

"Mi hija (My daughter), I'm talking to you." She reiterated.

"Well, mother. I'm happy to answer that question if you can explain your lies surrounding my father. Me dijiste que nos abandonó, pero no lo hizo, ¿verdad (You told me that he abandoned us, but he didn't, right)?"

Marcella stopped dead in her tracks & pondered carefully before uttering another word.

"Mi hija (My daughter)-?" she began, unsure of what to say.

"Mom." Scarlett pleaded in hopes of her father being the liar.

"He abandoned us by choosing a life he vowed to let go of." Marcella answered after taking a deep breath.

"& what life was that Madre (Mother)?"

"Who have you been speaking to? Tell me who was in that car!" Marcella demanded with guilt beaming from her soul.

"He was just a friend from school, & I saw Dad, okay! He told me-" Scarlett began.

"What did he say? What did he tell you? Where did you see him?" Scarlett's mother questioned in panic.

Scarlett knew not to say too much because come hell or high water, she was joining the drug cartel.

"None of those things matter, Mom. Don't you get it?! What matters is you lied to me! I needed my Padre (Father) all these years. You allowed me to feel rejected & unloved, why?" Scarlett cried.

"I'm so sorry, mi hija (my daughter). I was trying to create a better life for you. For us. I didn't know you felt those ways." Marcella shared.

"You never asked!" Scarlett yelled in response.

She continued to argue with her mother until they both grew tired. As the night came to an unbelievable closure, sunrise was making its big debut.

On Hempdale Dr., Sara was taking steps to heal from the loss of Bailey Brooks. She began with buying boxes to pack up Bailey's room, once & for all, but she simply could not do it. After her visit to Philadelphia Patients & Associates, she decided that she must fight for her daughter with the same gall, but tactfully so.

Sara had been so fractured that she became entertained & invested in the idea of working things out with Bailey's biological father, however, she knew he was no good for her. Sara only wanted him because he was the closest thing to having a resemblance to Bailey in her life. Her visits with Todd became toxic & draining; he wanted answers regarding Bailey's death that she could not give him. Things finally came to a head last week when he accused her of being so absent in Bailey's life that she felt neglected enough to hang herself in front of the entire school. Imagine his surprise when she rose from her side of the table to rip his head off & lick the bones afterwards. Multiple guards had to peel her off him, they swore Dracula made an appearance because there was so much blood. They carried her into the foyer of the prison & informed her that she'd be banned until further notice. She believed in whooping ass, "it's the only way some people learn to watch their mouths the next time around." She explained to the guards. Todd had scratches & bruises to recount that moment moving forward.

Meanwhile, in uptown Philly, Bennie & Bailey's Girls were meeting to hash out their expectations & kick off what's been anticipated to be an epic collaboration of minds.

"So, what are we talking here?" Naree asked Bennie.

"Believe it or not, I need to bring a different aspect to my cartel business. I need someone to look for the holes we miss when making our moves, el reparador, si quieres (the fixer, if you will). In layman's terms, I need an elite group that I can use to infiltrate every cartel operation there is, I believe that I can train you all to be that group." Bennie explained with his hands clasped together.

"What do we get in return?" Trinity responded, head cocked to the side.

"Well, besides your lives, my daughter tells me you all wish to become millionaires by Senior Year." He answered.

Scarlett cleared her throat.

"& she says you all are gunning to avenge your friend's death." Bennie continued.

Scarlett nodded in approval.

"Correct, her name is Bailey." Trinity agreed.

"So, what if we don't do this?" Emma questioned.

"It's simple. Te mato (I kill you)." He confirmed.

"Oh, I'm sorry, we don't speak-" Emma began.

"I kill you." Bennie translated.

The girls sat in silence for a moment.

"I guess we're in then." They all agreed in unison.

"Good. The ongoing mission is to force out drug cartels surrounding this region; once we do that, we can talk about your freedom or perhaps, taking over the world, one region at a time. My cartel organization is big, but I'm focused on an even bigger picture now. Beginning today, you work undercover for me. All operations are distributed by me. You report to me, me only. You work, I pay you- you cross me, I kill you, ¿Entendido (Understood)?"

"Si (Yes)." Bailey's Girls confirmed as they stood tall, overlooking the city from Bennie's high rise. It was time. Their time.

~~Chapter 5:~~

Smart Bitches

"We're officially funded!" Trinity announced, revealing the joint business account they all shared.

"Wow! It's truly happening." Naree sighed in disbelief.

"Yes! We've got so much to do! We can afford to have our company's entity established & trademarked now!" Scarlett shrilled.

"Our designs need to be protected as well. We cannot afford to be stolen from; this brand is far too personal." Trinity added.

"Correct, but since Mr. Perez gave us an advance, we also need to shift gears now. Trin, can you please conjure up something that'll keep our parents off our backs so we can attend the training camp for the cartel?" Emma began.

"Already on it, Em. I was thinking we could tell them we're all interested in attending a science fair or camp- something away from home, & that this camp or fair provides transportation- so they won't feel compelled to take us themselves." Trinity explained.

"Oooooo, yea, that sounds good, but our parents believe in doing their due diligence, they'll want to see some type of positive traction with this camp or fair. Could you-" Naree began.

"Create a site plastered with feedback from families talking this lovely place up? Sure can." Trinity smiled.

"Why must we even attend Cartel Camp? I've never heard of such a thing." Emma questioned.

"Nor have you ever been a hoodlum, honey." Naree explained.

"It's to prepare us for the unthinkable. We're intelligent, but we need to learn how to function like criminals who are in cartel gangs so that we can outwit them." Naree simplified.

"& maybe even kill them ..." Scarlett computed.

"No way. Perez didn't mention us becoming baby snipers- we're just going to be the magic behind *their* madness, providing them insight on how their operation could run much smoother." Emma stated with hopes that her outlook remained true.

The room became intense & final. Very quickly, they realized they weren't kids anymore. Tasks were delegated for both their company & the cartel. Trinity's responsibility lied in the completion of content to present to their parents for the hoax science camp or fair, Scarlett's task was to submit for their company's entity as a corporation & to trademark their brand's name, logo, & designs. Naree's job was to rub elbows with Perez to gain intel for their very first mission, & Emma, well she was officiated to launch part 1 of their revenge plot against Allision, Macy, & Kaylee.

Bailey's Girls worked hard to obtain some sort of normalcy at school & at home. At home, they communicated with their parents & spent time enjoying the little things, such as playing board games, arguing with siblings, doing homework, & watching their favorite television shows. Slowly but surely, they informed each parent of their elaborative plan to make a comeback for Bailey. Of course, they didn't provide the full ins & outs of their operation, but if the company were to be as grand as they expected, a heads-up would be in order. Their parents were supportive but naturally, their passion projected as a state of grievance; little did they know, these girls were grieving but they were also not playing around.

Continuing to attend Ulysses Academy felt like a betrayal to Bailey, especially when those simpletons still had the audacity to manufacture petty advances that made their lives a living hell. They knew they had to stick it out in order to execute their plan, effectively, so they dealt with the name-calling in front of their peers, speeches in the cafeteria meant to further demean them, & the altercations which often became physical. Allison had been spiraling lately, she was worse than usual. *Was it guilt?* The girls wondered. Too soon to tell, but they were going to find out.

Lately, Allison's father had been looking into Bailey's mother. He wanted to understand her obsession with his daughter. Initially, he didn't care too much to dabble in the logistics of female drama, but after he & his wife had to place a mental health warrant & a restraining order on her, they deemed her worthy of further investigation. Frankie rationalized Sara's deranged stunts as animosity from Bailey & Allison not getting along, but he knew there had to be something deeper. It was as if this family were toxically drawn to one another. Louise knew her daughter was no angel but considering their family secret; Allison racked up several passes to be the little shit she is.

While Allison trolled the hallways of the UA, Emma studied her & her crew for weaknesses. She determined the best strategy for revenge would be computing a cross-examination of everyone's whereabouts & encounters with Bailey before she died. "*Expose one. Expose them all.*" She jotted down.

The girls met at Wake-Up Philly to follow up on tasks delegated last week. Emma confirmed her grand plot was in motion, Trinity showcased the webpage for *Philadelphia's Science & Technology Tour;* a place where minds are empowered to elevate & pour into one another- only it didn't truly exist. Trinity passed out brochures so that the girls had something to provide to their parents before attending Cartel Camp. Scarlett provided documents of their company's submission to be trademarked, as well as incorporated. She also shared separate filings for protection of their designs.

Finally, the girls awaited Naree's report for their first mission. They were excited about the progress thus far, but their curiosity began to peek. Naree began to speak without sugar-coating a single thing.

"We have to swipe 10 million dollars from Perez's rival drug cartel." She announced.

"What?!" Scarlett laughed hysterically.

"10 million dollars- no way. We'd be murdered indefinitely if they ever found out." Trinity reasoned.

"I'm just the messenger." Naree stated.

"Actually, Trin, our lives are already at stake here. We've got to do it." Emma shared.

"Easy for you to say, I'm the hacker." Trinity snapped.

"We knew this wasn't going to be rubber bands & lollipops. We will back you, two thousand percent, Trin. We are your eyes & ears." Naree confirmed.

"She's right. He told me if you all don't cooperate, he's literally gonna kill you. I'd rather we fight to become bosses than for our parents to bury their children." Scarlett added.

"Oh, tough shit, Scarlett. He's not going to kill you, you're his daughter- so, why do you even care?" Trinity shot off again.

"I don't know that he won't kill me too, okay. Besides, no matter how much shit you give me about where I come from, I'm right here to the very end with you." Scarlett responded.

Trinity's heart sank to the bottom of her ass, she felt terrible.

"I'm sorry. I know you're in a tough spot. I just cannot believe we're doing this." Trinity expressed.

"Let's just continue to keep our future legacy & our company's mission in mind as we take these *assignments*. We cannot let Perez & his cartel come in between us." Naree explained.

"Let's keep Bailey in mind too." Trinity added.

"Right. We're only in this predicament because we were so hell-bent on avenging her death." Emma began.

"We still are." Scarlett confirmed.

"Then that's all that matters." Trinity declared.

"Well, I'm glad we could sort this out. We already know we must abide by Perez's rules to live. Let's just make life easier by working as a team. I've got intel right here on the biggest rivalry Perez has- their secret locations, residential addresses, & a list of police officers from Philly P.D. who are in their pocket." Naree shared.

"Dirty police officers? Why would we need that?" Emma questioned.

"Well, if we ever got busted, a little blackmailing could go a long way." Naree nudged.

"Riiight." Scarlett agreed.

"Oh my God, what have our lives become?" Emma asked.

"A motherfucking movie!" Trinity laughed. They all died laughing for a while together.

"Okay, it's game time girls." Scarlett established.

"Exactly, #GameOnForBailey that is!" Naree yelled as they cheered unanimously.

Although the town had been sleeping on Bailey's suicide, Bailey's Girls were not. After their meeting, they worked diligently to uncover all there was to know about Bennie's rival cartel, the Russian Mafia. Trinity hacked into their security surveillance cameras & sent the feeds over to Bennie. He was impressed with how quickly she got in, so he informed her he needed more. As she continued to dig, Benny sulked up every bit of the Mafia's drug operation. Emma was amazed at what Trinity could obtain by simply sending spam to the cell phone of Polina Orlov, daughter of the mafia's head & tale- Victor Orlov. Trinity also sent spam to Victor's right hand, Anton Orlov. She presumed he was into porn; her intuition was dead on. As soon as he clicked on the link she sent via email, she was able to monitor all data transferred through their network. She obtained the names they used for significant transactions, financial account information, & even email addresses from other big wig mafia members. They now had exactly what they needed to take what Bennie wanted- 10 million dollars. Emma provided new equipment requested by Trinity so that she could finalize the encryption needed to swipe the money without a trace. Scarlett purchased burner phones for cartel interactions only, she knew they'd need to cover their tracks one day. Their parents had begun to pry, so things were intense. Luckily, they always had an alibi.

Trinity's abilities were put to the ultimate test. The heat was on, & she knew she had to deliver- but could she really do it? Steal 10 milli from The Russian Mafia? ... after successfully sifting through emails of every mafia member, her fingers began to configure the logins. The girls surrounded her, sweating, eyes bucked, & on edge. Trinity requested Perez's Swiss account information & then made her final move.

Life was lonely on Hempdale Dr., Bailey's mother was fighting an internal war against herself. She wondered if there was any truth to Todd's backlash regarding Bailey's suicide. Before she began to sulk in her thoughts again, she heard the door rang.

"What are you doing here?" Sara asked as she opened the door.

"I just want to talk; I promise to leave as soon as you say the word." Riley answered.

Sara reluctantly opened the door & let him in. Their last encounter occurred after Bailey's funeral; she blew up on him- he was prepared for the same thing to happen, but she was *different* this time.

"I just want to see her room, if that's okay. I just really can't believe she's gone." He desperately explained.

"I understand. It's this way..." Sara said removing her hair from her face.

Riley walked into Bailey's room; it had been cleaned, & there were boxes stacked by the door.

"How have you been holding up?" He asked.

Sara sat on Bailey's bed & grabbed her favorite yellow, squishy pillow nearby. She clutched it to her heart & stared into his eyes.

"I tried to pack her things, I can't. My son hasn't been home since the funeral because my parents think I'm mentally unstable- which I clearly am not. My husband blames me for her death. I have a restraining order against me, as well as a hospital stay from Philadelphia Patients & Associates' psych ward on my record because I attacked Allison Parker." She unloaded.

Riley sat on Bailey's bed next to Sara.

"Was I truly not paying enough attention to my daughter?" She asked rhetorically, staring into the open air. "Bails, come back to me." she cried, plummeting to the floor. Riley kneeled & attempted to console her.

"Whatever I say may not comfort you at this time, but please know that you were a great mother to our daughter. I know that you loved her enough to call me when she needed help, that says a lot about your love. It's why I've always loved you." Riley admitted.

Sara sobbed hopelessly into his lap, she forgot how much she despised him. He stroked her hair & simply let her cry.

"Sara, you left me & raised her with someone better than me, so that she could have a better life. Look at what you gave her. I never had a room growing up, nor did I have things of my own. I've been in survival mode all my life, trying to grasp things that were never gifted to me. I'm just happy to know she had a roof over her head & was raised with love & freedom. You did that for her. I'm just sorry I couldn't have been more part of her story." He further explained.

"You were." Sara uttered as she wiped her face.

"She was furious when she found out I lied to her all those years, but she always asked about you. She wanted you around … I just couldn't bring myself to have you in my space again. I had my reasons, but had I known she was going to do this ... I would have never kept her from you." She cried again.

"She was such a beautiful girl. Her personality was bigger & brighter than anyone I know ... she was pure & sweet, rare. I let those girls ruin her." She went on.

"Ruin her? What girls?" Riley questioned, finally tuning in.

"Bailey was bullied & tormented by 3 girls for the past few years. I tried to take them on legally before she died but I lost. After she committed suicide, I went after every girl that bullied her. I cornered them at school, in parking lots, & at a place called The Social Bar. I tried to make them pay, but eventually, my antics imploded when the ringleader told her father on me ... & now I'm just... here." She unraveled.

He pulled her from his lap & hugged her tightly. He squeezed her the way he used to. She needed that. She hugged him in return & for a while. Time stood still; it was just them all over again. After their warm embrace, they immediately began to kiss one another. Each kiss felt like a door opening from the past. It got wider & deeper. They spilled into one another until their clothes came off. Passion was no match against a grieving woman, Sara unveiled her soul to Riley right on Bailey's bedroom floor. They made love, dangerous love- just like they used to. He was not finished with her though, he tossed her onto his mid-section & pinned her against the wall while glaring deeply into her eyes, it was as though they murmured "I've been needing you." She stared back, communicating with her eyes that she needed him too.

After quite some time reconnecting, they showered & began to fill one another out.

"I really didn't plan on this happening. I truly just wanted to have a piece of my daughter. I didn't get the chance to do right by her, ya know?" Riley expressed.

"I do, & maybe you would've if I didn't interfere. I have some albums of her, would you like to-" Sara initiated.

"Yes, I'd love to see them." He quickly answered.

Sara went into the kitchen & began to cook for the first time since Bailey's death. She prepared a nice meal from what was there & poured 2 glasses of wine for them to drink while they gushed over their beautiful baby girl.

"If only we could've done this together." Riley sang regretfully.

"We did." Sara responded as she took another sip of wine. For the first time in a long time, her house began to feel like home again.

~~Chapter 6:~~

<u>Target Practice</u>

"Ten million dollars. You just swiped ten million dollars." Naree announced.

Trinity double-checked the transaction & then blankly gawked at the computer screen.

"I just stole ten... million... dollars!" she said in awe.

"Tengo que llamar a papi (I have to call daddy)! This is amazing!" Scarlett shrilled as she took out her burner phone & dialed up Perez.

"Daddy!" She yelled.

"Yes, mi hija (my daughter)." He responded.

"It's done. Ten million dollars. I knew my sis would come through!" She screamed in excitement.

Bennie ended the call. Trinity lost her shit. She paced the floor in a manic state. The girls had never seen her like this before. Usually, she kept her cool about things.

"Trin, sit down, you're going to wake my parents. Are you okay?" Naree asked. Hell, she was getting nervous too.

Trinity didn't respond. She just kept pacing.

"Trinity!" Scarlett shouted.

"Shhhh!" Naree whispered.

"I'm sorry but she's freaking me out." Scarlett admitted.

"Trinity, STOP. You really need to chill out." Emma demanded. Trinity stared through Emma & sat down. Emma sat beside her & guided her through some deep breaths. Naree walked up to do what she does best.

"You did it, Trinity. I watched you pull off something that not even my father is capable of. Your encryption ensured there'd be no trace back to you or any of us- that was the most boss-ass move I've ever seen. You are untouchable." Naree explained, hyping her up.

"I have... never... saw that much... money... in my entire life." Trinity responded.

"Well, get used to it because we're in the big leagues now." Scarlett said as she began to feel herself.

"Pipe down, Sis. This was not okay." Trinity shared.

"What you did will go down in the history of cartel gangs. The Russian Mafia may be the biggest thing there is to fear, but how can they kill someone who's untraceable? You're a real badass, Trinity!" Naree finished.

Trinity sat upright & eyeballed the computer screen once more. She placed her hands on top of her knees &

rubbed them in a soothing manner. The girls surrounded her & began to hug & squeeze until she cracked a smile.

"I did it. I have no idea how I pulled this off." she said.

"The real mystery is what the hell Perez is going to do with ten million dollars & how he knew they had it. It's such a fixated request." Emma probed.

"Maybe they took ten milli from him, he'd never tell us anyway." Naree answered.

"After what Trinity just did for him, oh- I'm sure he'd tell us anything." Scarlett reassured.

Trinity snapped out of her shock.

"Okay, we need to tie up loose ends." Trinity announced.

"Oh shit. Who we gotta kill?" Ree questioned.

"No, fool!" Trinity laughed.

"I completed the transfer to Perez's Swiss account. Swiss accounts provide an exclusive level of privacy- its existence doesn't even have to be confirmed if the account holder doesn't will it to be. However, to keep the deposit from being flagged for any potential criminal activity, I need to get into their database & doctor the way this deposit was made." She further explained.

"Say what now?" Emma laughed.

Trinity laughed & shook her head. "I need to alter how Bennie received this money."

"But how would you do that? Like, do we need to physically go into the bank?" Scarlett asked.

"Everything's digital nowadays. You guys know my dad works in IT- he has equipment here that is top-tier- can't even be purchased in stores. I can sneak into the basement & grab a device I'm very familiar with. All activity *literally* goes undetected."

Trinity gave Naree the go.

"On it, Boss!" Naree confirmed as she made her way out of the room & into the basement. The girls continued to remain low-key, as they had been warned. Naree made her way back with devices only she & Trinity understood. This device was prominent for secret government agencies to use when completing highly classified missions, its name was secorà.

Trinity plugged the gadget into the computer. Shortly after, her fingers went ape shit on the keyboard. Before they knew it, she had gone into Perez's account, gained access to his bank's database & edited the entire transaction before it generated onto bank statements. It now reflected as a business grant from a private organization.

"Soooo, I guess you're officially a Black Hat Hacker now." Naree joked. Trinity laughed while Emma & Scarlett looked at one another in confusion.

"A what now?" Emma asked.

"I thought I was the geek here." Scarlett laughed.

"We're all geeks." The remaining girls chuckled.

"Alright, all jokes aside. We've gotta give our parents the brochures tomorrow because apparently, we start Cartel Camp in two days!" Naree reminded.

"Should we have given them the brochures earlier?" Scarlett asked.

"Nope. They can't have too much time to read into this. Anytime we have missions, we've got to keep a handle on the parents, they're like children- you leave em' sitting with something too long, they get curious & get to fucking up shit, real quick." Trinity explained.

The girls all laughed hysterically.

"So, does your mom know you're working for your dad?" Trinity asked Scarlett.

"Absolutely not. She didn't even tell me the truth about why he wasn't in my life. He didn't leave us, she escaped him after being part of his drug cartel too."

"Well, I'll be damned." Emma said in astonishment.

"Yea." Scarlett agreed.

"I wonder if our parents all have secret past lives they're hiding from us." Trinity shared.

"We have the dullest group of parents- no way." Naree chuckled.

"Right. My mom is so freaking noble, she'd probably send me to jail if she ever found out half the shit I've done." Trinity snickered.

"Oh snap!" Emma giggled.

"Yea, that part." Trinity continued.

The girls spent the night decompressing & cracking on their parents- meanwhile, Naree's mother was holding the grandest secret of all, & her daughter had no idea.

It was now time for phase 1 of their plan. Bailey's Girls presented all content to their parents for Philadelphia's Science & Technology Tour. They were enthused about everything the fair had to offer, so Operation: *"Fool Thy Parents"* worked out perfectly. The girls caught up in their group chat & confirmed that their parents were successfully deceived as they got rest for tomorrow's journey.

Anxiety settled in as they arrived to meet Perez for Cartel Camp.

"Right this way, ladies." Jase announced as they got out of his car.

"Thank you." They all responded as he walked them to the limo awaiting their presence. Scarlett glared up into Jase's eyes & remembered the vibe between them the last time she saw him. She felt a flush of warmth pour over her. *"Shit!"* she screamed internally.

Bennie sat with a glass of scotch inside the limo.

"Hola, hola (Hello, hello). Come on in." Bennie said as he raised his glass. He knocked a sip back & got right to it.

"I want to thank you girls for allowing me to take back a piece of the empire my family created when I was only 5 years old." He began.

"This takeover was crucial because it was personal. Because of how much it means to me, I could let you all go, but you have proven your value, so I can't do that just yet. For the next 48 hours, you will be in a sequestered location learning the art necessary to kill or subdue targets when required. Working in the cartel brings about many situations, I need you all prepared for the worst." He enlightened.

The girls awkwardly stared at one another as their limo drove away, its motion contributed to their heads spinning with this new information.

"So, we may have to kill someone? We didn't really-" Emma began.

"Sounds good." Trinity blurted out to save their asses. This was no time to deny Perez of his demands. They were in it for the long haul, so at this point, they *had* to be down for whatever.

"It's imperative you take heed to everything you learn from my men this weekend. There's a possibility you won't be able to think twice when placed in strenuous situations." He added.

"Understood." Naree stated as she nodded in agreeance.

The limo drove for over an hour & arrived at a 2-story cabin, tucked away in the deepest part of Maple Wood Forest. Bennie's men all stood in formation to assist with luggage & to execute orders given by Perez. They escorted the girls to their rooms & directed them to head out back in 20 minutes. Bailey's Girls took a moment to observe their surroundings, refresh themselves, & eat from the spread Perez orchestrated for them. They realized they were the only cabin for miles & miles, their nerves sat in their stomachs as they joined one another out back.

"Alright ladies, listen up. Grab a pair of earplugs & goggles. I'm going to hand you a gun. You are going to shoot that gun as quickly as you can when I say go. Simply aim for the target." Harvey instructed.

The girls turned to one another, shook as they stared into open space at the targets displayed to them. They grabbed their earplugs & goggles & then assumed their positions.

Scarlett laid flat on her belly, peering through the scope of a sniper rifle, prone position. Trinity stood legs spread, head & Beretta cocked to the right. Naree clutched her 9mm with her legs spread, head straight, & her eyes locked. Emma, poor Emma awkwardly paced with a G22 lowered by her right side, she wasn't feeling this task at all.

"One, two, three- FIRE!" Harvey ordered.

Bailey's Girls began firing at their targets but quickly became distracted by Scarlett's precision. They knew she was good enough for bragging rights, but this right here was some next-level shit. She shot the target multiple times in the head & heart, nonstop- she was on GO. Bennie walked closer & closer to Scarlett. He watched her demolish her opponent as he knew she would. He gave his men the eye & mouthed the words, "I told you so."

Scarlett pivoted between hunting positions & shot until she ran out of ammo, Bennie's men were impressed.

"Alright ladies, she's not the only one. I want to see you take your man down, now! LET'S GO!" Harvey yelled.

The remaining girls snapped out of their trance & began to fire again. Trinity & Naree did fair, they at least made flesh wounds to their targets. Emma kept dropping her gun, she missed every single time. Shots aimlessly flew, everyone ducked for cover. Emma finally clutched her G22 properly, but she could not stop shaking.

"Hold it." Jase yelled as he walked over to stand beside her. Emma halted but out of nervousness, she fired.

"Shit!" Carlos spat while grabbing his arm. Perez & his men laughed; Emma ran into the house in tears. The girls took after her, but Perez stopped them & sent Jase.

"I cannot do this!" She cried.

"It gets easier. You can't run during a mission when things get tough. You'd leave your friends behind?" He asked.

"I just SHOT a man who is probably ready to kill me, I am DONE." She cried harder.

"From what I hear, you girls have something to offer; the moment you don't, Perez will have Harvey reenact movies that keep you up at night." Jase warned.

Emma sniffled & stormed back outdoors. She located Carlos to apologize. He was on the sideline with Nest, getting the bullet removed.

"I am so freaking sorry." She began with more tears.

"No need to worry. I've taken many hits to the head, this is nothing." He responded. Emma was even more afraid of him now. She swallowed her saliva and half her tongue.

Perez allowed her some time to regroup with the rest of the girls but eventually instructed them all to go again. The girls reloaded their guns & went full force this time. Emma still struggled. Perez studied her closely.

"If you keep crying & shaking, you will be killed. Do you want to be killed?!" Jase yelled as he moved in on her.

"NO!" she yelled in response, still shaking & crying.

"Hold the gun, firmly. Do not let it go. Show the weapon you are its master. Your friends' lives are at stake, your family's lives depend on this very moment. FIRE!" he yelled in both an encouraging & terrifying tone. Her friends ceased fire. They felt terrible that she had been singled out.

Emma clutched her G22 & let it ring out multiple shots into the body of the cartel member on the target poster. She released a deep sigh of relief when she saw Bennie clap & nod his head in approval. She smiled nervously as her girls ran over to hug & squeeze on her. They performed their secret handshake & got back to it.

"You did great but here's a tip." Perez began.

"Sir?"

"Next time, open your eyes." Perez chuckled. Emma continued to shoot with ease as she kept her loved ones' lives in mind, but in the pits of her soul, she was still scared shitless, she realized she was not cut out for this.

Meanwhile, Scarlett & Trinity soaked up every bit of the action. Scarlett was used to shooting, so she was right at home with every weapon. Trinity? Trinity was a beast in the making, she let off round after round with no hesitation. Naree did well enough to get the job done but she was more so fascinated with what was to come. Bennie allotted a restroom break, the girls gathered themselves & returned for more.

Perez & his men rounded the girls up to educate them on the art of a silent kill. They acted out scenes that would require the snapping of someone's neck or a fatal blow to their spinal cord. Jase used Scarlett as an example, when he wrapped his arm around her neck, she tensed up, but she liked it very much. He began to pick up on what she was putting down, so he kept choosing her to showcase the skillset each girl must walk away with. Perez noticed Jase's gravitation to his daughter & forewarned him on the low that this infatuation would not be in his best interest. Jase understood that it wouldn't be tolerated, but he wasn't scared by a long shot. Everyone was dismissed to eat & get to bed. The girls ate, showered, & met up in one of their rooms to recap the day.

"So, I see Jase has his sights set on you. He didn't use us for role-play at all. We want to get killed too." Naree laughed.

"Oh, shut up. He doesn't like me. He works for my father." Scarlett deflected.

"It sure seems like he does. Child, when he put you in a chokehold, I didn't know whether to close my eyes or keep looking." Trinity added.

"Well, I did feel a vibe. Not sure if it's really what I think though." Scarlett confirmed.

"We'll see soon enough." Emma insinuated.

"So, how you feeling after everything today? I know things were rough. We wanted to come after you, but my dad sent Jase instead." Scarlett explained, hoping she wasn't mad at them.

"No, no. I'm okay now. I don't feel I'm the best candidate for this, but under pressure, I think I'll be fine. I love you guys." Emma reassured.

"We love you too." They said in unison.

They continued to chatter amongst themselves until Jase came to the door.

"Hey, Scarlett. May I see you for a moment?" He asked.

"Sure." Scarlett answered with her brows as high as her hairline. The girls covered their mouths & snickered under their breaths.

Scarlett followed Jase into a private area of the cabin. She noticed her dad & the rest of his men went to bed.

"So, what's up?" Scarlett asked.

"You tell me." He answered. She laughed & put her head down to keep him from seeing her smile.

"Don't hide. Let me see that pretty smile of yours." He insisted. She laughed.

"I don't really date boys. Well, I mean I literally do not date boys." She confessed.

"You date girls?" He guessed.

"I've never dated anyone." She laughed.

"Oh. Ha. Well, I feel a connection between us. I know I'm not alone." He exclaimed.

"Hmmmm you're not but can I think about this? I don't know how my father will react to my dating you." Scarlett expressed.

"What if instead of dating, we call it simply getting to know one another?" Jase pressed.

"Well, people get to know each other all the time. No harm there, right?" She smiled again.

"Not at all." He validated while moving in for a kiss.

"Cool it, Romeo. I'm not that kind of girl." Scarlett blocked.

"I respect that." Jase digressed. He had never been turned down before.

She stood on her tippy toes & kissed him on the cheek. He smiled in return & watched her walk away. Scarlett was on two thousand; she didn't want to come down from this high. She went back to the room she came from; the girls were sound asleep. She located her room & hopped into bed.

Nest walked through the house like a Drill Sergeant at 5 am, yelling orders for the girls to wake up. They were not happy at all, however, they managed to wake up & get with it. There was no time to freshen up, as they were rushed to make way to the living room. Bennie's men were lined up in front of a 98-inch OLED television. Bennie was held up in the second living room discussing business with a new contact. As the girls sat down, Jase slyly informed Scarlett that he adored her morning look.

"You all need to know what a dead body will look like." Carlos announced.

"Say what now?" Emma asked. Trinity tapped her leg to get her to chill out. Emma's face confirmed someone had her fucked up.

Carlos turned on the TV, it displayed a video feed of a room that held several dead bodies. The girls all gasped & held onto one another.

"To live with yourself after your first few kills, you must become desensitized to seeing people die." He explained.

"We've seen a dead body before." Scarlett coldly shared.

The girls immediately began to sob quietly together.

"We watched our best friend hang herself in front of the entire school. We're good on this little show you've all put together." Naree added.

Bennie's men paused & shared their condolences. Nest then requested the girls follow him. He led them to a room outside of the cabin. The room showcased on the 98-inch television was now live & in color, the girls were viewing several dead bodies- up close & personal; they were in shock, but they held their composure. Carlos escorted them around the room & explained in great detail who these men were & why they were killed; he shared they were traitors to Bennie. Bailey's Girls took heed.

"If this man say he gone kill you, HE GONE KILL YOU." Naree joked.

"That's not funny." Emma laughed.

Trinity & Scarlett laughed & shook their heads. Bennie's men chuckled lightly while Jase made eyes at Scarlett. He wasn't so sure he wanted to cross her father. Guess he needed a reminder of why not to.

Harvey took the girls to the yard for a very important sector, fighting. They trained all day. For hours straight, they learned how to fight to the death of them. Each man of Bennie's partnered up with the girls & allowed them to fight them like their lives depended on it- Bailey's Girls had finally been broken in. They learned how to flip, jump from high places & attack, as well as how to fight multiple opponents at once. They were tired but they were ready.

For the remainder of the weekend, they repeated all training & did not stop. Perez was pleased, so they were able to rest up nicely before heading back home. Each girl had been crafted into something bolder & brighter. They obtained something they never imagined coming from this shady getaway- confidence.

Chapter 7

Fearless

The UA's doors blew open with the wildest gusts of winds. In came waltzing Trinity, Naree, Emma, & Scarlett. They appeared to be the same but somehow the entire student body knew they were different; they stepped like royalty & smelled like trouble. Guess you could say the universe was letting them know all hell was about to break loose. The girls walked straight into the main hall, continuing to grab everyone's attention. They were dressed in skirts that hugged their curves; ones that hung low on one side but rose on the other, skirts that popped in fabric that wasn't even on the market yet because it was owned by their company. Between being given the side eye from rich kids to boys smiling & running into walls, they knew they were bitchin fashion!

"Allison Parker, Maci Karr, & Kaylee Lopez!" Trinity yelled as she took a stance in the center of the hallway. Naree, Emma, & Scarlett stood beside her. Everyone stopped abruptly, it was showtime.

"I know you're here. You'd never miss a day to raise hell. So, where are you? It's our turn." Scarlett rallied.

"It could never be your turn. Are you all high or something?" Allison responded as she made her way through the crowd. Maci & Kaylee followed behind her, per usual.

"I bet you'd like to think that, Allison. Funny thing though, we're here to let you know we're on to you." Trinity warned.

"Excuse me, peasant." Allison snapped with a little nervousness.

"You heard what she said. We're on to you. We know you drove Bailey to kill herself, but everyone here does not, do you?" Emma asked as she began to capture each face in the hallway. Every expression confirmed a story of its own. Emma spotted several people to target when this showdown was over.

"You came for Bailey's life, so we're coming for you. We just have the balls to tell you first." Naree added.

"Oh, are you kidding me? Bailey-" Maci began.

"Don't you EVER say her name!" Trinity bucked as she stepped to Maci's face. Shit got real all over again, except this time, Bailey wasn't here to see it. For once in their lives, Allison & her trolls were scared.

"Everything you've ever loved about yourself; it's all coming to an end." Emma warned.

"Alright, you've had your fun. What do you want? A check, I'll write you a wittle check. How much do you need to cut the shit?" Allison asked as she pulled out her checkbook.

"Oh, Trust Fund Baby, that's the thing. Money won't get you out of this ass whopping." Scarlett answered.

"It's been a long time coming." Trinity said as she shoved Allison into the wall before stepping through like a boss! Naree, Trinity, & Emma followed as Allison's back hit the lockers. Guilt flushed her face as she struggled to stand upright.

Allison & her minions were floored; no one had ever stood up to them like that. As they headed to their classes, they couldn't stop replaying what happened. They discussed losing respect & the fear they instilled in everyone.

"If those nerds can check us, who else will get the idea to step to us?" Maci questioned.

"Oh, there won't be any more of that. I was caught off guard today, it'll never happen again." Allison reassured.

"What could they possibly have on you though? It seems like-" Kaylee began.

"Oh, now you can talk, Kaylee? Where was your mouth when those broke bitches tried us a few minutes ago?" Maci asked.

"I'm starting to think you're not squad anymore. & what the hell were they wearing? I've been so distracted; I haven't had time to shop." Allison acknowledged.

"It's not that at all. It's just that out of everything we've ever done, this feels different. No soy un estúpida (I'm not stupid). So, say it. How can we have your back if we don't know what the hell is going on?" Kaylee addressed.

Maci felt Kaylee made sense, even though she was team Allison- no matter what. She stopped & looked at Allison as she began to squirm.

"I said it's nothing. It's either you're my friends or you're not!" Allison yelled as she stormed off with one tear struggling to find a way out.

"Now, you agree something weird is going on here, right? Allison doesn't freaking CRY!" Kaylee pointed out to Maci.

"But honestly, does it matter what she's hiding? We all have secrets." Maci admitted.

"Last I checked, you know all my secrets & when you get a splatter of wine in your system, you let it all hang out, so yea, it does matter. She just gets to soak up all nuestra mierda (our shit)." Kaylee expressed.

"Alli has saved us from so much, we honestly cannot be doing this right now, Kay." Maci pleaded.

"She's not God. She hasn't SAVED me from anything at all, Maci. Honestly, we followed her shenanigans & sent Bailey Brooks right to her grave! This obsession with her went on & on & on until-"

"STOP it, Kaylee. Damnit. Why can't you just STOP?!" Maci yelled before storming off.

Kaylee lingered in the hallway & stared into the distance at what she had been an accomplice to. She contemplated coming clean for her sins as she played back every scheme she adhered to. She even thought to apologize to Bailey's Girls, so that she could appease the guilt eating away at her, but she couldn't bring herself to face them yet.

As the day went on, Bailey's Girls plunged into their act of redemption. Emma informed them the best way to cross-examine Bailey's suicide was to interview students, teachers & each other. The girls split & put their words into action. They made quite the impression confronting the scariest bitches in school, so at this point, they knew exactly what they were capable of.

"That was pretty badass, what y'all did this morning." Joshua mentioned while preparing to enter the classroom.

"Oh yea?" Trinity asked.

"Yea, for sure. It's safe to say you stood up for us all today." He confirmed.

"I wouldn't say that. Not yet anyways." Trinity responded, gushing inside.

"It's just that I know girls like Allison, all too well. My sister, Jessica was bullied before we transferred here. She attempted suicide when she couldn't take it anymore, & it's like although she didn't die, we lost her because she was never the same again. We used to play pranks on each other, skip rocks down by the ocean, go to parties, & crack on rich white kids ... now all she wants to do is write. It's like she only lives in her head now." He revealed.

"Damn, I'm so sorry to hear that." Trinity exclaimed with her head hung low as she took a seat next to him.

"No, I'm sorry. I didn't mean to dump on you." He whispered.

"Oh, no. Please don't say that. I watched my best friend endure Hell on Earth, there's no way I don't feel you on this. I just wish that I could take them down, ya know? We deserve justice in every aspect. Girls like Jessica, girls like me & my friends, & girls like Bailey." Trinity declared.

"I'm really sorry about Bailey... she was always nice to me & my sister. When she died, Jessica became obsessed with her mother. She wanted to know how she was getting along but she-" he began.

"She what?" Trinity asked.

"Well, do you remember the day Mrs. Brooks was arrested?" he asked.

"Sadly, yes, I do. It was the day I saw Bailey for the last time." Trinity answered, shaking her head & choking back tears.

"I'm sorry. I know this is hard for you." He acknowledged.

"It's all good, I just wanna get them back, you know what I mean?" she reiterated.

"My sister has footage." He confessed.

"What do you mean, footage?" Trinity asked with her left brow raised & shoulders straight.

"Well, just as she was obsessed with Bailey's mother, she was obsessed with Bailey too. She has videos of Mrs. Brooks coming to the UA every day after Bailey's suicide. You & your friends hadn't returned yet, but Mrs. Brooks was here every day. She tried to tell us all that Allison & her friends were responsible for Bailey's death, but nobody listened. I wanted to tell her that we knew the truth." Josh unraveled.

"This is just... wow. So, Jessica was obsessed with Bailey as well? What makes you say that?" Trinity fixated. Josh hesitated but admitted, "She has videos of Bailey too..."

"What kinds of videos?" Trinity dug, boiling inside.

"All kinds. She's got videos of Bailey being bullied on various occasions, but she's also got good ones, ones where she's with you & your friends, smiling & laughing." He answered.

"Where were you when Bailey hung herself? Where was your sister? Trinity interrogated.

"I was in the auditorium; I don't know where Jessica was at the time. She's going to be meeting me for lunch after class, you can ask her. She'd do anything to help you take them down." He informed.

"I'll talk to her after class. Thank you." Trinity swallowed as she sat back.

"Anything I can do to help, I want to. I mean it." He shared.

"Can I ask- why didn't you help Bailey if you saw she was struggling just like your sister was?" Trinity blatantly inquired.

"To be honest, I convinced myself that it wouldn't come to suicide. That not everyone was as weak as Jessica. Not that Bailey was weak, I just-" he stammered.

"Bailey wasn't weak. She was tired." Trinity corrected.

"I'm sorry." Joshua expressed while placing his hand on top of hers. Trinity clutched his hand in return & waited for class to end. Her brain raced with thoughts; she couldn't focus one bit. She didn't even realize she held onto Joshua's hand the entire time. Class ended; she hopped up without thinking twice & raced to the lunchroom. Joshua followed behind her as closely as he could until they both made it to the double doors of the cafeteria. Trinity spotted Jessica sitting alone, she took a deep breath & went for it.

"Hey, Jessica, my name is-"

"Trinity. Hey, what's up?" Jessica responded.

"Hey Jess." Joshua greeted as he took a seat.

"I'd like to know your whereabouts before Bailey took her life. Could you please tell me where you were?" Trinity dived in.

"I didn't do anything, Josh, what the hell?" Jessica snapped.

"No, it's not like that. She knows you didn't do anything wrong." He explained.

"Actually, I don't- but I'd like to believe she didn't. Please. Where were you?" Trinity asked again.

Jessica took a deep breath & disclosed. "When Bailey left the auditorium, she went to the restroom. I know because I was in there. I heard her say over & over again, *'No one loves me like my daddy, no one loves me like my daddy, no one loves me like my daddy, no one loves me like my daddy.'*

She paused for a moment & then uttered the words, *'I'm sorry,'* & ran to the backstage of the auditorium. I followed her but everything happened so quickly, I didn't make it in time."

"Jessica, why didn't you say anything?! How could you let her kill herself? Did you get that on film too?!" Trinity shouted.

"Josh!" Jessica yelled embarrassingly.

"Trinity!" He snapped, regretting their encounter altogether.

"Bailey isn't here anymore! Don't you get it? I was supposed to graduate with MY best friend. We were supposed to attend college together & launch our business together, become millionaires- together. How the hell am I supposed to let that go?" She asked, tears chasing the crevices of the anger lines on her face.

Jessica ran off a hot mess. Joshua fled behind her. Trinity sat at the lunch table, sobbing in anger & defeat. Naree, Emma, & Scarlett entered the lunchroom & immediately sat down to console her. After sharing her latest cup of tea, Trinity made clear it was time to visit Bailey's father in prison. They discussed the importance of questioning more students & making them feel comfortable enough to be honest.

"I couldn't help but get pissed. I just don't understand why the hell someone would hold onto pertinent information like that. Like, you hear her have a nervous breakdown, & you do nothing. You say nothing. What in the actual fuck?" Trinity ranted, respectfully.

"But didn't you say Jessica went through the same thing too? We've all had a hand in this, one way or another. At least now, we know there's more to Bailey's death." Naree expressed.

"I'm scared to know what those things could possibly be." Scarlett stated.

"Me too, Scar, but we're rock'n out until the very end. Until we get justice for Bailey." Emma shared.

"So, let's do it." Trinity said while dialing Mrs. Brooks.

She told Sara they're serious about getting to the bottom of Bailey's death, & that students know more than what they've led on, so she wants to keep digging. Bailey's mother had so much hope, she was willing to help however she could. Trinity shared her need to see Todd. Sara was hesitant, but Trinity was family, so she informed her of the prison's protocol for visitors & asked her to come by afterwards. Before the call ended, Sara pleaded for Trinity to help Bailey's soul find peace & rest.

"I just want her to be free." She expressed.

Trinity ended the call & informed the girls that only 2 of them could go. She chose Ree & apologized to Em & Scar before admitting she had to have someone who could finesse if needed. Now was just as good a time as any, so, on impulse, Trinity & Naree agreed to skip the rest of the day, so they could make it to Windham Gates' Prison before visiting hours were over. Em & Scar were responsible for gathering any other information they could be missing. They set out to divide & conquer but life did what it does best when you think you've got it all figured out- slap the hell out of you & tell you that you don't!

Trinity & Naree left the cafeteria & began their mission to Windham City, which was a little over an hour away. They passed time by sulking in Bailey's favorite playlists & talking. When they arrived, a heap of discomfort fell over them. They didn't understand the downpour of uneasiness, but they pressed forward anyway.

"We're here to see Todd Brooks." Trinity announced as they approached the glass window.

"How old are you?" The guard asked.

"Old enough to visit Mr. Brooks." Naree answered.

"Identification, please." The guard demanded.

Trinity & Naree slapped their student IDs down under the glass & proceeded to the next phase.

"I'm not sure Mr. Brooks can have visitors after the latest incident with his wife. I need to check this out before I allow you girls back." The guard informed.

"Seriously? We drove over an hour to see him." Trinity responded.

"I understand but Mrs. Brooks is now banned from seeing him until further notice. This could also go for any other potential visitors as well. I really need to verify." He went on.

"Listen, Sir. With all due respect, this visit has nothing to do with Mrs. Brooks. We are here about his daughter, Bailey Brooks. She committed suicide & the last thing she murmured before she took her life was that nobody loved her like he did. We just want to be with whom held great significance to her; she was our best friend." Naree explained.

The guard paused for a brief moment & decided to press the button to let them through.

"I knew I'd need you." Trinity smiled as they walked through. Another guard met them on the other side & performed a search to ensure they weren't handling anything disallowed. They passed the search & were taken further back. Todd was surprised to find he had visitors; he went to the designated area & could not believe his eyes.

"Trinny?" He asked moving closer with the grandest smile on his face.

"Yes Sir, it's me." She responded with a blushing smile in return.

"Aww baby girl, it has been too long." He exclaimed, stricken with sadness.

"It truly has been. I'm sorry I haven't come before now. You've always been such an amazing bonus dad to me. To be honest, the only dad. Mr. Brooks, this is Naree Gem. She's-" Trinity began.

"I know who she is. Bailey told me all about you. It's very nice to meet you. What are you girls doing here? This is no place for children, & Trinny, honestly, no apologies are needed. I love you just as much as I always have. I remember when I first spotted you on the playground with Bails. You punched a little boy for taking her Ken doll, you were always so protective of her." He chuckled as he took a seat.

"Nice to meet you too, Mr. Brooks. Bailey spoke very highly of you." Naree responded.

"I appreciate that Mr. Brooks. Means a lot to me. I actually wanted to talk to you about Bailey, if that's okay." Trinity expressed.

"Sure honey, shoot." He smiled.

"We've been trying to understand why Bails would rip herself away from us. We knew things were hard, but we truly think something more was happening before she... you know." Trinity began as she fiddled with her fingers.

Todd hung his head low & immediately began to sob. He didn't want to say a thing, but he was tired of keeping secrets. After all, secrets are what ruined Bailey.

"Today, a student told me that before Bailey went backstage, she was heard in the girls' restroom, uttering repeatedly, *'No one loves me like my daddy loves me'* & then finally, she said aloud, *'I'm sorry,'* & then it was all over. She loved you, Mr. Brooks. I just don't understand why those were her last words." Trinity pried.

Todd broke down, instantly. He became a sobbing mess. So much so, that guards began to pay attention.

"Bailey isn't my biological daughter." He revealed.

Trinity & Naree's shoulders slouched forward. Their eyes became Pac men roaming the spaces in their sockets, running from ghosts & anything else unimaginable.

"That's not possible. Why would you say that Mr. Brooks?" Trinity questioned, trying not to lose every ounce of what she always believed.

"She's not, I mean... was not, my biological daughter. Sara was pregnant when I met her. I fell in love with her &

everything she came with, Bailey included, so I raised her as my own." Todd shared.

"So, Bailey didn't know this at all?" Naree questioned.

"I knew that Sara came with some baggage but when you love someone, wholeheartedly, you embrace that baggage. I'm a good man. I am here in this prison for only God knows what, but I am a good man." He responded, spaced out.

"You've been a great man since the day I met you, Mr. Brooks. Did Bailey know you were not her father?" Trinity asked for further confirmation. Todd took another deep breath & emptied the clip.

"Yes. She knew. When Bailey was 13 years old, we found out that she needed a bone marrow transplant. Bailey nearly died & although they had new technology that could help her, her chances were warranted as better if her biological parents could give her what she needed. For the first time in my life, I couldn't provide for her- so, Sara had to call her biological father, Riley. We came clean with Bails because she was so sick, we didn't want to hurt her, but her life was at risk. Riley came to her rescue. She peered at him from her hospital bed with such love & hate, he was her hero; he saved her life."

"All for her to recreate another tragic ending." Naree murmured, drifting away in pressing thoughts.

"I can't believe she didn't tell me this. I'm her best friend, Mr. Brooks. How could she not tell me this? Was I not her best friend? She was hurting & I missed that. How could I have missed that? Why would she keep this from me?" Trinity wailed as she held onto him.

Typically, the guards did not allow touching but in this instance, even they knew some deep shit was going down, so they permitted the moment.

"I'm so sorry, Trinny. Bails was diagnosed with depression; this secret dismantled her mental health. She wasn't herself for a very long time. The last time Sara was here, I blamed her for not paying attention, but truth be told, Bailey's journey of pain was no surprise. She had been fighting to belong & take back the betrayals we had given her. I guess it all became too much. I don't know why she discharged those particular words before letting go, but I sure which I knew. I wish I knew which father she was referring to." He sobbed.

"I think Riley was at the funeral." Trinity shared in shock. Todd sat in a state of distress, unsure of how to respond. Everyone cried simultaneously until visiting hours came to an end. Before they parted ways, they filled Mr. Brooks in on Allison, Maci, & Kaylee's evildoings known thus far. He sat with agony, grief, & regret. He told them he knows something is off with the Parker family & that Frankie may be the reason he's in there. The girls promised to connect those dots & to return to him soon.

The drive home was the toughest one yet. They couldn't even begin to grasp what they learned. Trinity dropped Naree off at home & decided to go & see Sara after all.

"What does Todd mean he isn't Bailey's biological father?" She asked as Sara opened the door. Sara gasped & held onto her chest. She didn't think Todd would share such intimate details of their lives with a teenager but since the cat was out of the bag, she decided to bare all to Trinity as well. Unbeknownst to them both, this was only the beginning of many horrors to come.

"Bailey isn't Todd's. Wasn't Todd's. Not biologically anyway." She confessed.

"I was filled in rather nicely Mrs. Brooks. How could you have kept this from Bailey?" Trinity pressed.

"I know. I know. Trinity, trust me. Please believe I didn't wish to hurt my baby. I was young once too, & in my past, I ran with the grimiest of men, Riley Hart being one of them. He's her father. Was her father. I don't know. All I know is that he got me & some tramp pregnant at the same time. We both ran for our lives. The only difference between her & I is that I kept my kid, & she didn't." Sara relinquished.

"Bailey wasn't his only kid?" Trinity questioned with a puzzled expression.

"Bailey isn't his only daughter." Sara corrected.

"She has a sister?! What the-" Trinity began.

"Trinity Michelle Woods, don't you dare." Sara finished.

"I'm sorry Mrs. B, but what the fuck?" Trinity spat out. She just had to.

"So, all this time, Bailey's had a sister she knew nothing about? Does Mr. Brooks know? He didn't mention this to me." Trinity pried some more.

"To be honest, he doesn't know much. Neither do I because as I mentioned, she was given up for adoption. She could be anywhere; the adoption was discreet. Riley hasn't met her. Doesn't know her. Hasn't seen the kid's mother since way back when." Mrs. Brooks explained.

"Well, how do you know he doesn't know anything now? We should ask him. You have to ask him. She's Bailey's blood. Maybe we could..." Trinity rambled on.

"Maybe we could what? He doesn't know anything, Trinity." Sara insisted.

"It's been so long since you've seen him, maybe-" Trinity continued.

"I..." Sara began but withdrew.

"Oh. I see. You already know the answer, Mrs. B." Trinity acknowledged with the deepest head nod known to mankind. Convicted, Sara sank in guilt.

“I’m sorry. I’ve been out here all by myself. No Bailey. No Brent. No Todd. No Sara. I am nothing without them, do you hear me? I’m nothing without my daughter. I’ve been nothing & no one without Bailey Nicole Brooks.”

“I feel you, Mrs. B. No judgments at all.” Trinity reassured, going in for a hug. “Family is family.”

Chapter 8:

The Fatal Kiss

Trinity went home with her heart & her mind heavy af. She didn't know whether she should share the tea with her friends or save face for Bailey's family. She arrived at school & forced a litty attitude when she met the girls at the front of the building. Her goal was to go with her gut.

"Naree told us about the visit. How you feeling?" Scarlett questioned.

Trinity's mood was shot to shit, she fired a look Naree's way. She wished she hadn't opened her mouth yet.

"You couldn't have given me time to process this before you said anything, Ree." Trinity snapped.

"I'm confused, Trin. Why are you mad at me?" Naree asked.

"I should've gone by myself. Bailey was MY best friend. I grew up with her family, you all did not! Now you're all privy to things I didn't even know yet, which doesn't feel right at all." Trinity explained, voice cracking into pieces.

"Woah, Trinity. I think you're losing sight of the mission here." Emma shared as she pulled her onto the side of the building. Trinity leaned against the wall & looked the other way.

"Trinity. You've got to understand that as we do this, shit is going to get real & you're probably going to regret traveling down this road because Bailey had secrets. You've got to ask yourself right now, are you ready for those secrets? If you're not, then we should just call it quits. Right now. Forget getting revenge for Bailey. Forget exposing bullies. Forget continuing We Bitchin Fashion & becoming millionaires! Forget #GameOnForBailey, the pact we've fought so hard to implement at this time. ALL OF IT!" Scarlett spat.

Trinity turned her head back toward the girls & looked Naree dead in the eyes & said, "I'm sorry."

"It's okay, Trin. I know that Bailey was your sister, so each blow hits differently. All we ask is that you remember she was ours too. We're in this for the good & the bad. We can't be spazzing out on each other, not now. Allison & her crew are waiting for us to fold. I refuse to give them the satisfaction." Naree expressed.

"You're right. I'm really sorry, Ree. Bailey was my sister, but y'all are my sisters too. We're family, always & forever." Trinity shared as she cried. The girls embraced her for a group hug. It was as though Bailey walked up & joined this legendary hug as well, her warmth surrounded them like the sun.

"As we continue to hunt down every secret that leads to Bailey's death, let's vow to never keep them from each other." Emma petitioned.

Trinity's heart sank into the pits of her stomach as she pulled away from their warm embrace. She took one good look at them & decided that sisterhood meant sisterhood, forever.

Allison breezed on by as Bailey's Girls continued to have their moment. Maci & Kaylee joined her on the steps, so they could enter the school together. They stood there for a moment, checking their hair & lipstick in their designer compact mirrors. As the front of the school became a ghost town, only two groups of girls remained.

"Bailey has a sister." Trinity spat out with her eyes closed. Naree, Emma, & Scarlett pulled her off even more to the side of the building.

"She what?! Since when? Mrs. Brooks is preggo?" Scarlett pried.

Allison & her crew crept closer to the side of the building to confirm the tea brewing.

"She has a what now?" Emma asked as she zeroed in on Trinity's squinted face. Her eyes were still clenched tightly & her mind was racing, she wished the words never left her lips.

"I don't recall Mr. Brooks telling us that. Are you serious?" Naree asked.

"Dead ass. I have a trusted source." Trinity confirmed as she finally opened her eyes to the face the girls.

"Spit it out, Trinity." Scarlett demanded.

"But I'm- ugh, it's Mrs. Brooks. She told me last night. Bailey's biological father stepped out on her & got some lady pregnant around the same time. The chick he knocked up gave her kid up for adoption though. I don't know anything else." Trinity confessed as she plopped down on top of the bricks holding up flower beds.

"Did you hear that? Bailey Brooks has a sister?!" Maci whispered to Allison & Kaylee as they crept even closer to the side of the building.

"Shhh." Allison whispered, she wanted to hear the rest.

"So, you mean to tell me that Mrs. Brooks informed you of an illegitimate child, but she didn't say anything else. What about Mr. Brooks? Or her biological father?" Emma asked.

"Mr. Brooks doesn't know much, otherwise, he would've told us yesterday. Aside from disclosing Bailey's health & depression to us, he somewhat hinted at being wrongfully imprisoned. Trinity answered.

"Wrongfully imprisoned? Did he not take part in illegal activities on an investment property he owned?" Emma questioned.

"Wait, wait, wait- wasn't the investment property also owned by Frankie Parker?" Scarlett asked, laughing at the audacity.

"Yes. After we painted every mischievous act bestowed upon Bailey by Allison, Maci, & Kaylee, he agreed that the Parker family was shady & that he thinks Frankie set him up." Trinity shared.

"He did say only God knows why he's in there & that he's a good man. I for one don't believe he's done anything wrong." Naree added.

"Mr. Brooks is an upstanding guy, I never pegged him to be part of anything he's been charged for, but clearly, we don't know anyone as well as think. Ree & I promised to dig into his speculations, but we can't lose sight of our mission for Bailey." Trinity explained.

"But what if our mission for Bailey is connected to Mr. Brooks after all?" Emma pondered aloud.

"I say we go for it all. Let's just see it all through." Scarlett suggested.

"Are you guys hearing this?" Kaylee asked.

"Yea, we like totally have to tell your dad." Maci suggested.

"We're not telling my dad anything. I've got this." Allison demanded.

"But what if they try to come for him? Shouldn't he be warned?" Kaylee asked.

"Face it. My dad is the most powerful man there is. My mother's position also solidifies fear & power; we Parkers are not to be trifled with. I am not worried about fake inspector gadgets. I will however keep an eye on them." Allison informed.

"What about Bailey's sister? Should we find out who she is?" Kaylee asked.

"I'm sure she's poor & demented as well. Besides, no face, no case." Allison expressed, laughing menacingly.

"But if Bailey has a sister who is looking for her, what if she comes after us? I know your dad can pull strings but if they keep running their mouths & spreading-"

"Lies. If they keep spreading lies, they will be dealt with accordingly. Period." Allison stated, abruptly.

Kaylee flared because she knew Bailey's Girls were spreading truth & not lies. She rolled her eyes, huffed, & then stormed away. Allison & Maci took their leave as well but not before making themselves known. Maci stumbled going up the steps, which quickly caught the attention of Bailey's Girls. They immediately scurried back to the front of the building, only to see Allison & Maci rushing through the front doors. Trinity raced toward them. Naree, Emma, & Scarlett ran to stop her.

"You bitches really ought to mind your business." Trinity shouted as she met up with them from behind. Allison & Maci turned around as they were all now in front of Strickland's office. Kaylee kept walking.

"Have you been injected with high-level street drugs? We could care less about anything involving you peasants." Maci lashed out.

"I second that. I find it hilarious that just because you bums received a morsel of attention from our student body, suddenly, you've gotten the gall to step to me... again. I wouldn't get too comfortable doing that." Allison expressed.

"Yea, like don't get too comfortable." Maci cosigned.

"You seem pretty pressed to me. I'd say we're just getting started." Naree acknowledged.

"For sure. You all think you're the baddest bitches walking in the UA, when realistically, you're just rich bitches who get away with everything." Scarlett pointed out.

"Sounds pretty bad to me." Maci laughed.

"Not when your rude awakening is near, princess."
Emma chimed in.

"How about we skip all the chatter & get right to it?
You're treading on very thin ice. I'd be mighty careful if I
were you." Trinity stated with her fists clenched, ready to
swing. Allison sized Trinity up & then took a step back.

"You really wanna fight, afro puff? I got your
number." Allison chuckled as she blew a kiss to Trinity.

"Yea bitch, I got your number too." Trinity responded
as she charged at Allison.

"Hey, you know what? We've got plenty of time for
this, but we've got that thing tonight. We need to collaborate
on that." Naree reminded as she stepped in between
everyone. Trinity froze instantly, she remembered their
second mission was active for tonight. Their job was to
infiltrate another rival cartel at a house party. After visiting
Mr. Brooks & Mrs. Brooks, her mind was all over the place.
She unclenched her fists & smiled.

"Guess I'll be seeing you soon after all." She smirked
as she shoved through Allison & Maci. Naree, Emma, &
Scarlett ran behind her again.

"You good?" Naree asked, briskly walking next to
Trinity.

"Yea, I thought you were about to whoop her ass."
Scarlett admitted.

"Right, I was ready to get some hits in on Maci's fake ass." Emma laughed.

"I'm good. I just can't play this little game anymore. We've all been bullied for so long by these girls. It drives me crazy to even see them at this point." Trinity responded.

"I feel you. They get to waltz to & fro like they own the place & everyone in it. I wanna end them as badly as you do, let's just be smart about it." Scarlett encouraged.

"I agree. As I said, their rude awakening is near, & we know that; since they don't, it puts us at an advantage over them." Emma explained.

Trinity stopped & took a deep breath. The girls halted & took one too because Trinity walks hella fast when she's upset. They decided to skip school to collect themselves & discuss tonight's undercover shenanigans.

They walked into Wake-Up Philly & could breathe again. They sat at their favorite booth without the fear of flashing back to the death of Nichola. They recapped Bennie's instructions & orchestrated their swag, of course, they'd be wearing SKIRTS! The girls were scared to be under the same roof as another drug cartel, but they were very excited, as this house party would be their first. Jase was appointed to escort them for safety & to apply pressure if needed. The girls were responsible for obtaining anything they could on the Mexican Cartel. They apparently had run-ins with Bennie's boys & now Perez insisted on having a pissing contest. Whatever the quest, Bailey's Girls were ready. They went home, relaxed, changed clothes, & then met back up at Wake-Up Philly to ride with Jase to Rittenhouse Square, which was a very nice area. When they arrived, they immediately presumed a body count if things took a turn for the worst. The streets were cold, music caressed the sidewalks, & drugs wafted in the air.

"I know you girls don't get out much, remember, we're undercover. Do not use your real names & you should probably use some of the drip I have here to at least look the part." Jase informed.

They all took one hard look at one another before sifting through what Jase had to offer.

"The skirts we keep, the rest can go." Scarlett announced as they grabbed makeup, luxurious velvet tops, high heels, & jewelry. They went from cute teens to Cartel Queens in a millisecond. They hopped out of Jase's car; he couldn't keep his eyes off Scarlett for anything. As they made their way into this extravagant party, they crossed paths with elite Mexican men & women. Everyone had on suits, nice dresses, & high-end jewelry. These girls were about to be broken in something serious.

Jase escorted the girls to the bar & then quickly appointed them to split up, so they could cover more ground; the goal was to get in & get out as quickly as possible. He took Scarlett to the west end of Santiago's mansion, one of the richest drug lords in all of Mexico. He ran different cities &

states, but Philly was his main territory. The girls worked the room & confirmed some guests were dancing, some were dining, & some appeared to be on lookout because they interacted with no one- Naree made those individuals her target. She pretended to be interested in the art displayed throughout the mansion & dredged up conversations with obvious guards to see who was friendly enough to say the wrong things.

Trinity briefly swept the halls with a devilish smile to gather intel through a tech device she wore which recorded various conversations within a 15-mile radius. She found her way to a study located on the east side of the mansion. She put on black gloves & slipped in to uncover what she could. There was a vaulted door inside, she knew the greatest source of intel had to be behind it. She immediately analyzed it to see how to get in. Its width had been customized; it was installed to swing in & had both a digital code & remote as options to open. She went into her purse & took out her 2639, this device was known to relay the password of any sort, but it needed time to go through all possible combinations. She placed it on the door & sat there as anxiety began to fill her chest.

Meanwhile, Emma roamed freely, fraternizing with women who were rich & unhappy- those women talk a LOT. She received earfuls regarding their husbands & baby's fathers, she knew it'd come in handy. Santiago's men rushed to the front of the mansion on high alert, she concluded there were uninvited guests. Santiago came from a private area of his home & stood in the center of his mansion, Tony Montana style. He analyzed each area from door to door & smiled as he soaked up the feeling of being King. Scarlett & Jase walked hand in hand, smitten by one another. Scarlett felt sexy & bold, she tugged Jase by his hand & pulled him closer to her. She glared up into his eyes & kissed him. She kissed him like she wasn't a novice at all. He most certainly kissed her back. They stood still in their magic, enveloped in one another, until gunfire ceased the moment. A fight broke out which led to bullets flying. They ducked for cover. Emma & Naree began to panic as they made their way towards one another. Trinity was the only body missing, they had no idea where she was. They paged her but with the screams, it was hard to get a clear tag on her location.

Trinity was still in the study, trying to clear the vault. She heard the gunshots, but her 2639 finally located the password- she was not leaving. She tied her hair up & punched in the code provided: 267922SM; it was now open season on the vault of Santiago's mansion. She quickly snapped pictures of the ledgers, drugs, & money inside. She pocketed samples of the drugs Santiago held & swiped flash drives that were depicted to be debit cards. She also took the liberty of swiping Santiago's drug operation; he had maps of their routes & locations behind the wall of a blackboard. She took pictures of that & every name for the route displayed. Gunfire began to get closer, so she rushed from the vaulted door, back into the study, & into the main area of the mansion to search for her crew. She paged Naree & Emma before going into a frenzy.

"Hey, Em, Ree, you there?" she shouted.

"Yes! We've been trying to find you for the longest, where have you been?! Are you okay? Meet us at the door!" Ree hollered back.

"We've got to find Scar & Jase, I'm on my way." Trin confirmed.

The lights shut off; Santiago's men grabbed their guns & began to fire again. The uninvited guests were men who were after Santiago. They wanted his head, but his men weren't having that, they lit the entire mansion up. Blood splattered the walls as the remaining guests ran for their lives, literally. The girls made their way to Scarlett & Jase, & they began to make a move to get out of the house.

"Scarlett!!" Trinity yelled as Jase jumped in front of her.

WHOOM WHOOM, bullets whirled into the chest of Jase as Scarlett turned around and saw his body hit the floor. She became someone she never thought she'd be so soon, a killer. Scarlett leaped toward the shooter & snatched his gun.

"SCARLETT, NOOOO!!" Emma yelled.

Scarlett used her left foot & kicked the shooter to the ground. She stepped back & shot the man right in the center of his forehead. His head slumped to the side; she knew he was gone. She towered over her prey in the darkness as Trinity, Naree, & Emma snatched her by the hand & guided her right back towards the door. She ripped from their grip & ran back to Jase. She knelt beside him & attempted to wake him from what felt like a nightmare to her.

"Jase! Please get up!" She cried as she felt his body for gun wounds. He groaned & began to move, he was alive. Scarlett pulled him to stand upright as they followed the girls through the front door & to the car.

"I'm okay." He reassured them after a deep cough. He raised his t-shirt & removed his bulletproof vest. The girls sighed & began removing everything they didn't arrive in.

"I'm so glad you're okay!" Scarlett responded as she grabbed his hand. She leaned over & kissed him again.

"I knew it!" Emma gasped.

The girls snickered amongst themselves & tried to forget the fact that they nearly died, as well as the fact that Scarlett killed a man tonight. Jase took them all back to Wake-Up Philly so they could debrief with Bennie & part ways. The coffee shop was closed, so they went around back. Harvey let everyone in & took them to Bennie's office. Jase stood in Perez's office with the girls, shirtless. Perez analyzed the bruises on his chest & poured a glass of scotch.

"Have a good time, Jase?" He asked while loading his Barrett M82. Jase already knew how Perez was coming behind his daughter, so he prepared himself for his wrath.

"Listen, Bennie, I-" he attempted to explain.

"No need to explain. Boswell saw you kissing my daughter tonight." Bennie confirmed before cocking his gun & aiming it at Jase. Scarlett ran in front of him & yelled.

"IS THIS HOW YOU TREAT SOMEONE WHO SAVED YOUR DAUGHTER'S LIFE?"

"What do you mean?" Bennie asks while lowering his gun.

"Papi (Daddy) they tried to kill me. I ran to leave the party. Jase dived in front of me & took every bullet, look at his chest! I should've died tonight." She cried.

Bennie braced himself & lowered his guard.

"I appreciate you saving my daughter's life. I will spare yours. A life for a life, but you are not to see her, touch her, or even speak to her. Comprender (Understand)?"

Jase's head hung low as he backed away from Bennie.

"Papi (Daddy)!" Scarlett cried.

"This mission was muy importante (very important). You have failed. I told you what happens when you fail." He expressed as he clutched his M82 closely.

Trinity walked up to Perez's desk & presented everything she swiped. She took a moment to show him each snapshot in her burner phone & then stepped back. Emma relayed the intel she gathered, & so did Naree. Bennie's face displayed pure satisfaction. He then looked at Scarlett & asked, "So, mi hija (my daughter), what do you have for me?"

"I killed one of Santiago's men tonight." She answered with her arms locked behind her back. Jase informed him it was Ricky- he was one of Santiago's good men.

Bennie walked over to Scarlett.

"Bienvenida a la familia (Welcome to the family), mi hija (my daughter). Bienvenida a la familia (Welcome to the family)." Bennie stated as he clutched the back of her head & held her closely. He knew his baby girl was an assassin at heart. Tonight confirmed she knew it too.

~~Chapter 9:~~

<u>Paris Trip</u>

Scarlett spent the next few days conflicted because she killed a man, & it was her first instinct to do so. She wondered if her grandfather trained her for that very moment all along- she even debated if he was part of the cartel too; she knew better than to ask.

Scarlett was also fighting the urge to call Jase; she heard her father loud & clear but in one way or another- he had her fucked up too. Trin, Ree, & Em comforted her & tried their best to bring her joy as she was now torn between two worlds. Fortunately, they were pressed to shift gears because they had to leave for Paris; Fashion Week was calling their names. Official documentation for their clothing line had finally been provided; We Bitchin Fashion was now recognized by the Secretary of State, & its brand name, logo, & designs were respectfully registered with the United States Patent & Trademark Office (USPTO). They also had a substantial amount of funding to implement every sector of their mission.

The girls foresaw that Paris could change the course of their careers, We Bitchin Fashion was going places, *literally*. Production was feasible because Emma devised everything with their mission in mind, she was innovative;

Bailey remained her muse as she recounted her love for fashion throughout their friendship.

The girls gathered their designs, marketing materials, & personal belongings, so they could set forth into Paris, France. Bennie was feeling godly, so he arranged for his private jet to transport them to Paris & appointed Nest as their security! He was secretly proud of them all. They arrived at Philadelphia International Airport with their parents.

The girls informed their parents of their adventure to Paris, but they told them the jet was compliments of a fashion house that held interest in them. Of course, their parents bid them a beautiful farewell & wished for them to be careful & to check in, or else they'd be popping up.

Since Bailey's girls begged to partake in this journey alone, their parents requested to always know their whereabouts; they agreed because with freedom came responsibility. As they boarded the jet, their luggage was stored away safely, & they were escorted to exclusive seats that turned into beds. In front of their seats, the chef prepared personal feasts of brunch.

"It's the esthetics for me!" Trinity shouted with excitement.

"It's the French toast for me." Emma screamed while pouncing onto her seat.

"It's the designer coffeeee for me!" Naree blushed.

"OMG we are living the liffeee now!" Scarlett shrilled. The chef came out & placed drinks beside their brunch, fruit was pouring from the glasses.

They waved from the jet as it prepared to lift off.

"So, do we have everything?" Scarlett asked.

"Ha! It's a little late to ask that question now, Scar. We're about to be in the air." Naree joked.

"I know. I'm sorry fam, my head has been all over the place. What have I gotten myself into?" Scar responded.

"I'm telling you. Worst shit could've happened. You killed someone who almost killed you, tbh (to be honest)." Naree explained.

"Right, it was a fair kill to me." Trinity added.

"But she like, has a soul, you guys. She means... we're not killers." Emma shared.

"I ain't a killer but don't push me." Naree laughed.

"No maim, no ham, no turkey. We're not doing that!" Scarlett cackled as she fell from her seat.

Emma laughed hysterically even though she felt a bit slighted. The girls were all on one accord when it came to uplifting their sister, but Emma still did not feel comfortable with the idea of killing anyone- she'd probably die first. She felt that if they targeted the righteousness of the kill, there wouldn't be room for conviction.

"Okay, trapper turned rapper! Let's focus, for real!" Emma giggled ferociously as the girls joined in, literally laughing until they cried.

"Okay, okay, okay- all jokes aside. Our domain is LIVE! I just need to add more content & finalize our search engine optimization. I must also ensure the host is enabled for purchases." Trinity shared.

"Layman's terms, please." Emma suggested with a snicker.

"The website needs to be upgraded to a plan that will allow transactions. Search engine optimization is what's used to help drive in more traffic. No worries, I got this!" Trinity ironed out.

"Okay, this is amazing! Once we land & settle in, you can finish that & then I can begin sketching designs for the upcoming seasons." Em responded.

"We should also be thinking bigger. Like, should we incorporate a production team? We don't want to cause a burnout in your skills, once people start buying as quickly as we know they will, restocking needs to be manageable." Scarlett shared.

"I feel you. I also vote for more team meetings. The cartel is clearly going to keep throwing curve balls, we've gotta stay two steps ahead with #GameOnForBailey & We Bitchin Fashion to prevent falling behind in our goal of avenging our sister & becoming millionaires. I'm so excited. I wish our girl were here to see this." Trinity smiled as she stared into the clouds floating out the window; each one took shape to Bailey's face, smile, & laugh.

"I can't believe it's almost been a year without her." Scarlett sulked.

"Yeah, time sure does fly when you're hurting." Naree added.

"We should celebrate her somehow." Emma said with a lightbulb.

"Yea, like maybe launch a limited-edition skirt called the *The Bailey*. Too corny?" Naree recommended, laughing.

"No way. Besides, she was corny. Ha, I remember she used to crack jokes & then laugh before any of us would." Emma laughed.

"Right. Ha, ha, ha. It's like she only told the jokes for herself." Trinity snickered.

"Sheesh! Before we get to crying, we need to get some rest after we chow down! We've got a long flight ahead, gotta hit the ground running when we arrive." Naree encouraged.

"Aghhhh, I'm so nervous. You're right, let's eat & knock ourselves out BEFORE WE GET TO PARIS!" Trinity yelled.

The girls dug into their platters of brunch while reviewing their itinerary. Shortly after, they turned their seats into beds, boy did they feel high-class. They slept until arriving in the city of love at Paris Charles de Gaulle Airport.

They were refreshed, excited, & ready to take on the world. As promised, the girls contacted their parents & let them know they arrived. They were then transported to Hôtel La Bourdonnais Paris with Nest in a private limousine, compliments of Bennie. He began to take a liking to these badass girls. A ruthless gangster he was, but he had a heart for these girls now.

They stepped from the limo at the hotel & immediately took in its essence. They raced in as Nest ensured their luggage was handled. Upon checking in, they sent texts to their parents to inform them of another safe arrival. They made it to their suites & could not believe their eyes; everything was extravagant. Beside their huge beds sat a round table with welcome champagne & macaroons, along with tour guides & menus for nearby restaurants. They showered & got ready to meet up. It was time to collaborate on additional content for their website.

Everyone showed up at Trinity's suite with their laptops, notepads, & pens. Scarlett used a menu to order room service as they dived right into business mode. Trinity logged into the account for the host of their website & began to hop into the section for SEO. While navigating the site's traction thus far, she noticed there was another website showcasing their designs. She stood from her computer, walked away, & then came back & sat down to double-check what she saw.

"What's wrong, Trin?" Emma questioned.

"Somebody stole our shit!" Trinity stated in pure shock.

"Come again?" Scarlett uttered as she dropped her laptop.

"Well slap my ass & call me Diamond because this is fuckery at its finest." Naree shared while googling all possible whereabouts of their content.

"I cannot with you right now, Ree. We only did a soft launch, who could've done this?" Scarlett asked.

"Apparently, a boutique in Philly is the culprit. What an insult." Naree informed.

"We did go to school wearing multiple designs from our new line. I know someone had to notice it wasn't on the market." Emma curiously inferred.

"You think we're *that* dope?" Naree questioned.

"Of course. But I also say that because in a school full of rich entitled brats, they'd notice if someone has something they don't." Emma explained.

"Exactly." Trinity cosigned while digging to locate the owner.

"Rebecca Lopez is who stole our designs." Trinity informed.

"Who the hell is Rebecca Lopez & how did she get our designs?!" Emma fussed.

"Doesn't matter because we're about to sue her ass! We're what - 5 hours ahead, right? It's 2:17 pm here, so it should be around 9:17 am back in Philly." Naree calculated as she dialed the number from the boutique's store page.

"Thank you for calling Fab Lives Matter, Rebecca speaking, how may I help you?"

"Lopez, Rebecca Lopez, correct?" Naree inquired.

"Uhm, yes this is Ms. Lopez, how may I help you?" she confirmed. Ree went for the jugular.

"Great. I just wanted to let you know that we know you stole our designs." Ree informed.

"Excuse me, I've done no such thing. I don't know who you think you are calling my shop with this absurd allegation. I do not play with children, comprender (understand)?"

"Allow me to help *you* understand. The designs you have plastered on pages 6 -9 of your website belong to We Bitchin Fashion. Our designs are trademarked & our business is registered with the state. Our company is legit; therefore, this is a verbal warning that you will be sued. You comprender (understand) me?" Ree spelled out.

"Sued? Okay, wait one minute. I had no idea these designs belonged to any brand. My daughter introduced me to a hot new teen line of fashion items that were tailored to my target audience. I am no thief." She explained.

Who's your daughter?" Ree questioned.

"Kaylee Lopez." Rebecca answered.

The girls all gasped in unison.

"Our clothing line is dedicated to Bailey Brooks! I'm sure Kaylee has told you so much about her. Please know that our lawyer will be in contact. Have a nice day, Ms. Lopez." Naree reiterated as she ended the call.

Rebecca immediately cleared her store out & informed everyone she'd be back later. She locked up & went home after texting Kaylee & telling her to be there if she weren't already. She flew home like a bat out of hell, mind racing, ready to confront her teenage daughter. She jumped out of her car & burst through the doors.

"Kaylee Marie Lopez!" she yelled.

"Sí (Yes) mama?" Kaylee responded.

"Why did you solicit me a stolen clothing line?"

"Qué (What)?"

"No qué, sabes exactamente de lo que estoy hablando (No what, ¡you know exactly what I'm talking about)!" Rebecca yelled.

"I don't know what you're talking about. I presented you nice drip. I can't believe you're accusing me of trying to bring you down." Kaylee deflected.

"Are you?! I just got a phone call informing me to pretty much lawyer up." Rebecca further explained.

"Really?" Kaylee questioned, looking crazy in the face.

"Yes really! & Who is Bailey Brooks? This clothing line is apparently for her." Rebecca questioned some more.

Kaylee began to look guilty, but she held her attitude.

"Bailey Brooks committed suicide at the UA last year. I told you about it, remember?" Kaylee answered.

"Oh no. Please tell me you had nothing to do with it?" Rebecca flared, pacing the floor.

"No Mamá." Kaylee responded storming through the French doors to her bedroom.

Rebecca wanted to believe Kaylee, but she knew that her daughter loved to talk- so if she was being short, it was for no good reason. She went into her study & began to search We Bitchin Fashion. She added a tab & searched her website beside it; immediately, she was taken aback because it was official- Kaylee had just lied to her face.

She sat there & took in the foolery. She felt so played, but she didn't stop there. She found tags on social media pages connected to Bailey Brooks. She began to click on them all. She read through posts regarding the nature of her suicide until she couldn't take it anymore. She closed her computer, left her home, & returned to her store. Kaylee sat in her room, swarming in lies & deceit.

After Naree ended the call, the girls sat in Trinity's room at a loss for words. It was like Bailey's life had been taken all over again.

"We did this for Bailey & they think they can just shit on it & sell what we have as their own? Kaylee's weak ass has it coming." Trinity snapped.

"I threatened to sue her, but we don't even have a lawyer." Naree admitted.

"Oh, no. I've got this." Scarlett reassured as she stood to her feet. She paced back & forth speaking to her father in Spanish. She was heated! That Italian came with the rah-rah today, she was ready for war!

She made him abreast of their current situation, and with no hesitation, he informed her that he'd appoint them the cartel's lawyer, Fernando Cruz. After Scarlett finished speaking with Bennie, she let the girls know it was being handled & that they must redirect their energy to Paris, because they were there for a reason. They left the hotel & visited fashion shows while touring the city. They toured to

Moulin Rouge, Palace of Versailles, Eiffel Tower, the Pantheon, the Latin Quarter, & Montmartre.

As night turned to early morning, they were all pooped. Everyone but Trinity returned to their rooms to recuperate. She was tired but she couldn't shake feeling played. She pulled out what she loved most, her computer. She didn't expect to hack anything in Paris, her tech devices that kept her off the radar were back in Philly. She felt unarmed but she couldn't let this mess slide. She began to search everything on Rebecca Lopez, she fell asleep on top of the keyboard before she knew it.

The sun rising was one of the most beautiful things to experience in Paris, they didn't get to see it today though; each girl slept in until the late afternoon, they felt sublime. They couldn't believe they were in Paris. They gathered themselves & joined forces in the lobby for breakfast. As they sat at the table, texts came through on their burner phones immediately. The lawsuit against Fab Lives Matter had officially been filed & served to fulfill its purpose. The girls held each other's hands & closed their eyes to have a moment of silence for Bailey. They took in deep breaths & let go. It was on. Rebecca was served while standing on the sales floor of her boutique. She was panicked but she knew who to call.

"Hola (Hello) Mr. Parker. Cómo estás (How are you)?"

Frankie smiled & responded, "I'm well, Rebecca. How are you?"

"No tan Buena (Not so good) Mr. Parker. I need your help." She pleaded.

"I'm sorry to hear that. How can I help?" He empathized.

"I was served today regarding a stolen clothing line. Could you please represent me? I honestly did not know these clothes were stolen. My daughter-" she cried.

"Say no more." Frankie confirmed as he prepared to do what he did best, represent. He quickly made a detour from his normal route & stopped by Rebecca's boutique to pick up the documents she was given. He analyzed them but not in true depth, he took them to his car & told her he'd call her soon.

The girls returned to their room & got dressed for a night on the town, limo vibes only. Before they left, Trinity had to get her hands back into the search she started. She stared through her laptop, *what should I hack first?* she wondered. She confirmed with herself that she needed to see Rebecca's business records. It was imperative she knew who they'd be dealing with, as well as how much money she'd made from their line so far.

Frankie entered his home with breakfast for his wife. He laid the documents on the bar & placed their breakfast next to it. Louise came from the kitchen & kissed him graciously. She enjoyed breakfast from Farrah's, & he knew it! She glanced over at the documents next to her order & noticed the business card attached.

"You're working with Fernando Cruz?" she asked.

"What, baby?" Frankie responded, not paying attention.

"Fernando Cruz. He's the attorney on the documents you have here." She repeated.

"Oh, okay. Yes, I just picked those up from Kaylee's mom, Rebecca. She told me she was being sued by a group of teenage girls." He explained.

"A group of teenage girls. This sounds oddly familiar." Louise acknowledged.

"Apparently, her daughter coerced her into stealing their clothing line." He explained, sharing the tea.

"These damn kids will be the death of us all, I tell you." She laughed.

"Not on my watch, Mrs. Senator." He confirmed in a frisky manner.

"Okay, Mr. Parker. You better be careful. This guy is currently under investigation for illegal dealings with the cartel." Louise informed.

Mr. Parker stood still in his tracks.

Trinity got into Rebecca's records. She navigated every document, saving screenshots & recordings as she went along. Trinity's computer alerted her that someone was in the queue, another user. She attempted to hurry as her moves were being noted. A message populated big & bold across the screen before she could close out.

"Gotcha." It said with a wink.

She recorded the last file, shut her computer down, & then jumped from her desk. She took off to the bathroom & became well acquainted with the trash can. Champagne & anxiety do not mix.

She contacted Naree & informed her she was headed to her room. When she got there, she let her know that someone experienced was on to her.

Naree encouraged her to keep her cool so they could have fun before attending the fashion show & meetings they had lined up. They didn't want to worry Emma or Scarlett, so they agreed to keep quiet until they made it back to Philly.

Their secrecy worked like magic because they had the greatest time of their lives. They invaded the town in style, wearing nothing but *We Bitchin Fashion*. They passed out marketing materials & took pictures everywhere they went. They had never been showered with so much love, it truly altered the direction of their energy- which was exactly what they needed.

Nest was completely worn out from posing as some tourist when he was undoubtedly a gangster who needed to get back to the bodies & the money.

Bailey's Girls turned in after turning up & then spent the remainder of their week attending fashion shows & collaborating with numerous brands.

They ended their bliss on the rooftop of a bar named ROOF Paris, they stared into the night & celebrated the fact that big-name fashion lines were now considering partnerships with their brand. They reflected on everything they went through to conquer this moment. That's right, We Bitchin Fashion would be sold from stores of highly anticipated calibers! They cheered to themselves & patted one another on the back for always checking in with the parents, no matter how chaotic things got, & they celebrated Bailey's life.

"Cheers to life, love, & sweet revenge." Naree sang. The clinking of their glasses rang greatness. The views from the rooftop were an introduction to the lives they always wanted. The lives in which they deserved.

Chapter 10:

Operation Hack

As their week of frolicking & gallivanting in Paris came to an end, Bailey's Girls were back to reality. It filled their parents with so much joy to see them beaming like the sun again.

They prepared for school & met at Trinity's to catch a ride. Ree, Em, & Scar all hopped in Trin's car, covered in their new drip. From their heads to their toes, they were bitchin fashion! Naree & Trinity decided to come clean with Scar & Em on their way to school.

"Hey guys, so when we were in Paris, I hacked into the business files of Rebecca Lopez's boutique." Trinity began.

"What?!" Scarlett asked in shock.

"Trinity, why would you do that when we have a lawyer who's going to provide those documents anyway?" Emma questioned, facepalming.

"That part doesn't matter. What matters is while I was digging through her accounts, another hacker sent me a message to let me know they saw me. I must've left some sort of digital trace behind. I didn't have my stuff with me. I fucked up." Trinity admitted as she turned around to face them at a stop sign.

"We know you did it purely on account of us. Don't beat yourself up about it." Em responded.

"Seriously, we know you don't do things recklessly. It's just frustrating because who the hell is trying to sabotage us?" Scar questioned.

"Well, seems like Kaylee grew a pair since we last ran into her. Maybe we should start there." Naree suggested.

"I'm with that." Scar agreed, popping her knuckles.

The girls arrived & exited the students' parking lot. They walked in sync as they blew through the doors of the UA. They smiled & continued to chat until approaching the devil's minions. They got closer & all hell broke loose.

"Kaylee Lopez!" Naree yelled.

"The peasants are calling." Allison yelled back.

"We know you stole several designs from our company." Trinity made known.

"Your company? Oh, cry me a river, Afro Puff." Allison laughed.

"Kaylee, you've got one second to explain yourself." Emma demanded.

"Kaylee would never steal from anyone. She's not even cut like that." Maci explained with disgust painted across her face.

"Yea, besides you bitches have nothing worth stealing." Allison continued.

Scarlett embraced her inner badass & grabbed Allison by her hair.

"I'm gonna shave your head & donate your hair to the cancer center if you don't pipe down!" Scarlett threatened.

Students began to laugh & record Allison's facial expression, she was downright speechless & embarrassed. Scarlett twisted her hair around her hand some more & then took her head & yanked it back against the locker. The girls panicked because this move was learned at Cartel Camp. They didn't wish to attract unnecessary attention, so they tried to stop her before she went any further.

"Scar, let her hair go. We can't do this right now." Naree spoke up.

"As much as I'd love to watch her kick your ass, you get a special pass today." Trinity educated as she placed her hand on top of Scarlett's. Scarlett took a deep break & scowled at Allison until Emma dragged her away.

"Girl, you were about to get it." Emma warned.

"For sure. I'd watch that mouth of yours moving forward." Scarlett reiterated as she knocked Allison's dangling ponytail from her shoulder. Allison flinched.

"Oooooooooo!!!!" a student yelled, jumping up & down in the crowd, dying of laughter.

"We cannot showcase any skills here, cartel or not. We must remain those special geeks until we get out of the UA." Trinity advised as they held hands, collectively.

They walked to class in style, they were the shit. No doubt about it.

"Funny how things change." Emma smirked as they carried along.

Trinity ran into Joshua on her way to first period. She stepped aside to apologize for her behavior with his sister.

"Hey, got a second?" She asked him as he tried to pretend he didn't see her.

"Uh, yea, sure." He said frowning to contain his joy that she spoke to him.

"So, I wanted to apologize to you & Jessica. I'm not sorry for being mad, but I am sorry that I spazzed on her when she chose to confide in me. I really want to get to the bottom of what happened to Bailey. I realize I can't do that yelling at people who do decide to open up to me during this process." She expressed.

"I appreciate your apology, but I already understood, trust me. If my sister had taken her life & anyone knew anything but never came forward, I would've been fighting mad too." He empathized.

"I wasn't fighting mad." Trinity shied away.

"Yea, you were. You were like AGHHHH." He chuckled lightly.

"Okay. Maybe I was fighting mad." Trinity laughed.

"Well, I'm gonna get going but I hope we can be friends." Trinity said with a warm smile.

"I wouldn't have it any other way." He responded. Yes, he would. He wanted Trinity to be his girlfriend. She was just his type.

"Okay, well I think you have my number. Feel free to hit my line, any time." She invited, walking away.

Her phone dinged, instantly, as he stood in a trance.

Josh: "Feel free to hit my line too." He texted.

Trinity turned around & winked at him as she continued to rush off to class.

Allison, Maci, & Kaylee sat in the girls' locker room, sulking in pity.

"How the hell did she just get away with that?" Maci questioned.

"I don't know. Maybe I'm just not feeling it today." Allison answered.

"Did you really steal their shit, Kay?" Maci asked.

Kaylee laughed & responded, "I wouldn't call it stealing."

"Oh snapppp!" Maci laughed as she stood to the floor. "Turns out you're one of us after all." She clapped.

"Actually, I do things bold & to their face. We could never be the same." Allison snarled.

"Oh, you're just pissed they showed you up again." Kaylee snapped.

"Yea, they've got bigger tits than I remember." Maci made known.

"Well, our tits are bigger." Kaylee stated as she hit the blunt they sparked, choking a bit.

Allison inhaled & exhaled before taking a hit.

"I've got something for their asses." She spoke.

"So do I." Maci confirmed.

"You better believe I do too. It's a party now." Kaylee added.

School wasn't heavy, it was actually quite okay. Students modeled so much respect for Bailey's Girls. More people started making small talk with them, inviting them to places, & asking to become their friends; there was a silver lining after all. The teachers spoke with them about their experience in Paris & asked them to share any delight they cared to express with their peers. Lots of kids had gone to Paris already because their parents were rich, but the engagement & experience differed completely because those rich brats were not business owners. There went those points once more, Bailey's Girls were climbing the social charts; they gained more followers & traction on their website, it was like a dream. They planned for revenge, not to become... popular.

"So, this is what it feels like?" they all embraced, succumbing to a newfound trace of relevance as they ended their day together.

Before making it to the car, alerts swarmed Trinity's phone. She looked down & began to read all incoming notifications; she dropped her phone.

"What's wrong?" Emma asked.

"Trinity began shaking & pacing the floors of the parking lot. We've got to go. NOW!" She yelled.

The girls didn't ask questions, they grabbed Trinity's phone & got in the car immediately.

"Someone hacked our business account." She informed.

"Wh-" the girls began.

"SOMEONE HACKED OUR FUCKING BUSINESS ACCOUNT! I HOPE THEY'RE READY TO DIE TODAY!" Trinity yelled as she clutched her steering wheel.

"No, no wait. We're not killing anyone else. Let's just go to your house while your parents are still working to figure out who did this. I know you can figure this out, Trinity. No one is better than you." Emma encouraged.

"THEN HOW THE HELL DID THEY GET INTO OUR BANK ACCOUNT?! I SPECIFICALLY LACED THAT MF WITH SOFTWARE! TO PROVIDE MORE PROTECTION! SO THAT I COULD PREVENT SHIT LIKE THIS FROM HAPPENING. IF THEY BROKE THROUGH THAT, I DON'T KNOW. I DON'T KNOW THAT I CAN FIND THEM." Trinity ranted some more, unsure of herself.

"This is just a formality. All the bigwigs undergo bullshit before elevating to greatness. We're being played. We need to figure out who the hell is gunning for us so that we can shut them down- straight like that." Naree explained.

"Formality my ass, Ree! They stole OUR FUCKING MONEY!" Trinity yelled.

"So fine. Fuck it. Let's get it back!" Scarlett demanded. On GO.

"Damn right, we're getting it back!" Trinity yelled as she pulled over to kick & scream at the dirt on the road. The girls got out, consoled her, & reassured her that they'd do anything to help her find the person screwing with them. They eventually got back in the car & managed to make it to Trinity's house, safely. Trin raced to the door & snatched out every gadget she could find. She plugged them into their proper places, adjusted her adapters, & pulled up their account. She began to go stir-crazy after a moment.

"What are you looking for?" Scar asked as she watched her scurry in distress.

"Digital dirt." She answered.

"What now?" Emma asked.

"I was messy when I hacked Rebecca's files. Someone saw me because I left traces of digital dirt." She explained.

Naree hesitated but asked anyway, "Well, do you see anything?"

Trinity didn't say a word, she kept digging. She sat in silence for nearly an hour. The girls knew to back off at this point because if Trinity could not locate the culprit, things would really take a turn for the worst.

"We were hacked by a source connected to Bell Enterprises. Bell Enterprises is owned by Jim Bell, Maci Karr's father." Trinity stated, punching through her

bedroom wall. She jotted something down on a sticky note &
wiped her eyes.

The girls were pissed too but they were speechless.
Trinity grabbed her laptop & gathered every device she knew
she'd need & told them to get up.

"I'm taking you girls on a little field trip."

"Where to?" Emma questioned.

"Maci's house." Trinity responded.

"You bet your sweet ass we're going to Maci's house."
Scarlett confirmed with murderous intentions. Trinity
snatched the sticky note from her desk. Maci's address was
written on it, along with the address of Bell Enterprises.

"Mama said there'd be days like this." Naree stated
with a smile.

"Days like what?" Scarlett asked.

"Days where you've got to show the workers who's
boss." Naree clarified.

"Period." Trinity confirmed.

The girls quickly ran out & sped to Maci's house.
When they arrived, they stepped out & rang the doorbell.

"Hello." Paula greeted as she opened the door.

"Hello, Mrs. Bell. We're here to see Maci. Is she home?" Trinity responded through gritted teeth.

"Oh, why yes. You friends with Maci? I've never seen you all before." She answered with delight. A scarf surrounded the center of her head. She had on red lipstick & a dress that flared at the bottom; it was like stepping into a Twilight Zone from the fifties.

"Yes maim, new friends." Scarlett cleared up.

"Well, it's nice to meet you all. Come on in. She's in her room upstairs, you may take the elevator if you like." She informed.

"Yes maim." They all stated in unison.

Paula escorted them to the elevator & informed them where to locate Maci's room. They hopped on, nervous but anxious to get to her. The elevator couldn't possibly get them there quickly enough. When they stepped off, they strolled down the hall & to the left. They didn't knock or anything, they ran up in her room like the police. Maci was sitting at her desk, drawn into her computer. She jumped back when the door flew open.

"What the-" she shouted.

"Shhhh" Scarlett instructed as she closed Maci's bedroom door & locked it. Maci had the fear of God in her eyes. She didn't know what to do, she was outnumbered.

"I think you know why we're here, so let's cut the shit, okay?" Emma directed.

"I don't." Maci responded with an attitude.

"I know someone connected to your father's company stole our fucking money, we're gonna need that back. NOW!" Trinity snapped.

"Or so help me God, I will air this place the hell OUT." Scarlett politely informed.

"Air this place out? Really Scarlett? Let's keep it cute, why don't we." Maci responded sarcastically before reiterating she didn't know what they were talking about.

"Okay. So, we wanna play stupid, do we? Let me break this down for you in a language only bitches like you seem to understand: If you don't get our money back to the account you stole it from, this *secret hacking company* your father THINKS no one knows about- will be exposed, indefinitely. I'll also leak every ounce of dirt I've located thus far." Trinity threatened.

"Pretty sure if you call her bluff, she'll have more time to dig- which means she'll also find more, & then your daddy's business will be donezo." Naree added.

"Literally." Emma laughed menacingly.

Maci's eyes bounced around in wonder as she braced herself.

"Wait! Alright! I did have someone take it, but I promise to give it back. I wasn't trying to fuck over my father." Maci explained.

"Oh, so you just wanted to fuck us over?! As if you don't have enough money already! You rich, arrogant, selfish, entitled fuck-face!" Emma snapped.

"I don't think you know who you're dealing with at this point." Scarlett smirked as she stepped beside Trinity.

"Call 'em & tell 'em to send it back, now! They have ten minutes. Oh, & while you're at it, let 'em know they mustn't attempt to cover their tracks this time because their security levels were breached." Trinity demanded.

Maci pulled out her phone in a panic & dialed an unsaved number quickly. Trinity watched her like a hawk.

"Don't try anything funny either." Naree suggested with her eyes scowled & arms folded.

Maci pressed the call button & let it ring for a while, no answer.

"Call again & put it on speaker." Naree instructed.

Maci hesitated but she called again.

"Can't talk right now, I'll hit you later." Jack informed.

"No, no, no, no, wait! This is important." She yelled.

"What's up?" He responded.

"The money I had you swipe; we've got to give it back." Maci spit out.

"Nah, can't help you there darling. I don't do that." Jack laughed. He wasn't one for juvenile games.

"You're gonna do it today." Trinity yelled.

"Who's that?" he asked Maci.

"Listen, the girls I had you swipe the money from are here. We've got to send it back so that my dad doesn't find out what we did. I go down, you go down too." Maci made known.

"Fine. But you still owe me my cut. I'm not compromising there. I did the job." Jack responded.

"Whatever. Just send it back, now. They gave us ten minutes. Please stop what you're doing & send it back! Now!" she instructed.

"Alright. We'll talk later." Jack confirmed.

"Now you can leave. He said he'll send it back." Maci smiled.

"I think I'm just getting comfy." Trinity said as she sat on Maci's bench.

"Yea, me too." Naree confirmed sitting on the edge of her bed.

"Oh, why the hell not." Emma laughed while taking a seat on Maci's vanity.

Scarlett smiled & cocked her head to the side.

"Let's get to know each other. I was trained to hunt animals; did I ever tell you that?" Scarlett grinned like a hyena.

Maci's eyes bucked & she stood from her desk chair.

"Please leave or I will call my-"

"You'll call who? Your precious stepmother downstairs? She's been drinking, so I'm sure she won't hear you now." Scarlett notified, moving closer.

"Girl, you tried it." Trinity chuckled.

"Yea. I could smell the liquor on her breath, good stuff." Naree smiled.

"This feels really good." Trinity laughed, clapping her hands together & throwing her head back.

"No. This is not funny. Just wait-

"Wait for what? You utter this visit to a soul & I will unveil the truth about your criminal ass father. I know he hires his hacking team to embezzle funds from other companies. Need I say more?" Trinity warned as she crossed her right leg over the left.

Maci stood in the center of her floor, hyperventilating.

"You're extremely overdramatic without your friends." Scarlett addressed.

"Yea, you should like BREATHE." Naree suggested.

Trinity received a notification on her phone.

"Money's back, all three hundred grand. Let's go." Trinity made aware as she headed towards the door. The girls followed but before leaving, Trinity stepped to Maci's face.

"Fuck with us or We Bitchin Fashion again, & you'll be sorry." She humbly informed as Emma unlocked the bedroom door.

Maci's face flushed red as she sat back down to pace her breathing. She was now in the hole $50,000 for a scam gone to shit. Today, she learned a valuable lesson: Never poke a bear that's been dying to eat you.

~~Chapter 11:~~

<u>Game Changer</u>

Bailey's Girls had been feeling great about themselves, lately; they were literally sitting on top of the world. Life was flowing smoothly for a change. Their company was thriving; they now possessed many options for exclusive partnerships to showcase We Bitchin Fashion. School was better than ever, not because Allison & her minions were dead but because they acquired new friends. They gained friends who directly connected to their personal interests & religions- those things never got in the way of their sisterhood, it was just dope to vibe with people who understood the logistics of hunting, hacking, mathematics, or communication, directly- no breaking out the layman's terms because they get it, ya know.

They collaborated on cartel work & their company, but they also began making room for potential boyfriends & social lives. Friday was here! Emma informed the group she'd be meeting the mathletes at Wake-Up Philly. Trinity let her girls know she'd be going out with Joshua, their texting had gotten a little heavy, so they figured it was time for a date. Scarlett gave them the tea; she was going to meet Jase behind her father's back for dinner at some fancy-schmancy restaurant. Naree told them she'd be attending a sleepover at Byeol's house, a Korean girl whose name meant *Star*. As they all set forth in different directions, they did their secret handshake & bid one another a temporary farewell. Scarlett hopped in the car with Jase, he took her to an Italian restaurant in Downtown Philly.

"How you been?" Scarlett asked, interlocking their fingers.

"I could be better. Not being able to have you in my reach kills me. What are we gonna do?" Jase questioned with worry. He never bothered with relationships because he was dedicated to Bennie's business, but he was far too intrigued with Scarlett to walk away.

"How about we simply enjoy the moment? We can worry about the rest later." Scarlett encouraged.

They kissed & analyzed the menu together.

Trinity went home, changed clothes, & then drove to meet Joshua at Martha's Steaks. They both were craving Philly cheesesteak sandwiches with curly fries & a coke! Martha's was the best place to go because no matter what you order, it's going to giiive what it's supposed to give! Trinity stepped inside & found Joshua sitting in a booth with their orders.

"Aww you ordered for me." She smiled.

"Of course. As long as I know what you want, I'll always order for you." He responded with a smile, dimples just dimpling.

"Well, aren't you the perfect gentleman." She complimented as she took her seat.

"Only for the perfect lady." He admitted, bashfully.

"I'm no lady." Trin laughed.

"Oh yea, then what are you?" He asked, hormones going bonkers.

"Guess you'll find out soon." She chuckled mischievously. Trinity wasn't giving up a thing, she just loved flirting with him.

They sat & ate but could not stop staring at one another. They were so stinking cute. Trinity never had a boyfriend before; this was all foreign, but she felt "why the hell not." They had been cup-caking for a while which consisted of confiding in one another about their personal lives & sharing encounters they had with bullies, i.e.- rich kids. Their date was just the buttercream they needed. They became so close in one sitting. Trinity was certain she could trust him, & he, her.

Naree settled in at Byeol's house. Instantly, it felt like home; she was quite comfortable being somewhere that embodied her family's culture & traditions. Naree & Byeol connected over their religion: Buddhism & discussed plans to visit home again. They both have been in Philly for nearly half their lives. As they flipped through family photo albums

& ate ice cream, they quickly realized they were on to an amazing friendship.

Emma was chilling at Wake-Up Philly with the mathletes, they were discussing upcoming events. She was thrilled to be part of such an elite group of minds. They too had already been accepted to Ivy League colleges, talk about being "locked in." Emma excused herself so that she could step away & check in with her parents.

She exited the coffee shop & dialed her mom. While pacing & talking, she recognized two black SUVs that had been sitting there since she & the mathletes arrived. She thought the cars were empty, but caught glimpses of movement, & realized they had been scoping her the entire time. She attempted to end the call with her parents, but her mother would not stop talking. She began to sweat, profusely.

Panic imploded upon her. She jogged to the side of the building to see if Perez was in his office- big mistake. The first big body busted a U & drove down the alley, facing Emma. She immediately looked behind her & saw the other big body coming from the opposite direction; they were blocking her in. Cartel Camp did not prepare her for this. Thoughts flooded her mind; she quickly informed her parents someone was after her before dropping her cell at the scene. She took off toward the back door where Bennie's boys usually stood. Two men jumped out of one of the SUVs with a black hood & snatched her.

Emma screamed while being thrown into the back of an unfamiliar place. She was threatened to keep quiet, but she didn't. She snatched & pulled at her hood & began kicking everywhere around her. They gave her free rein as they sped away with their prize. Both SUVs sped from the alley & hit a right to haul ass. As they drove away, Emma screamed & yelled at the top of her lungs. A large man leaned forward & socked her dead in the face, bye-bye birdie. They arrived at an undisclosed location where Emma was carried in & held captive. She was still quite out of it, but she could hear one of the men speaking. "We've got Perez's daughter. Make the call to Bennie, so we can do what we need to do." Mateo said.

"We kill her when he say kill her." Tony responded. Emma began to sob quietly while pondering her next move, she wasn't prepared for this at all. *"Mr. Perez wants to kill me?! No, he wants to kill his own daughter! What is life right now?!"* She contemplated while sizing up each of the men through the thin fabric of her hood. She took in their profiles-insatiable, reckless, & ruthless; she was kidnapped by a group of mercenaries.

Meanwhile, back at Wake-Up Philly, the mathletes began to worry about Emma; they scurried around the area in attempt to locate her for over an hour. Emma's parents were unsettled enough to contact the police. When Emma dropped her phone, they called her back-to-back to see if she was okay, her mother's gut confirmed she was not because she never answered.

Emma's parents reported her as missing. Philly P.D. educated them on filing missing person reports, which didn't sit too well. They had to wait 24 hrs. Laura phoned everyone she knew to put their minds at ease, no dice. Em's sister, Karra asked where she was because they were due for a sister-date at the movies. Laura didn't even know what to say. She hit her best friend, Marcella & shared the way her call ended with Emma. Without delay, Marcella contacted Scarlett, & asked her whether she was with Em. Scar freaked because she could not say she was with Jase. She told her mom she was at the park, 'just chilling,' but that she was going to look for Em & then come home immediately.

Scarlett blew up Em's phone, no answer. She blew up her burner, no answer either. She knew working for Perez would come with its pains, but Em going missing wasn't anticipated whatsoever. She 3-wayed Trinity & Naree & dropped the bomb regarding Emma's disappearance. They all agreed to cut their evenings short & head straight to the coffee shop to investigate the true whereabouts of their best friend. Scarlett was smart enough to call her father too. He rounded up his men & told the girls to get over to Wake-up Philly, asap! Scarlett informed her mother she'd be home soon & promised to keep her posted.

Wake-Up Philly was now occupied with cartel members & 3/4 of Bailey's Girls. Bennie took the lead as his men stood & Bailey's Girls sat, seeking to gather direction. Bennie's cell rang right before he opened his mouth.

"Hola (Hello)." He answered.

"We've got your girl." Santiago informed.

"Who the hell is this?" Bennie questioned, staring at his video surveillance.

"Scarlett's life will come to an end if you don't drop 20 million at Dilworth Park. You've got 1-hour, pretty boy." Santiago instructed. Bennie paused & looked at Scarlett sitting in the flesh. He became pissed at the audacity.

"When I find out who you are, Estas MUERTO (you're DEAD)!" He yelled.

"She killed one of my good men. Shot him dead in my mansion. You didn't think I took that lightly, did you?!" Santiago explained.

"Santiago!" Bennie yelled.

"You call the police & she's dead." He informed before ending the call. Everyone stood afoot awaiting instruction.

"I want Banks back now! Ray, Jase, Carlos, & Nest you all are to accompany Scarlett, Trinity, & Naree. Guard them with your lives! Also, no police involvement, they'll kill her if we slip up even once." Bennie made known.

"I can hack the footage from each traffic light surrounding the area." Trinity suggested in a frantic state.

"I'll investigate, see if there's anything here that can help. I know the mathletes said she left her belongings, so she had to be snatched from here." Naree enlightened with her thinking face.

"Why did they take her?" Scarlett asked with a fist full of tears.

"Mi hija (My daughter), we have no time." Bennie reminded.

"Dad!" Scarlett shouted.

"Mission 2..." he answered.

"This is my fault?" She cried.

"No, no, no mi hija (my daughter). We only have 1 hour before they kill her. Let's stay focused, so we can retrieve her, quickly. Gear up." He directed.

Scarlett wiped her face & followed Bennie's men to the back room to grab a gun. She was ready for war. Jase shot her a few looks to showcase his compassion, privately.

Trinity got onto her laptop & began to retrace Emma's steps by viewing her interaction on the feed of the coffee shop & then cross-referencing her activity on the feeds from cameras surrounding the coffee shop. She saw Emma pacing the sidewalk, on the phone. More importantly, she saw two black SUVs in the same footage across the street from the coffee shop. She watched them observe Emma & saw them take off when Em ran to the back. She then jumped to cameras from the alley & saw them back there as well. She witnessed Emma's kidnapping. She lost track of them after they left the alley, so she hacked into the video feed of red-light signal cameras on every corner. She continued to track their vehicles for as long as possible while jotting down street names & landmarks. Bennie watched her in action, amazed. He lit a cigar, poured himself a shot of Whiskey, & walked the floors of the coffee shop, plotting revenge. *"20 million dollars, huh? More like 20 million bullets."* He thought.

Naree ran back inside with Em's phone & waved it in the air. "She wanted us to know she was here!" She reported in excitement.

"I've pinpointed where she may be. Two black SUVs took her to some warehouse near Columbus Blvd. Let's go!

I'm wiping the footage to cover our tracks, but I have it saved to my computer for future referencing." Trin announced.

Everyone solidified their gun of choice & rolled out together. Bennie had Ryan cover the shop due to their departure. The police arrived & began to question Ryan. They were forced to take Emma's kidnapping seriously after her mother went down to the police station, bet they won't try her again.

Upon arrival, the gang took their positions & moved in. They saw Emma tied to a pole from afar & two OPs standing on guard nearby. The remaining mercenaries walked toward the front after hearing movement. As soon as they stepped into open space, they were free game. Bennie's boys came in deep & lit their asses up. They opened gunfire & instantly eliminated Santiago's men on the spot.

Bailey's Girls ran to Emma through the smoke & flying bullets & began untying her. One of the OPs on guard near Emma raised his weapon & prepared to blow her away, but Jase got to him first; he killed him within a millisecond. The last mercenary ran full fledge with a knife toward Emma. Naree turned around & used her leg to trip him. He fumbled his weapon & fell face forward onto the blade of his own knife. The girls paused & gasped at the sight of what emerged from his skull. They took the black hood off Emma's head & squeezed her tightly, she was in so much shock that she couldn't even showcase her level of gratitude.

Trinity & Scarlett helped Emma walk from the warehouse to their vehicle. Jase & Ray collected evidence. Carlos & Nest swept the warehouse for gun shells and casings. Naree educated the men on retrieving bullets from dead bodies. They were familiar with simply killing to get the job done but with her mother working in the medical field for so long, she learned enough to kill someone & cover it up, entirely.

Quickly, she managed to remove the bullets from each man & swipe their identification to follow up on who they were specifically. As they exited the warehouse together, Jase initiated operation "torch the place." They sped away & headed back to the coffee shop.

Emma sobbed silently & recounted her kidnapping, the second worst day of her life. Scarlett contacted her mother & let her know that Emma was okay & was on her way home. Marcella had so many questions, but Scarlett cut her short & told her she wanted to call Mrs. Banks to put her mind at ease as well. Upon calling Mrs. Banks, they had to formulate the proper story. Emma contacted her mom & immediately broke out into a cry like no other. She told her mom that she was okay & that Trinity would bring her home shortly. Emma's mom informed her the police were there & would await her arrival, so they could ask her some questions.

Emma let everyone know the police would be at her house, so they orchestrated to meet at the coffee shop, swap cars, & let Trinity be the one to take her home. They arrived at Wake-Up Philly & gave Bennie identification from all the men they killed. He was elated with this victory & thought quickly to have Trinity do her thing. She got onto her laptop & deleted all footage from red-light signals to & from the warehouse location. After successfully doing so, she drove Emma home where she came face to face with cars from Philly P.D.

Before Em could even exit Trinity's car, her mother came out running. She clutched her tightly & obsessively kissed all over her face before escorting her inside to speak with the police.

"Hi there, Emma. My name is Hank & this is Sean. Are you okay?"

"Yes." She responded meekly.

"Could you tell us what happened today?" He went on.

She put her head down & began to fiddle with her fingers uncontrollably.

"I went to Wake-Up Philly after school to meet with some new friends. After chilling for a bit, I stepped outside to check in with my parents & while I was pacing the sidewalk- in my own world, I noticed this weird man was watching me. I panicked & tried to run but he got me. He really got me. He threw me in his car & took me somewhere, but I can't recall where because I was so distorted when trying to run for my life. I managed to get away from him, but I never saw his face. He had a black hood covering my head the entire time." She explained, rattled with fear of the actual truth.

"Oh, baby. I'm so glad you're okay! I want you all to find this man & throw him under the jail, do you hear me?!" Mrs. Banks yelled.

"Mom, I'm okay." Emma reassured while fighting back more tears.

"You say you were snatched from the sidewalk? We went to the coffee shop before coming here. We reviewed their footage; it does not show you anywhere in the vicinity. Are you sure you were taken from there?" Officer Sean asked.

"Yea, could you have possibly been somewhere else?" Officer Hank added.

"No. I was at the coffee shop. My belongings are still there. I'm shook, not stupid." Emma snapped.

"Okay, okay, Emma. Thank you for that. What happened to your face? Did he hurt you?" Sean pried.

Mr. Banks looked up from his wheelchair. His soul cringed at the thought of someone touching his daughter.

"He hit me. I wouldn't stop screaming for help." She confirmed.

Mrs. Banks fell to the floor. She was so blinded by Em's return that she didn't see the bruise plastered across her face.

"Do you know if he drugged you or possibly took advantage of you?" Hank questioned.

"I don't think so." Em responded.

"Maybe you all should go down to the ER. We can follow you to ensure a rape kit is ordered. They can also run some blood tests to trace any unusual substances." Sean suggested.

"Mom... do I have to? I don't want to leave. I just want to be here with you, Dad, & Karra. Where is she?" Em responded.

Mrs. Banks pulled herself together to be strong for Em. "She's with Marcella for the night. I couldn't look her in the face & lie. Honey, let's just go to the ER to put potential what-ifs to bed. Dad & I won't be able to sleep without following up properly. I'm sure you won't either." Her mother insisted.

Emma nodded her head in agreeance. A lump migrated to the pit of her stomach as the police wrapped up their notes. Hank handed a card to Mr. & Mrs. Banks in the event Emma remembered anything more. She was taken to the ER by her mother, Hank & Sean trailed them in their swat cars. Mrs. Banks encouraged Mr. Banks to stay home so he wouldn't have to go through the typical difficulties of getting in & out of the car- he was not about that wheelchair life, sometimes he just had to be.

Emma spent hours at the hospital, she was already restless but having to be poked & pried at didn't make things any better. Hanks & Sean continued to press her for information, but she stuck to her story until they got the memo. They were able to confirm no foul play via rape kit and bloodwork. Mrs. Banks filled in Mr. Banks; they were grateful for this news. The doctor put Emma on fluids & had her rest for the time being.

She texted her girls & let them know what the police were up to so they could continue to cover their tracks. Trinity reminded Emma that the police could never have a lead on someone she eliminated in plain sight. Em felt more at ease. Their night came to an end, but the games were only beginning. Bennie was ready to take out Santiago, Santiago was ready to go to war with Bennie & his men, Bailey's Girls were prepared to get some shit popping, & the Russians-well let's just say they finally found out they're missing 10 million dollars.

The next day, Hank & Sean set out to tie up loose ends because they didn't believe Emma's story at all. They reviewed feeds from red-light signal cameras surrounding the area & even re-visited Wake-Up Philly, still no trace of Emma or her mysterious kidnapper. This dead end forced them to close the case as their minds swelled with wonder.

~~Chapter 12:~~

<u>Once Upon a Laugh</u>

Principal Ritton contacted Louise regarding Allison's behavior; he enlightened her she needed to meet with him today or Allison would be facing disciplinary action for her latest encounter with a student by the name of Elizabeth Smalls. Ritton had no qualms looking the other way when it came to Allison, but this time, she was screwing with someone whose father was also a major contributor to the UA.

Louise flew in, dripping in diamonds & designer. She sat down with Principal Ritton & shared some intimate details about their family's background & how she understands Allison has inexcusable behaviors, but to simply bear with her. Principal Ritton explained the position he's been placed in, as he has forcibly written her off for years now. He warned her that Allison's next altercation would result in actions stipulated in the UA's student code of conduct. Louise left his office flustered. Before exiting the school, she located the nearest girls' restroom & contacted her husband. She laid her phone on the sink & hit speaker.

"Hey Lo, everything okay?" Frankie asked.

“I’m over at the UA. Ritton summoned me because Allison’s behaviors are out of control. I just ugh.” She explained, sniffling.

“That’s our baby girl.” Frankie responded in a joking manner.

“She’s not & I’m starting to think that’s the problem.” Louise admitted.

“Not this again, Lo. Every child goes through a stage of rebellion.” Frankie rationalized.

“Yea, simply imagine the shitstorm that emerges when she finds out she’s not our biological daughter. I love her to death but I’m at my wits end with her blatant disregard for this family’s name. We give her everything & she tromps all over it. I have so many obligations, I cannot continue to coddle her tomfoolery.” She explained, tearing up again.

“Calm down, Lo. We can have a serious chat with her today. Maybe even begin implementing decreases in allowances if she persists. I know you were scheduled to provide insight on the federal budget, try to see if you can still make it, & let me worry about our daughter.” Frankie insisted.

“I love you. We’ve had quite the journey with Alli. I am drained. She’s about to step into the real world, she won’t survive like this.” Louise expressed.

"You're right. There's one thing my father made clear to me. It's either you let me teach you & beat you or the world will." Frankie informed.

"Maybe we should investigate her background more; see if her biological parents can help us make sense of who we've been trying so hard to raise." Lo suggested.

"We don't need to do that. We did our due diligence when we adopted her. She is just like any other child, I promise you. We can talk more over dinner later, try to have a good day, baby." Frankie encouraged, smiling through the phone.

"You've got it, boss." She confirmed.

"You know I like it when you call me boss." He jived.

"Oh, Mr. Parker." She laughed. He was good at doing that. Making her laugh.

Louise exhaled & ended the call. She wiped her face, touched up her makeup, & brushed her hair. As soon as she left, two familiar souls danced from their restroom stalls.

"THAT BITCH IS ADOPTED!" Trinity yelled.

"Shhhhh" Naree laughed.

"No seriously, this is GOLD!" Trinity carried on.

"Oh, baby you have no idea!" Naree agreed.

"Oh, but I do." Trinity said rubbing her palms together as if gathering warmth in the wintertime. It was about to be a cold, cold world, alright. She had a glacier up her sleeve!

"Not only does she torture us, her poor mother is sick of her shit too." Naree acknowledged.

"This has truly made my day! I can't wait to tell Scar & Em!" Trinity raved!

"Right. Best tea ever!" Naree amened.

"Period!" Trinity shouted as she washed her hands.

"Shall we stir the pot, my lady?" Naree asked.

"Oh, we shall." Trinity answered, displaying a devilish grin.

Bailey's Girls met at Bennie's high-rise location after school. When Trin shared the breaking news, their hearts sang revenge again! Bennie was elated to see their spirits lifted. Trinity got on Perez's desktop & began to create unique flyers- she went to town on that keyboard & hit print-print-PRINT! They boxed up each batch of flyers & distributed them evenly. They couldn't wait to go to school tomorrow, more importantly, they couldn't wait to go tonight.

Bailey's Girls told Perez they'd see him later. They loaded each box of flyers into Trin's car & made way to the

UA. Operation: Check That Bitch was in motion. Trinity utilized her 2639 to break into the UA's security system. She hacked the feed to delete their presence after the deed was done. They all went home & slept like babies, they even smiled in their sleep- talk about being in sync with one other. These girls were family. A family on the verge of destroying another.

Thursday morning arrived. The wind was whistling, birds were singing, & the sun was shining; it all felt right. It was officially game time. The UA was gleaming with its green trees, rustic build, & rich vibes. Each student breezed past one another on their own high, unaware of the drama unraveling before them. As they entered the building along with the educators, students began to gasp one by one. Bailey's Girls waltzed in wearing all-black everything- black skirts, black boots, black mesh tops, & black garter belts; they were bitchin fashion.

As they continued further, the wind blew their hair in slow motion. Their perfume wafted in the air, slapping any bystander in the nostrils. Their faces- pure perfection, as they were beat for the gawwwds! They observed Ritton & Strickland in an uproar trying to tear down the flyers but there were just so many- it was impossible. They continued to storm through, unbothered. Allison, Maci, & Kaylee came in from the side doors; unbeknownst to them, Allison's world had blown up. They paid no attention though; they were used to students sizing them up, so they continued to walk like they owned the place. Everyone went to class & the whispers began. Allison received awkward looks, but no one had the balls to ask her about what they'd seen. By the time lunch was in session, the entire school had seen the flyers. Ritton instructed educators to confiscate all flyers; they cleared the main halls, classrooms, & restrooms- but they missed a spot.

Allison & her minions went to their hideout to smoke, the girl's locker room. When they stepped in, they saw the walls covered with the same flyers from this morning, Maci read one. "Allison Parker, you weren't born into a rich family, more like adopted by one. That's too bad."

"Still caught off guard?" Maci questioned as she slapped the flyer into Allison's hand. Allison coughed on her smoke. Kaylee's eyes were at attention. She ran to the wall & grabbed one too. "You're adopted & now, everyone knows." Kaylee read aloud.

"Maybe we should create a website for you too, since you're actually poor. Your adoptive parents want to send you back where you came from. Sheesh!" Maci read.

"Is this a joke?" Kaylee asked Allison.

"You're kidding me, right? It's obviously bullshit." Allison laughed.

More girls came into the locker room. They couldn't escape the postings, they read them too. After doing so, they all stared back at Allison. She didn't know whether to leave or keep smoking. She kept her cool & laughed as she choked on her smoke again. She got up & left the locker room.

"Come back." Maci yelled, taking off after her. Kaylee grabbed several flyers & then followed. The halls were swarming with students who were headed to lunch. When Allison stepped into the hall, she immediately felt outed.

"Hey, is it true you're adopted? I am too." Ann questioned with the widest smile on her face.

"Ugh, I am not adopted, you mindless idiot." Allison shrilled.

"So, you're not even rich? Like, where they do that at?" Elizabeth Smalls laughed.

"You better watch it, thot, or I'll take Jasper from you, again." Allison scowled, boiling inside. She didn't believe she was adopted, but she was bothered.

"Allison. Please slow down." Maci pleaded.

"Leave me alone." She grunted, dashing out of the building. Maci & Kaylee stood behind the glass doors, wondering if there was any truth to those flyers. Allison sat in the parking lot & finished her blunt. As she sat there swimming in her thoughts, she decided to hop on social media to take her mind off things. She scrolled & liked pictures she loved & then responded to some DMs. She was used to lots of DMs but today, people either asked if she was adopted or told her they knew she was. It was official, Allison was pissed & she was unhinged. She ran back into the school & looked for Trinity. She ended up on the balcony area of the cafeteria.

"I know you did this, bitch!" She yelled right before slapping the black off Trinity.

Trinity cocked back & caught her with a right hook. It was on. They fought like animals over prey until the UA's security hauled them to Principal Ritton's office. He contacted their parents & informed them their children were being suspended.

Bailey's Girls & Allison's minions stood outside of Ritton's office, awaiting the chance to move in. They stared one another up & down but Maci & Kaylee didn't try anything. Ms. Woods arrived. Shortly after, Mr. & Mrs. Parker arrived. They sat in a conference with the principal, security, & their children.

"Trinity Woods is spreading lies about me! She's jealous." Allison explained.

Trinity didn't utter a word.

"See, she did this. I know she did it. She wishes she were me." Allison continued.

"Watch it, blondie." Trinity smiled.

"Oh, you watch it, afro puff!" Allison yelled. Trinity stood from her chair & whopped Allison in the back of the head. Security detained them both.

"I can't be held accountable for this. There's no proof. Isn't that how it works Mr. Parker?" Trinity questioned, using his own foolery against him.

He didn't respond. Mrs. Parker raised her brows at Trinity. Ms. Woods shot Trinity a look. She didn't like the Parker family, but she didn't tolerate disrespectful children on any front.

"She's correct. We cannot hold her accountable for the flyers. We must however suspend you both for fighting. You can return to school in 3 days. Please reflect on your behaviors to prevent further action." Ritton shared.

Security escorted the girls & their parents from the building. Their friends sulked against the wall after being told to report to their next class. They walked away with their phones in hand, ready to text about the drama.

Ms. Woods took Trinity home & didn't say much. She knew if her daughter fought, it was because someone hit her first. Trinity was still fuming, so she went to her room & jumped into the next phase of operation: #GameOnForBailey.

Allison was taken home. When she arrived, she located the butler & made her demands for dinner. Mr. Parker cut her short & took her to his study.

"Baby girl, I know things have been hard for you, lately. I just want to check in, see how life's been treating you." He began.

"Very well, Daddy. I have no complaints." She responded.

"How do you feel about those flyers? Kaylee showed us copies on our way into the office." He pressed.

"I don't care. It's not true." Allison shrugged.

"What if it were?" He pressed again.

"But it's not." She reiterated, shrugging her shoulders once more.

"But what if it were?" He insisted, consumed with guilt.

"But it isn't." She repeated, pretending to be unfazed.

"What if it were true though? What if you were adopted?" He attempted to ask again.

Daddy, tell me it isn't!" She yelled.

Frankie dropped his head to align with her eyes. He stared into them as if latching onto her soul.

"You are the greatest thing that's ever happened to your mother & me." He said, bereft.

Allison stood up.

"It's not true! Daddy, tell me it's not true!" She wailed in anger.

"It is." He confirmed. She hurriedly backed away, devastated. The back of her head kissed the edge of his mounted bookshelf. She fell into his arms, jolted & betrayed. He held her like a wounded bird & apologized repeatedly.

The wings that carried Allison to social dominance suffered an attack today; *baby girl* had been downsized a bit.

Chapter 13

<u>Breaking Point</u>

Allison reluctantly embraced her new truth during her suspension. Her mind imploded with a disturbance that left her more of a deviant than before. She shut down completely; she wouldn't speak to her parents, nor would she leave her room. Mr. & Mrs. Parker tried many ways to appease her, *but she was not here for it*. They offered her an increase in her allowance, a shopping spree to any store per her liking, a new car, & even an opportunity to work alongside her mother as an assistant. There was one thing Allison loved more than money- power, but she turned that down too. TBH, they didn't know whether she was truly devastated or if she was plotting to return the betrayal. They did everything but get on their hands & knees & beg for her forgiveness.

"I won't apologize for raising you. I won't apologize for falling in love with the little human I met who had no mother. I will however apologize for keeping this secret from you. I feared that telling you meant you'd love us less, & some people you've never met before, more." Louise spoke as she walked away.

Allison stared into the empty space of her room, conflicted on how to feel exactly. She still said nothing. She was now the outcast in a world she sank her claws in to become Queen of. Every kid at school viewed her differently, friends included. She poked fun at anyone that needed a handout, when lo & behold, she had been provided the ultimate handout of all- she was adopted by one of the town's richest families. It didn't matter how sorry her parents were, she grew more & more despondent. She began to wonder who the hell her real parents were.

After Bailey's Girls set it off at the UA by launching their illicit prank, they proceeded with Bennie's instructions to activate mission 3. Luckily, Trinity wasn't on punishment for being suspended. She confessed to her mother that she posted the flyers & backed it up with a million reasons as to why; although Reece didn't agree with outing Allison's adoption, she understood the malice; she knew that Allison bullied Bailey, her friends, & only God knows who else- she had it coming, respectfully.

Reece had a heart-to-heart with Trinity. She begged for her to place her pain somewhere else before she ruined every opportunity in progress for her future. Trinity displayed compassion, but she didn't agree to let sleeping dogs lie because the bitch in her was very much awake, & she was not finished yet.

Trinity shifted her focus & hacked into HR's database at the Four Seasons Hotel Philadelphia at Comcast Center. She added an interview for Naree on the calendar of Rosalie Gonzales, the general manager. She also ensured Naree's resumé & application were on file for referencing. Naree's job was to work undercover at the hotel & report to Bennie who was stealing cocaine from one of his busiest locations in the nation, Miami, Florida. Naree attended her interview & rocked it with her amazing communication skills. Guests approached the lobby for assistance, so she immediately dived right into hospitality. Although Rosalie didn't recall pulling Naree's application, she hired her on the spot because she admired her willingness to help. Naree was in & officially working undercover as concierge. During her hours of training (after school), she evaluated the ins & outs of the hotel. Trinity, Scarlett, & Emma visited frequently throughout her shifts to gather intel for Bennie as well.

Naree retrieved the blueprint to the hotel & took note of the cartels that operated there. She created a list of members who utilized the hotel's private jet services; she figured one of them had to be responsible for stealing Bennie's cocaine. She reported that each jet only went off route while servicing cartel members & that hotel security neglected their posts on nights when cartel gangs met up-MAJOR RED FLAG! Every other night at 10 pm, the ballroom enveloped various schemes. She got into the surveillance room & confirmed these gangs not only partied together, they collaborated on drug transactions & shared hookers from time to time. Naree fixated her gut on the ballroom, she insisted it was their target area. Little did she know, the Russian Mafia ran the Four Seasons & door 5 was prohibited, even on the blueprint. Employees are made aware that Door

5 is off limits during orientation, but Rosalie was so caught off guard with Ree's onboarding, she failed to mention it. Door 5 had been established as a no-entry/exit door; it's used to suss out anyone who doesn't belong.

After nearly 3 weeks, Naree submitted her final report to Bennie & informed him she heard whispers that numerous cartel gangs were meeting at the Four Seasons tonight. He appointed the girls to tap in but do nothing, he needed fair confirmation of who to kill. Naree shared Bennie's demands with the girls; they understood the assignment, so they headed to the hotel. Trinity flew in barefaced & snatched for the gawwwds! She bodied a brown catsuit with brown thigh-high designer boots. Her hair raged in coils & curls- she presented bomb-ass melanin under pressure. She rushed into the ballroom & quickly set up audio & surveillance.

Near showtime, Scarlett & Emma arrived, serving face & giving body ody ody in their luxury gowns; they were tasked to interact on the inside. Trinity finished planting her bugs & cameras & then met with the girls in the surveillance area since it had been cleared. They hovered to watch the magic happen. This was their biggest mission yet! As the men started rolling in, Naree checked her list to confirm the identities of them all. The scene was filled with drugs, guns, & bad intentions. Scarlett & Emma left the surveillance area & entered the ballroom through its main entrance. Trinity watched them mingle accordingly.

After listening to high-end criminals deliberate who controlled what area & what drugs were being sold, Naree grew tired, so she hopped up to make her entrance as well. She realized she still needed to cover her position as concierge, so she helped some guests, & then proceeded to the ballroom after changing clothes. She changed from her uniform & into a gown Scarlett bought for her. It was as though Cinderella recreated herself once more; all eyes were on Naree when she entered the room. Scarlett & Emma were so proud, but they stayed away to prevent inclusion. Rosalie happened to be there tonight, so she introduced Naree to everyone & talked her up to the Kingpin, he was intrigued. Naree smiled & did what she did best; she charmed the pants off those men & their Kingpin with her mouth & her mind. She was pretty worn out, so she left to find a restroom.

Naree poked her head into the surveillance room & made sure Trinity was good. She told her how sleepy she was & then continued down the hall to the restroom next to the ballroom. She wiped her eyes with her left hand & used her right hand to pull the door open. She waltzed in, trying to wake herself up. Sadly, this wasn't the restroom. It was door 5.

A cartel member by the name of Dmitri instantly drew back his Lebedev pistol & rang several shots into Naree's chest. Her body blew back into the hallway. Trinity, Scarlett, & Emma all gasped & immediately began to panic. It happened so fast; they didn't know what to do. Scarlett whispered into her mic for Trinity to stay hidden, so she could debug the room & get the rest of the footage they needed. Emma began to hyperventilate but she knew she had to get to Naree. Trinity wanted to get to Naree as well, but she knew they couldn't get caught, so she stayed put & told them she'd catch up ASAP.

Victor Orlov ripped into Dmitri in their native tongue. He was pissed that Dmitri shot a staff member; they were like family to him; they kept his luxurious hotel in demand- a public shooting could ruin the reputation of the Four Seasons. He ordered everyone to leave, every cartel member fled the scene as Scarlett & Emma approached, dialing 911. Emma had no idea she was in the presence of the mastermind behind her kidnapping, & Scarlett had no idea these men were still after her. That's right. Santiago and the Russian Mafia were in business together.

Naree fainted after losing so much blood but not before seeing Scar & Em by her side, & hearing Trinity in her ear. Emma thought quickly & grabbed the bud from Ree's ear & hid it in her bra to avoid suspicion.

Trinity ended the recording & hurried from the surveillance area after deleting everything they witnessed tonight. She rushed to the ballroom during the frenzy, swiped her devices, & stored them in her duffle. She then ran back to the surveillance room to delete her activity. She slipped out through the main door, just in time to catch Naree being rushed to the hospital. The policemen on the scene attempted to ask questions but the girls were too rattled to speak, so they left. After they left, Trinity knew what they had to do.

"Hey, let them take her. Y'all ride with me. We can follow." She insisted as she stood at the opening of the ambulance door.

"I love you Naree! You're going to be okay." She shouted, hoping these words were true.

"I already know what's up. Em, ride with Trin, & I'll go with Ree, we can't leave her alone." Scarlett insisted.

"Okay, fine, but we've got to go, now!" Emma yelled in tears. She didn't do well under pressure. Luckily, Scarlett didn't open fire this time, it would've been a bloodbath for damn sure because they were outgunned.

The medics worked on Naree & attempted to ask her questions; her eyes opened & shut a couple of times, but she was unresponsive.

"Ree, please say something. I don't know what I'd do if something happened to you." Scarlett cried as she clung onto her palm for a sign of life.

Trinity phoned Bennie & informed him of Naree's multiple blows to the chest. Immediately, he felt gutted.

"¡Los mataré! ¡Quiero quién hizo esto! AHORA! (I will kill them! I want who did this! NOW!)" He yelled before throwing his phone. Bennie grew to love the girls just as much as he loved Scarlett; the fact that one of them was down meant war to him. Trinity cried & ended the call. She turned to Emma who was a mess & tried to corroborate their story for tonight.

"Okay, Em. We've got to get ourselves together. People are going to be asking us questions, we've gotta know what to say." Trinity began.

"Ree was shot. Right in front of us, that's all there is to say. I don't know what more to say than that! I'm sick of this shit. What really happened?! What the hell happened?! I don't even know who shot her!" She cried.

Trinity understood that Em was the baby of the group & that she needed a moment, but she was a wreck too.

"The hotel's halls were pretty clear. We can tell them she was robbed. She tried to fight the guy off, so he shot her. I didn't get to see who did this, but you better believe we've got the footage to find out." Trinity said choking back heavy sobs.

"But what about-?" Em began.

"I deleted it." Trinity finished.

Emma nodded her head in response. They arrived at Thomas Jefferson University Hospital. The medics rushed Naree in as the girls ran behind them. Her condition had already been dispatched, so the nurses on duty were prepped to respond accordingly. Trinity demanded help from the front desk, but they couldn't help at all. Eventually, Doctor Stanton came out & informed the girls immediate surgery would be needed to save the life of Naree Gem. Trinity phoned Ree's parents right away & then contacted her own. Scarlett called her mom & Emma called her parents as well. They all raced down with fear in their hearts & only the worst of realities in their minds. *Were Bailey's Girls about to lose another sister?*

"What happened, mis amores (my loves)?! Marcella asked, arms wide open as she approached the girls. She saw blood all over Scarlett & Emma, but not Trinity. She didn't think too much about it though.

"That's what we'd like to know." Detective Morales stated as he approached the girls & their families. Alongside him were Officer Bennett & Hank.

"Excuse me, I'm Naree's father." Jun intercepted.

"Yes Sir. We're trying to follow up on your daughter. We need to know if the girls can tell us what happened tonight." Detective Morales reiterated.

Scarlett looked over & attempted to speak but Trinity cut her off. "Someone tried to rob her at work. She tried to fight him off, so he shot her. I don't think he got the chance to take anything though."

"Yea, when we came to meet her, he ran away & there she was... lying in a pool of blood." Emma confirmed.

"I notice you two are covered in blood but not you, could you tell us where you were?" Officer Hank asked Trinity.

"I went after him." Trinity answered in the calmest tone. Unbothered.

"You what?" Trinity's mother asked in shock.

"He shot my friend. I acted on impulse. I know it was a dangerous thing to do, but I had to try to catch him." Trinity explained. Still unbothered.

"I remember you all. Emma how are you holding up? I know this can't be easy after what you just experienced." Officer Hank acknowledged as if he were on to something again.

Emma was nervous but she responded with ease. "It's a lot but this isn't about me. My best friend, our sister, is fighting for her life." She responded.

"Of course." Officer Bennett interjected, sizing Hank up like an idiot.

"So, did you all get a look at him? We're going to follow up with hotel security, but we'd like to know anything you may remember." Officer Bennett added.

"We didn't see his face. He was wearing all black. We were more concerned with the body on the floor, Officer." Scarlett answered.

"No, no. Of course. But you, you say you went after him. What did you see?" Officer Hank asked, staring at Trinity.

"Blood." She answered with the face of a killer.

"I think that's enough, Officers, Detectives." Mrs. Banks shared.

"Understandable. Well, we're going to follow up with hotel security & then get back with you folks. Stay put alright." Hank informed.

"What are we? Suspects?" Trinity questioned with an attitude.

"Not at all. Until we're able to get a better idea of what happened, you're Naree's only hope at catching who did this." Detective Morales expressed with compassion.

The girls all shot each other a look & embraced their parents. As they stepped back to talk amongst themselves, someone familiar came panting through the door.

"Mrs. Brooks?!" Trinity acknowledged, running over for a hug. The girls & their families exchanged hugs with her as well.

"I came as soon as I heard. It's all over the news." She said, unwrapping her scarf & taking a seat with everyone.

"How is she?" Mrs. Brooks asked.

"We don't know yet. She-" Scarlett cried.

Dr. Stanton came into the main wing & asked for Naree's parents. Code Blue alerts sounded all over the hospital, everyone on duty ran to Naree's room. Bailey's Girls & their parents stood to the floor with their eyes in disarray. Dr. Stanton informed everyone that Ree was unresponsive. "We're doing everything in our power to help her." He further informed before advising Mr. & Mrs. Gem to follow him. Her parents were floored but they carried one another through the double doors of what felt like the other side. Naree was currently being resuscitated, once they got her stable, Dr. Minchew stepped away & enlightened them on her condition.

"I'm Dr. Minchew. I've worked on your daughter for a while now, she is not responding to any treatment. I'm sorry to say this, but Naree Gem is in a coma. It's unclear as to when she will wake up."

Every word he said thereafter faded into the air. Mr. & Mrs. Gem ran into her room & cried for her to come back. Mrs. Gem began analyzing her vitals, checking the equipment, & thoroughly reviewing her lab work.

"He's right. He's right. Our baby is in a coma." Mrs. Gem cried. Mr. Gem broke down, Naree was his favorite, although he'd never utter it aloud. After they cried for as long as they could, they stepped into the waiting room to tell everyone else. The entire waiting area filled with melancholy & confusion. Mr. & Mrs. Gem phoned home to Ari & Jin & informed them of their sister's state. A neighbor transported them to the hospital. When they arrived, they went to visit their sister. They didn't know what to make of it all, but they were devastated.

Detective Morales rushed a warrant over to the Four Seasons for hotel footage. He & Officer Hank arrived to review said footage but found nothing.

"There's something off about those girls." Hank said, shaking his head as he rewound & fast-forwarded, only to end up empty-handed.

"What are you saying? They had something to do with this?" Morales inquired.

"You know that case with the kidnapping at Wake-Up Philly? Same thing happened. I pressed for info- nothing. I went to obtain footage- nothing at all. I never come up empty-handed. It's like it's all connected." Hank explained.

Detective Morales laughed. "Darla put you out the house again, didn't she?"

Hank rolled his eyes. "Man, that's got nothing to do with this. I'm telling you something fishy is going on here. The footage was wiped. Can't you tell?" Hank further explained, annoyed this time.

"Yea, yea, yea, & my sac itches. Let's close this thing out." Morales commanded.

"I'm not letting this go. I'll take the case." Hank pressed.

"Have it your way. My wife actually *wants* me home." Morales chuckled as he handed Hank the paperwork. Hank sat in the room for hours, reviewing footage back & forth; he couldn't pinpoint anything exactly but as he sat there, he decided to go old school. He went around the hotel asking guests questions & began interviewing staff on duty. He decided it'd be a cold day in hell before he let go of his hunch this time. Nevertheless, he found absolutely nothing. No one at the hotel saw anything & if they had, they weren't going to say because they knew snitching on a cartel member meant a bullet to the head. Hank was done.

The nurses allowed Naree's friends & family back, two at a time; Trin, Em, & Scar disregarded that rule to stand beside their sister. They towered over her bedside the same way they did Bailey's casket & cried harder than they could've ever imagined.

"Ree, wake up. Please wake up. We're waiting for you. You've got to come back." Trinity wailed as she scooted onto the left side of Naree's bed. She laid her face upon hers & cried some more. Scarlett got in on the right side & held onto Naree's hand. Emma took her place at the foot of the bed & curled around her feet. They all cried & prayed until they fell asleep. Nurse Joe & Belamie saw them when administering meds to Ree, but they decided to be nice & let them stay.

"I wish you loved me like that." Nurse Joe said to Belamie as she stood in the doorway, admiring what she saw.

"Aw Joe. You know this love is rare. These babies are sisters, & last I checked you still owe me $100." Belamie recalled with laughter.

"See what I mean. If you loved me enough. You'd just let me borrow what I need without wanting it back." Joe shared.

"But then it's not borrowing." Belamie explained.

"How about we just call it that?" Joe snickered.

"That's okay, I'm just gonna adjust your timesheet & let Uncle Sam have my $100." Belamie stated, dying with laughter.

"Bitch!" Joe laughed.

"Girl, get out of here before we wake them up." Belamie laughed as she shoved Joe out the door. Bailey's Girls slept until they heard Scarlett's phone ring. It was Bennie. He asked Scarlett to fill him in on Naree's condition & told her he needed them to get down to the coffee shop asap. Scarlett woke the girls & informed them they had to leave. They sat in silence for a while, taking in the fact that Naree wasn't coming with them. They stared at her body, & even tried to wake her, but there was no response. The girls went out to the waiting room & encouraged their parents to go home. They informed them they'd be right behind them.

Their parents were okay with this. Mr. & Mrs. Gem thanked everyone for their support & retired to Naree's hospital room with Ari & Jin. On the way to Perez, the girls were quiet, they couldn't even listen to the music. They entered Wake-Up Philly through the back. Bennie opened his arms & embraced them all. He took a step back & then asked, "What happened?" as he shook his head repeatedly.

"Honestly, Perez, I don't know. I was looking but she was in a blind spot. I'm going to review what I have until I get you an answer." Trinity responded with disappointment growing within her.

"Padre (Father), I. We." Scarlett stammered.

"I know, mi hija (my daughter). I know." Bennie empathized.

"We were working the room, trying not to look like we knew each other. She came in & was paraded around by the hotel manager; they loved her. I don't know who shot her." Emma recounted in a daze.

"We did what we were supposed to do. This shouldn't have happened." Scarlett stated, becoming angrier by the second.

"I want you girls to get home. I will notify my men to investigate this. Lay low for now. Only go to school & to see Naree until I tell you otherwise." Bennie commanded as he gifted them all their very own handguns.

"Yes Sir." They confirmed in unison.

"These are ghost guns, meaning- they're unmarked, untraceable, & do not have serial numbers. Keep them nearby." He ordered.

Yes Sir." They responded in unison, again. Bailey's Girls departed Wake-up Philly with a darkness lingering behind them. It was now time to seek revenge for not one but two sisters.

When they made it home, their parents took a moment to just love on them because life was short & they didn't know how short it'd be for Bailey. I mean *Naree*.

Sleeping was the hardest thing to do. Trinity texted Josh, but he never responded. She stayed up all night reviewing footage from the Four Seasons, too exhausted to make any sense of it. Her eyes closed when the sun rose.

Scarlett called Jase; he comforted her & reassured her that once Ree's shooter was identified, attempted murder wouldn't be the case.

Emma only managed to do one thing when she crept away from the love of her mother & father- an impromptu movie night with her little sis, Karra. For just a moment, time stood still.

~~Chapter 14:~~

<u>She's Awake</u>

Nearly 3 months had gone by, Naree Gem was still in a coma. Trin, Em, & Scar visited her every day. They went to school & attempted to savor the remaining semester as best they could, but they were losing hope; they feared having to let her go. Doctor Stanton reported an increase in her brain activity, but he stated that she wasn't expected to wake any time soon. Naree thrived in a land that only she could see.

"Bailey." She shouted, smiling ear to ear.

"Reeeeeee! What are you still doing here? You've got to wake up!" Bailey encouraged, shining brighter than ever before.

"But... I like being here with you." Naree responded.

"It's been so long. I can't let you go again." Ree added.

"I miss you all so freaking much, but I ended my time because I was ready. You were made to do wonderful things. For one, WE BITCHIN FASHION! I am such a big fan!" She cried, wiping each tear away.

"But Bailey." Ree attempted to plead.

"No. You have already lost me; they have lost me; they can't lose you too." Bailey insisted as she hugged & squeezed Naree. Naree nodded in agreeance but not without squeezing her back. She spent so much time catching up with Bailey that she forgot she truly ceased to exist. As her father, Jun sat next to her, dragging back his tears, he felt her arm twitch. He was warned that these responses were more of reflexes & not to let them fool him, but her arm twitched again.

"Doc! Somebody get in here, NOW! I think she's waking up!" He yelled, alarming his wife & kids. They scurried around, waiting to see if it were true this time. Jun experienced this same panic, daily; he always alarmed someone that Naree was waking up, but she wasn't. It became a terrible game that only the Devil himself could play. Doctor Stanton entered the room with Nurse Joe, prepared to report the harsh truth, yet again. He had Joe check Ree's vitals as he analyzed her closely. Naree batted her eyes. He alerted more staff to look alive.

"Naree. My name is Doctor Stanton, if you can hear me, squeeze my hand."

Naree squeezed his hand. Stanton looked over at her father with hope in his eyes. "Let's get her prepped for lab work, please." Stanton instructed.

Naree returned. Stanton suggested a resting period & educated her family on what to expect during recovery. Everyone was elated, they had so much to say but opted to simply stare at her in peace. Naree wasn't strong enough to speak yet, but she was awake. She moved her hands & feet as if they were a grand discovery. Her family surrounded her & smothered her with so much love.

Sena took a moment & contacted her friends to share the news; in no time, they darted through her room door to see for themselves. They gathered around her & played her favorite music & told her about all the things she missed. They didn't leave her side. After a while of fading in & out, Naree began to speak.

"Bai-" she murmured.

"Shhh. Just rest. Don't push yourself." Trinity whispered, lying against her bed rail.

"Bailey." Ree spoke again.

They all stared at one another in bewilderment.

"Bailey's not here, Ree." Trinity sadly informed.

"Oh God, what if she has amnesia?!" Scarlett shrieked.

"Shut up!" Emma gasped with her hand covering her mouth.

"Should we get help?" Trinity questioned, standing at attention.

"I saw Bailey." Naree finally managed to get out. They all stared at one another again but teared up this time around.

"I'm not crazy." Naree followed. They chuckled lightly & confirmed within themselves that Ree was back for real. They sat closely & listened, patiently. She told them she danced with Bailey all around New York & that she was a fan of *We Bitchin Fashion*. They couldn't even fathom the reality of this conversation. Their movie-like moment was interrupted by Officer Hank & Naree's parents. Detective Morales received notice of Naree's recovery from her parents, so he raced straight to Thomas Jefferson University Hospital.

"Hi there. My name is Officer Hank. Girls, you mind if I have a moment here with your friend?"

"I mean, her family just left so that we could finally see her but yea, you can have a moment." Trinity responded, brow raised & tude on spicy! Em & Scar's stance projected the same energy.

Ree's parents knew how protective the girls were of each other, so she let them all stay.

"Do you remember what happened to you at the Four Seasons?" Hank went on. Naree's eyes bounced around the room, she didn't know what to say. Even in her weakest moments, she knew how to finesse.

"I don't understand." She responded.

Hank looked at her parents. He tried again.

"Nearly 3 months ago at the Four Seasons, you were shot several times. Any idea as to why someone would do this to you?" Hank blatantly pressed.

"I don't know." Ree answered, but she knew everything. He pressed a little more.

"Someone from the hotel shared a statement today. In hopes of identifying your shooter, she'll be returning to the station to meet with our sketch artist. I just wanted to check in with you to see if you could add any details." Hank shared with a smile, finally on to something.

"She said she doesn't know." Trinity reiterated with her head cocked to the right.

"No. I understand. I just-" He attempted to continue.

"No actually, she *just*. She *just* doesn't know. She *just* woke up. She *just* discovered she's lost 3 months of her life laying in this hospital bed." Scarlett interrupted.

"Listen. I understand that this is a very delicate matter, but I cannot help her get justice if I don't ask these questions." He explained.

"Who came forward? We weren't made aware of a witness." Sena probed.

"We tried calling this morning but couldn't get through to anyone. A young lady employed by the Four Seasons says Naree left the front desk, changed clothes, & then entered a party with known drug cartel members & criminals." Hank shared.

"My goodness!" Sena exclaimed, clutching her pearls & her husband.

"Why would there be criminals at the Four Seasons?! Drug cartel members?! My daughter would NEVER intentionally enter a place with such affiliations. What are you all doing about this?" Jun interrogated.

Trin, Em, & Scar all looked at Naree simultaneously. They couldn't permit anyone the opportunity to expose them. They were all ears at this point.

"We're following this case very closely. I assure you of that. I personally want to get to the bottom of this." Hank enlightened.

"Did this girl see anything else? Who is she?" Sena questioned.

"I can't disclose her name, but I will say that she told me she followed Naree because she looked nervous, she wanted to see where she was going. She tracked her through the hall & right to the door where she was shot. She confirmed that she saw the man who shot her." Hank reported.

The room became filled with mixed emotions. Everyone wanted justice for Naree, but the girls were desperate to get their own kind.

"Wow. That's amazing. So, like, did she tell you any features of this man? Did she describe him in any way?" Emma asked on the sly.

Hank hesitated to answer. He felt pretty confident with his witness, so he decided to share what he knew.

"This young lady didn't provide a precise description. She told us she wasn't too clear on what he looked like, but that she remembered exactly what he wore. She'll be back this afternoon to meet with our sketch artist. When they complete the sketch, we'll submit it into the database so that we can track him down."

"Thank you so much, Officer." Scarlett coughed up.

"Yes. We truly appreciate your efforts." Trinity added, slyly.

"Okay, well we're going to let Ree rest. *If* she remembers anything, we'll give you a call." Sena shared. Her husband cosigned as he escorted Hank from the hospital room. Her parents walked over & kissed on her after realizing she could speak. They hugged her & told her how much they loved & missed her so.

Trin, Scar, & Em shared a temporary goodbye to catch up on some homework. They had some "homework" to catch up on, alright; they were on a mission to locate the employee who's been singing like a canary. Scar & Em hopped into Trin's car, phoned Bennie from a burner, & made him aware of what their next move should be, he approved. Trinity pulled into the vicinity of Philly's Police Department. She needed to be close enough to hack their surveillance footage. She located their IP address & logged in after utilizing her software to generate the proper password.

"Access granted." She murmured aloud, sucking her teeth. She was now able to view & potentially control the feed of the police department's CCTV cameras. Scar & Em sat next to her, awaiting further instruction. She rolled back the footage to early morning & began scanning for any young female.

"He kept emphasizing "young lady," so I'm thinking she has to be between 18-21." Scarlett shared.

"What are you? A Profiler now?" Trinity laughed.

"No, but if she was willing to come down to the police department & snitch on known cartel members, she's some kind of young & dumb." Scarlett rationalized.

"But we're young." Emma reminded with laughter.

"Yea. But we're also different." Scarlett informed.

"This is true." Emma confirmed.

"Shh. SNAP! I got her ass!" Trinity shouted.

"She wore her freaking uniform to the damn police station." She continued.

"How can we find her though?" Scarlett inquired.

"I have software installed for facial recognition. I'm gonna get her. I'm gonna get her." Trinity reassured.

"She's a bad Mama Jama!" Emma sang.

"Oh, yes, she is!" Scarlett laughed.

"Terri Moore, DOB: 12/24/2003. She's 19 years old, lives at... Four Seasons Hotel Philadelphia at Comcast?" Trinity reported in confusion.

"Say what now? That can't be right. What do you mean she lives there?" Emma frowned.

"Maybe she uses their address? Could there be a possible malfunction with her facial recognition?" Scarlett suggested.

"Hell naw, I only operate & partner with the best. She's got to live there. Only one way to find out." Trinity confirmed as she started her engine again.

"Wait!" Emma shouted.

"Oh shit. Look who just came to us." Scarlett acknowledged.

"Shit, shit, shit! Okay, let me get back into their feed; we need to see & hear everything we can. Call your dad!" Trinity rattled off.

"On it!" Scar confirmed.

"Should we go in?" Emma asked, unbuckling her seatbelt.

"Of course not. Bennie will tell us what to do." Trinity answered.

Scarlett pulled out her burner phone, called up Bennie, & put it on speaker.

"Ohla, mi hija (Hello, my daughter)." He greeted.

"Ohla, padre (Hello, father). So, we've got eyes on the witness. Her name is Terri Moore, she's 19. Trin is pulling the video feed from the police station to monitor & track her activity. She's walking to meet with their sketch artist right now. What should we do?"

"When she leaves the building, you all take her & bring her to me." Bennie commanded.

"Take her? Like kidnap?" Scarlett questioned.

"Si, mí amor (Yes, my love)." Bennie confirmed.

Every eye connected as they took in a deep breath.

"Shit's about to get real." Trinity established, shaking her head from side to side.

Scarlett ended the call & responded, "We can't get caught."

Trinity & the girls reviewed the footage & tracked Terri leaving the Detective's office. Trinity turned up the audio.

"Hi, I was told your sketch artist isn't here yet, I'm going to run to the grocery store to get some things. I'll be back later."

"No problem at all, we apologize for the confusion." A clerk responded.

"No worries at all, see you later." Terri responded, making her way out of the building. She was met at the entrance by the sketch artist, Jackie. The girls held their breath, but Trinity prepared to gather every detail she spilled.

"Shit, shit, SHIT!" Emma panicked.

"Shhh!" Trinity griped. They listened to Terri sit down with Jackie. "Tell me everything you remember, okay? If we ever need to stop, just let me know."

"Just let me know." Trinity sang.

"Just let me know." Emma sang.

"Just let me know." Scarlett laughed & sang as well.

The girls snapped out of it when Terri's mouth began to run like the motor on a foreign car.

"He was tall. Wore a very expensive designer suit. I think he was Russian, most of the guys were. He had a cold black goatee with hints of grey." She described.

Is that all you recall?" Jackie asked.

"Well, he... had on a hat & had a long ponytail, shoulder length to be exact. I can't remember anything else but the girl at this point. I think she may have been there with friends." Terri went on.

"Damn, does she know what happens to snitches?" Scarlett questioned. The girls were pissed but they notated her description of the culprit, so they could find him before the cops did. Terri's session ended with the sketch artist; she told her she had to run to the grocery store before work but reassured her that she'd return shortly to tell her everything else she knew. She stepped out of the police station, unaware there were several eyes on her.

"Follow her!" Emma charged. Trinity crept off quickly & stood by until Terri got into her vehicle.

"Scarlett, get the license plate, make, & model- she's in a green Mini Cooper." Trinity informed as she continued to follow Terri down the street & around the corner to Wilma's Whole Food Store. The girls' nerves were kicking in.

"OMG, we don't know how to kidnap anyone! We didn't learn that in Cartel Camp." Emma expressed.

"No, we did not, but you were kidnapped. You remember how it happened, don't you?" Trin questioned.

"Every bit of it." Em confirmed.

"Use that." Trin ordered as the car became a heap of cartel energy. They pulled further into the parking lot near her vehicle & analyzed their surroundings. There were people there, but not too many at all. Terri was sitting in her car on the phone, she was preparing to exit her vehicle.

"We've got to get her before she makes any transactions. If she ends up using a card & then goes missing, they could track her last location here, & that will be a problem. We've got to work with those blind spots." Trinity recommended.

"I'm not ready!" Emma shouted, waving her hands midair.

"Em, do it now!" Scarlett yelled. Emma took off her hoodie & jumped out of the passenger side of Trinity's car. Scarlett hopped out too. Trinity popped her trunk. Emma walked up to Terri's backside as she reached to close her door. She covered Terri's face with her hoodie. Terri began to scream, so she yanked her head back & banged it on the hood of her car; Terri got knocked the hell out.

"Oh shit!" Trinity said in shock. Emma dragged Terri to the trunk & Scarlett assisted with dumping her body in; she was out cold. The girls coordinated for Scarlett to drive Trinity's car to the coffee shop & for Trinity to drive Terri's car after completing the task of deleting footage showcasing their arrival & Terri's kidnapping. Within 2 twerks of a thot's bottom, it was done.

On the way to Bennie's, Em's adrenalin rushed from her palms to her head. She heard screams coming from Trinity's trunk. She tried to shake them, but they imploded her soul. Terri screamed for dear life, all the while knowing she wasn't going anywhere. Emma shook her head from side to side, struggling to drown out every cry that called out to her. Scarlett looked over & noticed Em wigging out.

"Hey, babe, you did an amazing job back there. Don't freak out on me, okay?" Scarlett comforted.

"But the screams, Scar. I can't get her screaming out of my head. She won't stop screaming!" Em replied.

Scarlett double-checked her rearview mirror & looked over at Emma. "She's not screaming, sis."

Emma grabbed her head.

Scarlett switched to driving with one hand only & laid her right hand on Emma's left.

"I understand this isn't what you signed up for. We'd probably be much better off without the latest of our cartel adventures, but this is where we are & this is who we must be... until my dad says otherwise. You were badass back there, just now. Let's rock with that, okay?" Scarlett encouraged.

Emma's world became sound again; her ears gathered Scarlett's pep talk & the music from the radio. She smiled.

"Alright, well if you rocking, I'm rolling. I was pretty badass, wasn't I?" She responded, chuckling lightly. Upon reflection of her own kidnapping, she realized the screams she heard were hers. She wasn't okay with putting anyone through something she couldn't fathom herself, but she understood the assignment. They continued until reaching their destination.

Trinity started the cooper after hacking into Wilma's video feed. She sped away & stuck her landing at Wake-Up Philly. When she arrived, she hopped back onto Wilma's surveillance & deleted her exit from the parking lot. She walked through the doors of Wake-Up Philly, high from adventure & noticed that Terri was still out, lying on the floor of Bennie's office. They stood amongst themselves, staring at her young, impressionable body.

"So, what are we going to do?" Trinity asked on behalf of them all.

"We have to kill her." Bennie responded plainly.

"Couldn't we just keep her?" Emma questioned.

"She's not a dog, Em. No, we cannot keep her." Trinity cosigned.

"But-" Em began.

"Look, at the end of the day, it's either Terri or us- can't be us. On top of that, she's spilling any ounce of tea she has regarding Naree's shooting that night. We can't have that. Naree just woke up, she's lost nearly 3 months of her life, baby girl gotta go." Trinity explained.

Scarlett looked over at Terri & then stared her father directly in his eyes. "Dad?" she questioned, awaiting confirmation for something more.

"Si, mi hija (Yes, my daughter)." Bennie responded.

He walked over to hug them all. Their faces fell into his flesh, sobbing with tears. They didn't want to take an innocent girl's life, but they knew that they had to. Bennie promised to take care of her because they had done enough. They informed him that her vehicle was in the alley, he sent Carlos & Vest to get rid of it. Before the girls could exit the building, Terri awoke from being knocked the hell out. Her eyes danced around her sockets in confusion. She looked at everyone in the room, terrified. She struggled tirelessly to beg for her freedom, as she faded in & out from her head wound. She recognized Scarlett & Emma. "You're her friends." She pointed. She asked them what she did wrong, which seared into the souls of these Cartel Queens. Each cry she let out opened a wound they'd never be able to close. Her recognition of them solidified Bennie's commands. She had to *go*.

Terri grew anxious when she realized her cries weren't enough, she began to wail & scream as loudly as she could. There was business booming at the coffee shop, so Bennie had to pull his cartel card. He grabbed his Beretta & a silencer & walked over to Terri. He stepped dead in front of her & fired a kill shot, put a bullet right through the center of her forehead. Brain matter splattered across the floor of Bennie's office. Blood danced across his shoes. Emma flew to a trashcan & made herself at home as she threw up, ferociously.

It was at that moment that Scarlett knew she was her father's niña (little girl). Terri had finally been silenced; Bailey's Girls had been too. Bennie encouraged them to make haste so that Harvey could dispose of her body & clean up. They gazed at Terri & mourned her, together, before taking their leave. Bennie explained to them that he would do it again & again if it meant keeping their identities a secret. His impactful statement solidified their understanding of Terri's murder. She had been killed but they remained alive to love, fight, & avenge Bailey's death yet another day.

When the girls were out of sight, Bennie sat at his desk & took back shots of tequila, he made a phone call.

You know the sketch artist down at Philly P.D.?"
Bennie asked.

"Yea, Boss." Carlos confirmed.

"She has a sketch that can't be released. I need you to
retrieve it & take care of her." Bennie instructed.

"I send her to meet her maker by sunrise." Carlos
confirmed.

"Entendido (understood)." Bennie responded.

Chapter 15

Hide & Seek

After the kidnapping & murder of Terri Moore, the girls found it imperative to spend more quality time with Naree- it settled in that their sisterhood was more important than anything. They grieved the loss of Terri but with Bennie's new instructions to go undercover yet again, they were forced to keep it moving.

Scarlett & Emma were directed to go back to the Four Seasons & locate Naree's attempted murderer. They knew she graced the presence of many men that night, so a simple one-and-done undercover mission wouldn't do it- they had to go deep. Emma decided they should pose as agency workers. To protect their true identities, Trinity created a mock site that hosted their credentials, documentation, & resumés; Desired Staffing, LLC is who they "worked" for. Their identification presented photos of them in wigs, lots of makeup, & false first & last names. They prepared to keep up the proper façade for this hotel mission.

Naree had been undergoing occupational therapy & physical therapy so that she could practice her fine motor skills, strength, & endurance; making progress wasn't easy, but she was definitely on the way to popping her shit again. Most people fade away when showing up becomes an inconvenience for them, but not for Ree, she was surrounded by friends & family, daily; they never left her alone. Today, she was finally going home. Ree's family, Bailey's Girls, & their parents all stood proudly in the hall to watch her walk through what felt like the gateway to Heaven. She lost a little over 40 pounds during her stay at the hospital, even though this worried her parents, she enjoyed the slim thick Asian she saw stepping. Everyone cheered & recorded her epic road to freedom- talk about inspired. Every parent choked back tears as they held onto one another & Bailey's Girls danced in unison like they were on top of the world. Today was a good day. They begged Ree's parents to take her home, Mrs. Gem hesitated but agreed after they pulled the sister card. Naree had so much joy in her heart, she never knew it was possible to be this happy. She was placed into a wheelchair & escorted to her whimsical carriage, Trinity's car. They helped her in, & before she knew it, she transformed right back to the life she once knew.

"We're so happy you get to go home! We've waited so long for this moment." Emma expressed.

"Like, for real! Even Bennie's been worried about you." Trinity shared.

"Really?" Ree questioned.

"Yea, he actually came to see you, often." Scarlett answered.

"Sure did. He also had me set up footage so that he could monitor your progress & make sure no one came to finish the job. You were all over the news, girl." Trinity shared.

"The news? What? I'm a star?!" Naree asked, blushing. Everyone laughed. "No. Seriously. I'm lost for words. I can't believe you all made this big a fuss over little ol' me." Ree continued.

"Little is right, girl have you seen you?! You are SNATCHED!" Trinity giggled, serving a right-hand swipe underneath her chin.

Naree blushed & chuckled as loudly as she could.

"We'd go to war & back over you, Ree. I thought you knew that by now." Scarlett shared.

"Yea, you have no idea." Emma added with a sigh. Trinity & Scarlett shot her a look. Naree caught it but she didn't read too much into it.

"I'd do the same for you all as well. What's been going on? I feel so lost. How's the cartel business? How's We Bitchin Fashion? Do I need to go & see Bennie?" Ree rambled on.

"First of all, we're going to keep our word & really take you home. Since the shooting, your parents have been wired- understandably so. I don't think we should raise any further suspicions. Bennie also thinks you should lay low for a little while. The summer will be over soon." Trinity explained.

"But I left so many loose ends on my mission. I didn't get to find out who was stealing from him." Naree explained.

The girls sighed regretfully.

"We've been working undercover at the Four Seasons." Scarlett informed her.

"You what?!" Naree asked as she struggled to lean up.

"Bennie wants us to find out who almost killed you." Trinity clarified.

"Damn." She responded. Being shot sank in all over again.

"That's not it." Trinity began. Naree looked over at her & waited for her to spill the tea. Trinity prepared herself by inhaling, exhaling, closing her eyes, & then reopening them again. She looked at Naree in the most solemn way she could & said-

"We killed Terri Moore."

"Who's Terri Moore?" Ree asked, frowning.

"She worked at The Four Seasons. She was there the night you were shot." Trinity explained.

"Is this the girl the cop was referring to when I woke up?" Ree probed.

"Yes." Trinity confirmed. Naree's head dropped in disbelief.

"But we had to." Scarlett blurted out.

"Of course." Ree responded. She couldn't bring herself to say anything more.

"I mean WE didn't actually kill her though." Emma stated.

"If that makes you sleep better at night." Trinity chuckled. Emma sulked immediately because she knew the truth.

"We kidnapped her & took her to Bennie after we found out who she was. She provided intimate details of the Russian who nearly killed you. She even recognized Scar & I. She had to go. She knew too much & was willing to keep talking." Emma confessed.

"I know how we coming behind each other. I would've made the same call too." Ree admitted.

"We love you Ree." They all said in unison.

"I love y'all so much more." She said as they drove away in peace, vibing to the best shit.

Trinity pulled up to Ree's home. They all got out to see her inside. When she walked in, her siblings made it rain with confetti. They hugged & squeezed her like a brand-new puppy. Ree's parents were so elated to have her back in their grasp, they couldn't stop crying. The girls were invited to stay for dinner because the kids ordered Ree's favorite pizza. Naree saw "Welcome Home" banners draped from the ceiling & gifts lined across the table. "I need to get shot more often." She acknowledged with a light giggle while tearing through all her new clothes & shoes. The more she analyzed the brands, she realized it was all new merch from We Bitchin Fashion! Naree's excitement took her to her happy place, Fashion Ecstasy. Before she knew it, she & the girls all smiled & yelled, "We Bitchin Bitches!" Sena laughed & shook her head, "Just what am I going to do with you girls?"

Naree cackled hysterically & spent the rest of the evening modeling their new line, singing karaoke, & chowing down on pepperoni pizza.

Scarlett & Emma's bliss seeped through the corners of Naree's home & into the night. Reality sank in that they had to attend another cartel party at The Four Seasons tomorrow. They were extremely uneasy, but they knew they had to do it to find Naree's shooter. Ever since Bennie gave them guns, they stayed strapped up everywhere they went; this party would be no different.

Their inner thighs would be rocking their firearms, in case anything popped off. When the sun arose, Trin & Ree could tell Scar & Em didn't sleep a wink. They ordered some breakfast via Bennie's Chef, Mozart; he delivered a beautiful spread per usual. Along with him was Jase, who accompanied the chef to bring Naree's arrangement of long-stem roses from Bennie. "What a beautiful gesture! Y'all think I'm playing when I say I need to get shot again. This shit is lit!" Ree joked, stuffing her face into 36 of the grandest assortments of roses she'd ever seen.

"Damn. I thought those were for me." Scarlett joked while glancing at Jase inconspicuously. Everyone kept quiet because they knew Mozart's loyalty to Bennie, he'd rat out Scar & Jase- indefinitely! "Say less." Jase responded as he turned his head & smiled before walking away. He exited Naree's bedroom slowly to get one more look at Scar, his gaze solidified that he had fallen. After he & Mozart left, Bailey's Girls immediately became enveloped in every bit of tea there was involving Scarlett & Jase.

"Chyyylllee if Perez finds out about these sneaky links- Jase is gonna be the one suffering the consequences. Whatever Perez does will be worse than what the fire challenge did to our generation." Trinity bluntly depicted.

"Fire challenge?" Emma questioned.

"Yea girl, I know you've seen those viral posts of teens rubbing flammable liquids on their asses & then setting them ablaze! Some of em' ended up in critical condition." Trinity explained.

"Well, let's skip critical condition- Jase's ass just gone be dead. Period." Naree added.

"Ugh, please don't say that. What am I supposed to do? I think he loves me." Scarlett piled on.

"Do you love him?" Emma asked with the brightest smile.

"I haven't thought that far." Scarlett answered in deep thought.

"Maybe you should & then decide if it's worth putting his life in danger... like on some real shit." Trinity suggested.

"No, like seriously. I think we should plan his funeral. What's his favorite song? Maria Maria?" Naree joked as she sang.

"Shut up!" Scarlett laughed before grabbing a pillow & tapping her against the head with it. It was on! The girls were full-fledged pillow-fighting with no remorse. Naree tried her best to keep up, but she dropped to the floor after a few minutes. The girls ran to her aid. They felt terrible all over again. They realized she wasn't the same anymore, she used to put them on their asses when pillow fighting, something this small seemed so unfair.

"We're going to find him." Emma consoled.

"& I'm going to put a bullet straight through his skull." Scarlett informed.

"I'm so sorry, Ree. Are you okay?" Trinity empathized.

"I haven't had a pillow fight in months. Trust me, I needed this moment with you guys. I wish I could go to the party tonight. I could probably find him. Maybe Bennie will let me." Ree propositioned.

"No maim, no ham, no turkey. Absolutely not. Daddy already said you cannot go. We're about to start school, you need to be in full recovery." Scarlett firmly informed.

"I'm not handicapped. I could fight you right now." Ree responded.

"Are you serious?" Scarlett questioned, awkwardly.

"No, ha-ha it's the drugs talking. I'm sorry. I popped some hydrocodone before Mozart delivered breakfast." Ree explained.

"Ha, yea, the breakfast we just slaughtered with our pillows!" Emma laughed.

"I'm still gone eat this food." Trinity giggled.

"Me too. Let's get it!" Scarlett cosigned.

The girls ate their delicious breakfast & tried not to wake Ree's family. Eventually, they left Ree to get some rest & went home to prepare for the cartel's gala tonight. Scarlett & Emma couldn't hide their fancy drip this time, they were dressed to KILL, literally. To ensure this mission flowed smoothly, Trinity printed up exclusive invites for a fashion gala at another hotel nearby; the girls convinced their parents they were cordially invited to an event for only the elite in the fashion industry. Their parents trusted them at this point, so the prying ceased but they informed them not to sign anything without their consent, as they were still minors. The girls agreed.

Scar pulled up to pick up Em in a rental orchestrated by Bennie. Em walked out, ripping the runway; wind was blowing in her mind but there was no such thing at all. It was hot as hell, but so was she, & she knew it. She hopped into the car with Scar & they headed straight to the gala. When they arrived, they went into their duffels & grabbed their wigs & guns. Trinity was on standby at home, reviewing footage from the night of Ree's shooting. She also had a live feed going to report current activity to Bennie.

The girls hopped out & went right in. They grabbed some wine & worked the room. Emma thought some of the men looked good, but she kept her eyes on the prize, *wherever he was*. Scar noticed her feeling herself, she reminded her they were there to do one thing & one thing only. Em responded, "A little staring never hurt nobody." They laughed until finally crossing paths with a familiar face. They knew him but he did not recognize them. They hit Trin's line & told her to get dressed & come to them, ASAP! She didn't question them; she was always on GO. She grabbed a nice designer gown & laid them edges like a mother putting her child to sleep- she laid them tf down! She didn't have a wig to wear, so she showed up, drip sick, & on point as herself.

When she arrived, she made her way to the ballroom, undetected. She kept her distance from Em & Scar but quickly recognized a face she refused to run from, Trey. She sized him up as he consorted with the enemy. As soon as his conversation ended, she grabbed him by the arm & pulled him into the hallway. There were knots in her throat, but she had to know why he was there.

"Bro, what the hell you doing here?" she asked, getting straight to the point.

"I could be asking you the same, sis. This is a known cartel party." Trey responded, folding his arms.

"Some friends from school told me it was a dope party going up tonight, so I came." Trinity covered.

"It's a dope party, alright." He mumbled under his breath.

"What?" Trin asked, playing stupid.

"Nothing. & what the hell do you have on?" Trey deflected, finally sizing her up too.

"I'm damn near grown, don't come at me like that. Again, Trey. Why are you here?" Trinity pressed.

"A loyal customer of mine from the diner invited me, so I decided to slide through." He enlightened.

"Oh okay, well maybe you should slide right on up out of here. I can't be partying with my brother around." She encouraged.

"Hell naw. I'm older. You go home." He fired back, hoping sis would just tear her ass. He was there to work for one of Bennie's rival cartels; his homebody put him on, so he was considering the connect to make extra money for his family. Little did he know, his sis didn't need him to hustle for them, she already had it in the bag.

"Don't get to talking out the side of your neck, Trey. This party's lame anyway. I'm outta here." She popped off, throwing her gown behind her. She exited the building & immediately hit Scar & Em to tell them their plan wouldn't work tonight.

Scar & Em aborted the mission on the low as well. They hopped in the rental & met up with Trin in the parking lot. They conversed about how wild it was seeing Trey there; Trinity took it upon herself to notify Bennie. "I guess you could color me surprised too. Keep an eye on your brother, so my men won't have to." He responded before ending the call. Trinity knew she had to keep her brother in check, he wasn't getting killed on her watch.

Bailey's Girls rode off into the midnight, unsuccessful- but in hindsight, they had just struck gold.

~~Chapter 16:~~

<u>First Day as Seniors</u>

It was the first day of Senior year. The summer catapulted many things; an intense amount of elevation included. Bailey's Girls shut the entire scene down when they arrived at Ulysses Academy in their brand-new convertibles.

Trinity, hair bigger & bolder than ever, stepped out of her Mercedes-Maybach 6 Cabriolet; it was all black, outlined in chrome. She was bitchin fashion & giving Black Goddess.

Scarlett swayed from the inside of her red Mercedes-Maybach 6 convertible; it spoke to the ether dwelling within her soul. She was bitchin fashion & giving Italian Mommy.

Naree & Emma both fell for Aston Martin's DB1 (Volante). Ree's Aston was dark green & Emma's was all white. They were bitching fashion & giving every bit of Rich Bitch energy!

Every student's mouth plummeted to the pavement, because what the hell?! Bailey's Girls were exiting from exclusive student parking- the same parking lot they witnessed Allison & her trolls step from for years; it was all theirs now. They were finally able to afford it. The first 4 spots were paid up for the entire year. Trinity was on her petty shit- so much so, that she hacked into the UA's system & pushed those bitches' spots to the very back of the parking lot- Yahtzee! Bailey's Girls were the new baddies & the entire school knew it. Allison & her girls exited their vehicles pissed because they had to walk further than usual. They weren't acknowledged by anyone. After seeing a crowd form at the entrance, they took off to see what the fuss was about.

"Let's get into it. Geeky & overlooked are the last things they are this year." Kensington whispered to another student as Bailey's Girls walked by.

"I conquer. They're giving sassy, confident, & top-tier! I didn't see this coming at all. Did you see their cars?!" Rico responded clapping his hands.

"Super swanky! I LIVEEEE! You know they're millionaires now? I saw their clothes being sold at the department store I work for- you know it's high end!" Kensington praised.

Rico & Kensington stood in awe as other students eyeballed the girls in slow-mo. Each of them had on enough drip to drown, We Bitchin Fashion was in the building, TOUGH!

Ree popped her shit with her new body, those curves were talking & the boys were listennning! They also rocked their own designer hardcovers & backpacks- who needs another brand when you've got your own to serve in?! They were unquestionably covered in their fashion line; the back of their shirts read "We Bitchin Bitches." As they strolled together through those double doors, they witnessed the reckoning they always imagined. Allison & her minions were furious! They couldn't believe the come-up before them, talk about devastated. Staff were staring at them in shock, they couldn't believe their eyes either- Bailey's Girls had finally arrived & this time, they weren't leaving until they finished what they started.

As the day went on, the girls were treated with more respect than ever- they had officially become one of the elites, but they were destined to redefine what elite meant at the UA. During lunch, they took a moment to utilize the attention they drummed up for themselves.

"Attention class of 2022!" Trinity announced as she tossed her hair behind her shoulders. She stepped up on one of the cafeteria tables. Ree, Em, & Scar all mounted a table of their own too. Trinity continued.

"If you have ever been bullied before, we are treating you to lunch today!" Trinity announced.

"Yes! If anyone has ever made you feel like scum or less than because they have more- we are here to let you know that you ARE everything! You deserve a nice lunch today & every day, anything you want!" Scarlett added.

"Has Allison, Maci, or Kaylee ever offered to be kind or buy your lunch?" Emma questioned as loudly as she could. Each student directed their attention to Allison, Maci, &

Kaylee's table & shook their heads no. Hell, even the staff on duty shook their heads no. One student stood from her seat & clapped. Several students followed until the entire cafeteria was on their feet & applauding Bailey's Girls. They were so happy to see the cool chicks before them; this change- they deemed to be a damn good one. During the applause, Allison & her girls had been torn asunder. Kaylee got up from their table after much discomfort & walked out. The crowd went wild; they cheered, whistled, & even threw food- this moment had officially gone down in bad girl history. Kaylee had already been conflicted when it came to Allison but today, a change of heart was finally in order. The first day of school went so well that Trinity decided to visit Bailey's mom. She stopped by in her fancy new car, Sara was taken aback by the young lady before her.

"Oh, my goodness! Bailey would've LOVED this car!" She said as Trinity made her way to the door.

"That's exactly why I got it." Trinity smiled, going in for a big hug. Sara invited her in & sat down with her to recount her first day as a Senior. To no surprise, the waterworks began as they took in that it was or would've been Bailey's Senior year as well. Sara cried uncontrollably; Trinity backdoored & couldn't help but do the same. When they both gathered themselves, Trinity asked to see Bailey's room, of course, Sara obliged. Trinity walked in & took a deep breath. She laid across Bailey's bed & stared at her room in full detail, it was exactly the same. She inadvertently cried some more. She didn't know whether Bailey's room should've been cleared at this point or not, but she understood why Sara refused to let her go. She tucked her hands underneath the pillow to cozy herself up for a nap but felt something there. She pulled it out & confirmed it was one of Bailey's diaries. She began to read it. Lumps the size of horse nuts formed in her throat.

Trinity found herself in attendance to Bailey's story, starring treatment from the girls who hated her most. Bailey composed tragic encounters with her bullies from beginning to end- surprisingly, she barely mentioned Kaylee. Trinity's eyes sprang from her head when she saw that Bailey wrote: 'Kaylee bullied me directly in fear of Allison Parker. She's afraid of Allison Parker, & so am I.'

Trinity rose from her bed & continued to read. Those bitches & their reputations were done for. Trinity knew exactly what she needed to do. She scanned each page of Bailey's diary into the notes section of her phone & sent a copy to Scar, Ree, & Em. Their group chat was heated, it was only the beginning.

When school was in session the following day, they stepped out just as sassy & classy but with more spice than ever, they were saucy! They stepped to Allison & her minions at the back of the parking lot- compliments of Trinity Woods.

"Care to explain to us why your names are all up & through Bailey's diary if you had no dealings in her suicide?" Trinity questioned as Scarlett recorded their reactions for further embarrassment. Allison & Maci stood with the blankest of expressions. Kaylee's face pled guilty, but she didn't utter a word.

"You're reaching." Allison responding.

"Nah baby. You're so bland. You didn't think we'd find out. Took some time but it's all where it needs to be. You will be prosecuted for the turmoil you caused our sister." Emma informed.

"I don't have time for this." Maci responded.

"Of course you don't, but you will. Please note: if you were ever the slightest confused, you're reckoning is here." Scarlett made known.

"Oh, but don't worry, Kaylee. We'll take it easy on you. Bailey barely mentioned your name, but you were still an accessory to her demise, so you shall suffer as well." Naree added.

"Just like she did." Trinity continued.

"Vibe check." Allison shouted.

"All good." Maci cosigned as they walked away.

"Oh wait. Since we're checking vibes & all, can you tell us what your vibes were in the footage we have of you physically assaulting Bailey Brooks?" Trinity questioned as she cocked her to the side. Allison's eyes danced around her sockets in a panic, she responded, "Funny, I don't see a video." & kept it moving.

"How's that adoption thing going?" Emma asked to add fuel to the fire.

Trinity, Naree, & Scarlett looked at Em in shock.

"Damn, Em. That was a low blow." Trinity snickered.

"When it comes to Bailey, I'm with all the shits." Emma addressed, staring Allison dead in the eyes as she fumed. Allison retracted her steps & charged at Emma. Trinity & Scarlett stood in front of her.

"I dare you to touch her." Trinity threatened.

"Yea baby, I'm waiting." Scarlett added.

"Your reign is over." Naree laughed as she sashayed in front of Allison & Maci. Kaylee remained neutral & didn't say a word.

"I remember my first day at the UA; you all embarrassed me in front of the entire school. Remember that? I do. Hmmm yea, you assaulted me & then used the blood from my nose to paint a memory on the skirt of someone who later became my best friend. My sister. You called me fat, & even posted nasty things about Bailey befriending me all over social media- seems like yesterday. But I tell you what. Don't worry about fighting Emma. Don't worry about laying hands on Trinity. Hell, let's even toss Scarlet to the side too; how about all of you run that shit back?" Naree encouraged.

A crowd formed in the parking lot when they noticed it was clique against clique. Naree walked even closer to Allison & pushed her. "Come on. I speak English after all, see?!" She said before pushing her again.

Allison didn't do squat. Scarlett continued to let the camera roll since everyone was putting on quite the show.

"Peasants." Allison murmured as she pulled Maci's arm to walk away.

"Did you forget that quickly that you're the real peasant? Hold on y'all, she forgot. The money you've been rubbing in our faces isn't ACTUALLY yours, Alley Cat. Comprender (understand)?" Scarlett educated.

Everyone laughed hysterically as Allison's crew walked away. Allison replayed every event of her childhood in her mind; she knew they were right- the life she proclaimed as hers all along didn't even belong to her, *technically*. She began to think of how her parents could make it up to her. *"I take my apologies in thousands & millions,"* she pondered to herself.

"I got it! I'm going to throw a huge party for my birthday next weekend. That's how I'll fix this. Become top dog again." She informed the girls.

"Are you sure?" Maci hesitated.

"Oh no worries, I'm sure it'll be bussin!" Kaylee sarcastically added.

"But I mean really though, we're not in a prison. Top dog? It's not that serious. We should focus on our Ivy League opportunities. If they truly have footage of any terrible things we've done, we'll all cease to exist." Kaylee continued.

"Like I said. I'm throwing a huge party next weekend. I could care less if you come. I need to reinstate my status before prom. I will be the Queen." Allison reiterated.

"Well, operation extravaganza is in progress!" Maci cheered. Kaylee rolled her eyes & decided to level with Allison.

"Okay. Fine. Say you reach "Queen status" again. Imagine the blow to your ego when shit hits the fan & everyone finds out you did in fact torture Bailey Brooks? That you rammed that poor girl into suicide because you couldn't fathom that your-" Kay spat before being cut off.

"Look! I'm getting really sick & tired of your shit. Pick a side, Kay! Pick a motherfucking side!" Allison yelled as she stormed away. Kay turned around & went back to the parking lot. She decided to skip school & do some soul-searching. Before she made it to her car, Maci sent a reminder text.

"Don't forget you played a hand in Bailey's suicide as well. Stop pretending to be holier-than-thou & get on board for Allison's birthday party. Chow." Kaylee threw her phone & reflected on whether she sold her soul to the Devil himself.

Chapter 17:

Expose the Bullies

"Anybody can get it at this point." Trinity declared, hype as hell. She & her girls were in the flesh at Allison's birthday party.

"You got the stuff?" Naree asked.

"Hell yea, I got the stuff." Trinity confirmed.

"What stuff? Why are you both talking in code?" Scarlett questioned.

"Right! *You got the stuff?*" Emma mimicked with laughter as the girls died laughing too. They got on the elevator & pressed the button for the penthouse floor.

"Bright idea to crash this party, girls! Em & I have been raving about this opportunity! I can't believe we're finally going to lay her shit bare tonight!" Scarlett shrilled. Trinity stumbled upon some intel relinquishing the identity of Allison's birth mother.

"Sometimes you've got to use what you got to get you want." Trinity responded.

"Isn't that in reference to giving up the nookie?" Scarlett questioned as she chuckled immaturely.

"Depends on what you want." Naree laughed.

"This is the longest elevator ride in history; we've got time to talk about 'stuff,' nookie, & whatnot. No wonder Allison thinks she's on the top of the world, sure does feel like it at this point." Emma giggled.

The elevator finally dinged. They performed their secret handshake simultaneously & stepped out like the badasses they were. Bailey's Girls entered the party in style, bitchin' nothing but fashion! Instantly, they spotted Allison at the photo booth, taking pictures with her sidekick, Maci. Surprisingly, Kaylee was on the other side of the room, sipping what appeared to be a martini.

"Funny how rich kids do whatever the hell they want." Trinity remarked.

"Right. We still check in with our parents!" Emma cosigned.

"& DO!" Naree laughed.

"Y'all are so extra!" Scarlett cackled.

Music floored the penthouse, eyes locked on Bailey's Girls when they stepped in; the DJ stopped spinning & the Photographer fumbled his camera. Ironically, Allison & Maci missed their entrance because they were so full of themselves. The girls used their vanity to their advantage as they slipped into the crowd long enough to activate their grand scheme. Trinity targeted the projector; it was playing a slideshow of photos & videos for Allison. Each slide took a trip down memory lane. She waited for the perfect moment & switched out the flash drive in place of her own. As Allison stood obliviously at her table designated for gifts, the crowd began to gasp, for they saw what she did not.

The Photographer captured each moment of Allison's fascination with her new designer bags, fragrances, & jewelry. Allison's smiles turned to frowns upon noticing the misdirection of her audience's attention. "Are you all blind? It's MY birthday! All eyes on me!" She yelled. She took her hand & swiped it across her throat, signaling for the DJ to cut the music as she made her way to the other side of the room. Her parents followed. Those claws came to a screeching halt when she approached the projector screen & saw a video of a meth-head with the hashtag, #AllisonsBioMom. She literally couldn't move. The video proceeded to show this woman, her mother, in a disturbing light. She was smoking meth, snorting it, injecting it, & hell, there were even slides of her eating it.

"Anthony, turn it off, NOW!" Louise screamed as she shoved through students, friends, & family. She hired him to operate the projector so that the good times could keep on rolling. He stepped away to drink & mingle- big mistake. Allison remained motionless. Her mouth stayed open long enough for flies to enter & make a new home. Her nose flared as her father approached her, Frankie attempted to comfort her, but he was caught off guard with her question.

"Is that her?" She asked humbly. He looked for Louise, seeking approval to answer, but she was scolding Anthony. He turned back to Allison & instantly, she knew the truth. "You have got to be kidding me." She murmured in disbelief. Anthony still hadn't managed to end the slideshow because he was too busy being fired. Allison got closer & locked eyes on the hot mess she had for a mother. She analyzed her hair, her pale white skin, & those blue eyes. She wondered if being her kid made her smile as wide as the meth did on the footage she saw. When the slideshow ended, she remembered she was standing in the middle of her own birthday party. She gazed around the room & was immediately flushed with embarrassment. Bailey's Girls approached from opposite directions & joined forces. They stood in front of her & said "Happy Birthday, Alley Cat!" in unison.

"How'd you peasants even make it through the door? Glad you're finally getting a taste of what having money feels like." Allison responded.

"Oh no. You're mad? No worries. I hope you enjoyed the birthday present from yours truly. Much better than the show you gave us of Bailey, don't ya think?" Scarlett seconded.

"You basic bitches have some nerve." Maci stated, folding her arms as she stood next to Allison.

"Good boy, now sit. Sit. If you sit, I'll give you a doggie treat." Naree sarcastically stated, speaking dog to Maci. Maci rolled her eyes. Kaylee saw there was a standoff, but she didn't engage. She grabbed her purse & took her leave. Allison & Maci spotted her escape, they were not pleased.

"Guess Kaylee's tired of being your lapdog. I'm so glad Maci does enough licking for the both of them." Emma acknowledged.

"She's weak & also none of your concern." Allison responded. "How about we settle this once & for all?"

"Yea, how about that? Let's say you come clean for torturing Bailey, maybe we can let you make it." Trinity suggested.

"Let me make it? Do you know who I am?" Allison asked.

"To be honest, I don't even think YOU know at this point." Scarlett enlightened.

"We're giving you a countdown. You come clean or we will do it for you. You've got 24 hrs." Trinity informed.

Allison's parents shut the party down & began to escort everyone out. "We'll be seeing you." The girls said in harmony as they gracefully exited as well. They boarded the elevator & chatted about tonight's shenanigans while they waited to reach ground level. When they got off, they saw Kaylee standing in the lobby.

"Something's off with them. She's the key." Naree said, slowing them down.

"Yea, but we can't ask her, she's the enemy after all." Scarlett pointed out.

"What if she's not?" Emma questioned.

"But she is though." Scarlett repeated.

"Right. I know Bails didn't say much about her, but she was still front row to every antic, including shit with us. I'm not fucking with her." Trinity explained as she exited the building. Kaylee overheard them & decided to finally say something. She caught up to them in the parking lot.

"I know why Allison bullied Bailey Brooks!" She blurted out. The girls quit bickering.

"Well. You've got our attention." Scarlett informed.

"She was jealous of Bailey." Kaylee began.

"We're listening." Trinity responded, head cocked to the side.

"She was jealous of Bailey because of her boyfriend, Chase. Chase had the biggest crush on Bailey Brooks & he didn't care to hide it. But, because he & Allison's families are locked in, he's forced to be with her." Kaylee continued.

"Wait what? All of that over some boy?! & What you mean their families locked in?" Trinity asked.

"Well, Chase isn't just *some boy*. He's *the* boy, & it's a rich people thing; his family ranks the wealthiest in town & their power trumps all. Chase & Allison's families approved of them dating one another, there's not much room for error or do-overs. He used to like Allison, but Bailey shut that shit down without even trying, which drove Allison crazy. She couldn't stand how beautiful Bailey was, nor could she grasp the fact that Chase was really smitten by her. When rich families set their children up, some sort of trust fund or mutually beneficial deal is on the line. It's like do or die sometimes." Kaylee explained. Bailey's Girls stood in the parking lot, speechless.

"We gave that bottom feeder 24 hours to come clean, but it's on now." Trinity confirmed. Bailey's Girls were outraged! Allison drove Bailey to suicide over a boy who didn't even want her, how pathetic is that?

Trinity spent the entire weekend creating Allison's final reckoning. She conversed with Josh & was able to retrieve every bit of footage she needed to tie this all together, but she wanted more. She called Naree & told her to go & pay Allison's bio mom a visit. She wanted to out her father as well. Naree spent her Sunday bargaining with meth to get information out of Cassandra Nicholson. Ree had the girls in her ear as Trinity's job was to search any names she dropped. They just needed the proper tea to get this job done.

"So, you'll give me that if I tell you who the father of my child is?" Cassandra asked, scratching & twitching.

"Yea. But it's gotta be legit. Give me a name." Ree demanded.

"He cheated on me with another woman. It's been so long ago. I can't, I don't know." Cassandra contemplated.

"I know you want this. You're having withdrawals. Tell me more & you can have it." Ree pressed.

"Oh! I remember! His name... was Hart! He was my heart but then he cheated on me & got her pregnant." Cassandra informed.

Trinity's eyes widened; this story sounded all too familiar. *"Hell naw, not possible."* She pondered, shrugging her thoughts off.

"Okay, so his name wasn't Hart? He was just your heart? Please tell me you know something else." Ree pleaded.

"We sold drugs together. Now, he's the reason I can't live without them." Cassandra further expressed.

Naree sulked & gave up.

"She's been doing drugs all these years, there's no way she's gonna remember. She doesn't even know where she is. We've got to try to talk to Bailey's mom, again." Ree explained, walking out of the trap house.

"Did you give her the drugs?" Emma asked.

"Naw. I couldn't do it. I'm going home. I'll call you all later." Ree went home flustered & upset, she wanted to help but she felt inadequate.

"What's wrong honey?" Sena asked, hugging her closely.

"I think my coma changed me. I used to be so good at communicating with people. Now, I just... I don't know. We found out that Allison bullied Bailey because her boyfriend had a freaking crush on her! Is that what this life is about?! Driving someone to suicide over the simplest of things?!" Ree cried.

Sena's head hung low & she began to stew in guilt of her own.

"Mom. You saw Bailey last at the hospital, how did she? What did she? I mean, like- could you tell me if she was in pain anymore?" Ree questioned, struggling to find closure.

Sena took the deepest breath she could find & bared all honesty. "Bailey appeared to be at peace, but I found something that told me she was more disturbed than anything." Sena confessed.

Naree looked up from her pity party. Sena exited her bedroom & returned with a document in a plastic bag. There was blood on it. She handed it to Naree & sat beside her bed for what was to come.

"What is this?" Naree questioned as she began to read it. She analyzed the document & confirmed it was Allison's birth certificate. Her biological parents were Cassandra Nicholson & Riley Hart.

"I don't understand. Why would this disturb Bailey?" She asked her mother.

"When Bailey was delivered to the hospital, I had to remove her clothing & place her personal belongings in a bag to give to her family. I found this & knew right away, she had been harboring way more than she led on. Riley Hart is Bailey's biological father." Sena revealed.

Naree was LIVID! "So, you mean to tell me that Bailey's long-lost sister is the demon that drove her to kill herself?! Mom, how could you keep this from me?! Why?!" Ree yelled, storming from her bedroom. She grabbed her car keys & hauled ass to Trinity's home. Sena knew not to run after Naree because she was pissed, as she should've been. Naree arrived at Trinity's- winded & pounding on the door like a mad woman. Luckily, Trinity's mother & brother were at work. Trinity opened the door in a panic.

"What the hell? Are you okay?" She asked.

"That bitch is Bailey's sister!" Naree yelled, retching for air.

"Slow down. What?" Trinity questioned.

"Allison Parker is Bailey's sister! Allison's father is Riley Hart! Bailey's father is-" She heaved.

"Riley Hart!" Trinity finished.

"WHAT THE F---" Trinity yelled when it registered.

"Exactly!" Ree amened, clinging to her chest for more air. She stepped inside & gave Trin the play-by-play. At this point, Trinity had exactly what she needed to blast that little witch once & for all. She & Ree stayed up part of the night, struggling to make sense of the conundrum that just occurred. *"How could this terror be Bailey's sister? Her blood? No way."* Trinity deliberated amongst herself; her brain became dismantled as she rummaged about her racing thoughts. She couldn't even begin to delve into how she was going to address this matter, but she was damned to let this shit ride.

Naree went home after a while, but Trinity stayed up the rest of the night, she was HEATED! When Ree made it home, she gave her mother the silent treatment & cried herself into a deep sleep. Scarlett & Emma were oblivious to the newest storm brewing, they didn't know why tomorrow would be the worst day of Allison's life. When the sun rose, Bailey's Girls did too. They dressed in their million-dollar brand to spark good vibes & took off to step- as they should, together. They pulled up & walked into the UA on their best shit. To their surprise, the educators were escorting everyone into the auditorium.

"Damn, did we miss something?" Scarlett questioned, lingering behind her friends. She saw posters for an emergency assembly.

"I don't recall any event occurring today. Then again, we have been preoccupied lately." Trinity responded.

"True. As long as my GPA doesn't drop, we're all good." Emma joked.

"I'm still stuck on this beef Allison had with Bailey. Like, over a boy? Seriously though?" Scarlett expressed. Trin & Ree gave each other the side eye but didn't utter a word yet.

"Yea, it's giving bum if you ask me, because if she was really "that bitch," she would've cuffed somebody else-period." Trinity shared.

"I've honestly lost respect for her. I mean I knew she was dry as hell, but I never imagined in a million years she'd let some dusty ass boy ruffle her feathers so hard." Emma admitted.

"Bailey was a baddie though. I see why the bitch was so pressed." Trinity laughed pettily.

"Right this way, girls. Please come in & have a seat." Counselor Strickland directed as they scurried along. The auditorium was packed. When everyone was seated, counselor Strickland took the stage.

"Thank you all for moving so quickly. We have a very special guest here today. Her name is Morocco Santana. She has an important message regarding the awareness of bullying. Please refrain from using your phones at this time; this message impacts us all." Strickland announced. The lights were dimmed & the show, well it began. Bailey's Girls immediately felt uncomfortable. *"Oh, now they want to talk about bullying?"* They all thought. As the slide showcased various forms of bullying, they sat, stewing in heartache. When the presentation ended, Santana stepped to the mic.

"I know that some of those images were hard to see, as I'm sure you all have encountered bullying in one way or another. To recap, bullying can be spreading rumors, mean mugging/ giving someone distasteful looks, or antagonizing someone to the point of embarrassment, public humiliation, or exclusion- & that's only all under the social radar. Bullying can be physical, verbal, or via electronic devices, such as social media. Let's try something. If you have ever been bullied, stand up." Santana instructed.

Everyone hesitated as they peered over at one another to confirm their acts of bravery. Nearly every student in the room crept to their feet.

"Wow. This is the largest crowd to stand before me. Typically, students are afraid to stand because it solidifies that there was once a weakness lurking inside them. Please know that being bullied doesn't make you weak- it means you were a target. You were targeted because someone liked something about you so much, or there was something they just didn't understand about you, & we fear what we do not understand, yes?" Santana explained. Every student nodded in agreeance.

"Okay. Sit. Let's try something else. If *you* have ever bullied someone, intentionally or not, stand to your feet." She instructed. Some students stood, snickering with their friends, & some sat, brewing in their guilty pleasures. Allison & Maci stood in high fashion & low vibrations as darkness fell upon them. Kaylee did not sit with them, she sat across from them. She looked directly at Bailey's Girls & stood to the floor after taking a deep breath. She almost passed out with those eyes glaring at her, but she felt standing meant accountability, so she did it. Santana looked over the audience & spoke with no sugar.

"I understand that admitting something so terrible is forbidden in this generation, but I said that if you have bullied someone, intentionally or not- to stand." A few more students stood to their feet. "That's more like it. Take a good look at yourselves." She directed as she grabbed the mic & walked closer to the edge of the stage.

"My meeting you today is no accident. I have followed this academy since the report of a student taking her life on this very stage." Some students attempted to sit.

"No, do not sit. Please stand. Hear me when I say that Bailey Brooks has not been forgotten. She took her life one year ago, today." Trinity, Scarlett, Naree, & Emma all gasped. *"She's here for Bailey."* Trinity cried as she stood & clapped. Her girls followed. Santana continued to speak.

"This presentation may have seemed impromptu, but I have been planning this visit since that beautiful soul hit my radar. I know that Bailey's GPA was a 4.0 & that she loved fashion & real estate; she was going places. Do you all have any idea what it would feel like for your parents to find you hanging from this stage? To bury you? To let you go? Imagine that for a second." She paused. "Doesn't feel too comfortable to picture, does it? What if Bailey was your friend or family member? This pain is real & it hurts. Sit down. There's a bully out there called life & it comes for us all, all too often. Please note that the way we treat others finds us one day." The educators clapped. There were mixed feelings in the room though, she spit some real shit. Could they handle it?

"I've got something to say." Trinity initiated. Naree spookily glanced over at her, she didn't know what was about to go down. After all, they had a secret. "Sure, come on down." Santana invited. Trinity walked briefly until she made it to the stage. She began seeing flashbacks of Bailey's body clinging to the rope that once dangled from the ceiling. She saw her body, lifelessly, draping like the curtains she longed for. She saw Bailey. She choked on her tears & reached for the mic. Santana handed it over.

"Bullying doesn't only hurt the people you do it to, it hurts those around them because the light that once dwelled within that being- burns out. Bailey's light beamed as brightly as it could until she decided... no more. I have a presentation I've been waiting to share." Trinity stated as she pulled a flash drive from her pocket & inserted it into the projector's input. It was a collection of encounters recorded by Joshua's sister, Jessica. Scarlett, Naree, & Emma got up & made their way to stand below the stage in solidarity of Bailey. As they stood, facing forward, they embraced the reactions of educators & students in the room- Allison & her girls were on candy camera.

"Allison Parker led a crusade against my best friend, my sister, Bailey Brooks- all over a boy, Chase Valentine. In these videos you see, she & her friends tormented her, endlessly. Today, she's finally being laid to rest as you all now know her truth." Trinity revealed.

"She's lying!" Allison screamed.

"Trinity, this is not how we do things." Principal Ritton regretfully informed as he jogged down to the stage.

"Right, because the UA doesn't do anything at all! We grieve Bailey every day! This school never grieved her, not ONCE!" Trinity yelled. Ritton walked up to the stage to take the mic & cut the footage. Trinity refused to let go of the mic & she blocked the input with her bottom to keep Ritton from removing the flash drive.

"I SAID I HAVE SOMETHING TO SAY!" She shouted. Principal Ritton stood aside, he knew her wrath was unmanageable at this moment.

"Allison Parker. You killed my sister, just know you killed yours too." She announced. Allison frowned. The brows in the crowd stood in amazement.

"Oh, just in case you're having a blonde moment- Riley Hart is Bailey's bio dad, unbeknownst to us all, - he's your bio dad too. Bailey Brooks is your biological sister. I hope you can live with yourself, you trifling, jealous-ass bully!" Trinity notified. She handed the mic over to Ritton & angrily walked away.

"What?!" Scarlett shouted. Naree filled Scar & Em in on last night's session of tea. They couldn't even respond clearly.

"It's true. Allison made us torture Bailey because Chase was feeling her." Kaylee declared as loudly as he could. Trinity stopped dead in her tracks. Scarlett, Naree, & Emma all turned around. Allison & Maci were flushed with embarrassment.

"What in Sam Hell do you think you're doing?" Allison asked as she charged toward Kaylee.

"Something you'll never have the tits to do." She answered. She pushed Allison down & walked toward Bailey's Girls.

"I'm sorry. I'm so sorry for everything I ever did to Bailey. To each of you. I am a coward & inhumane, but I promise, I'm ashamed of who I've been. I pray you all will forgive me one day. Bailey was so lucky to have friends like you." Kaylee continued.

Allison's mouth hit the floor like wet panties; she couldn't believe Kaylee finally turned against her. "You are the weakest fucking link!" She cried as she stormed out of the auditorium. Maci ran behind her to the same restroom Bailey cried in before she died. Allison was found on the floor of a stall, crying her eyes out. *Had she finally been broken?*

Bailey's Girls thanked Kaylee for apologizing & then walked away. The room once empty, felt so full. Bailey's Girls exited the auditorium, no one stopped them. Santana & every educator in the building were mortified, the students were speechless. They were finally done with Allison & her crew.

As the day went on, Allison felt the shift in her social status, it declined worse than stage 4 cancer. No one spoke to her, they talked about her to her face, posted about her behavior on social media, & ignored her when she attempted to speak. She was in shock. She cried uncontrollably & lashed out when she felt the need. She was no longer the "it-girl" & to add insult to injury, Chase dumped her via text & changed his status to SINGLE on all major platforms. She figured he was just throwing a fit, so she gave him some time, but he was done.

Allison's rise to Queendom was null & void. She walked out of her fifth-period class because she couldn't handle the heat. Maci's loyal ass fled the scene as well.

Bailey's Girls were pulled into the office during 7th period, but they were not in trouble. Principal Ritton apologized for his lack of attention to Bailey's suicide & informed them he will continue to bring awareness to bullying every chance he gets. They were grateful. They left Ritton's office, mission accomplished. It was one year later; Bailey's soul was finally at peace.

Bailey's Girls felt empowered by their win. Now, it was time to make some other wrongs- right.

Chapter 18:

Strike Back

Allison spiraled. She had been humiliated one too many times by Bailey's Girls; since her ego had been bruised, she was forced to face the music. What a miserable tune it was. She went to her adoptive parents & laid out the lyrics before her. They allowed her to spaz on them & attempted to provide peace- there was none.

Allison took her dad's credit card & purchased a room at the Four Seasons. She held up there for a while- no school, no friends, no parents. She used the time to reflect on her journey to this point & realized she had been a pawn in this game of adoption all along; she acknowledged that her parents knew of her connection to Bailey. There was not an ounce of shock when she presented her embarrassment to them, she settled in on how they more so comforted her- like "there, there, you will get through this." She decided she'd get through it alright, by confronting her birth parents once & for all. She utilized the information accessible to her but came to a dead end because although her parents were blasted, she didn't know their whereabouts & she was damned to ask her parents for help. She left her hotel suite & went searching for a familiar face.

"Hi, Mrs. Brooks." Allison greeted.

"What the hell are you doing at my front door? You've got some nerve!" Sara replied.

"Chill... I come in peace." She responded, rolling her eyes. She felt Sara was being overdramatic.

"Allison Parker, you are now an adult who is on *my* property. I could rock-a-bye baby your ass right here on my front lawn, & I wouldn't be charged at all. With your dad being a lawyer, you know this right?" Sara threatened as she began closing the front door in her face.

"Riley Hart is my father!" she yelled with tears pouring from her eyes. The once creaking door came to a halt. Sara looked at her & didn't see the monster that killed her daughter, she saw a little girl. She invited her in.

"What do you mean Riley Hart is your father?" Sara questioned, giving a side-eye.

"This just in... I'm adopted. Turns out, my birth mother is Cassandra Nicholson. Trinity Woods & her friends exposed her identity & the fact that she's on drugs at my 18th birthday party." She cried relentlessly.

"During an emergency assembly the other day, Trinity announced that my birth father is Riley Hart, & that he's Bailey's birth father too?" She glared up, seeking further confirmation. Sara nodded yes with the blankest expression. The downpour of Allison's waterworks became a thunderstorm. She was a hot mess. Sara contemplated her position in this matter; she didn't want to show too much compassion to Allison Parker- it'd be a betrayal to Bailey. She got up & grabbed Allison some Kleenex. Allison's mask had been cracked & the face behind it revealed itself.

"Wow. Trinity dished it out like that, did she? I can't say I'm not proud. All too often, we spend time ruining others, but when it's our turn- we can't handle it. It hurts our feelings. It breaks us. We weren't prepared. You must pick yourself up & embrace what life has given you. I have Riley's number; I'll write it down. I don't know much about your mother, except that she & I were pregnant at the same time because Riley was unfaithful. I knew that her child was given up for adoption, but I didn't stick around much longer. I moved on. Guess you're Bailey's half-sister, didn't see that coming at all." Sara expressed; brows raised.

"I envied Bailey." Allison pulled from within herself to say.

"Of course, you did." Sara responded, trying to keep her snazziness to a minimum. She didn't want to kick the girl while she was down.

"My boyfriend really, really liked her. I was humiliated, I wanted her to feel the same. I am truly, genuinely so sorry. I just didn't want to take that L." Allison admitted.

"So, you made me take one? Sara shook her head. "I'm not sure what you want from me."

"I came here because I feel so lost. My life has been a lie. I don't want to be around my parents or my friends. I thought to reach out to my older sister, but I don't trust her. She wouldn't understand." Allison answered. Sara deescalated from within & realized Allison was in the same position Bailey was in when she found out that Riley was her father.

"The greatest thing about being lost is that you get to be found. Bailey didn't get the chance to be found. To work beyond her trauma, but you have that opportunity. You think taking an L is losing a boy you like, live a little longer, honey. Taking an L is losing your only daughter. Your home. Your husband. Your son. Your job. Parents. Your only transportation. Yourself. Taking an L is working to satisfy employers who will not pay you your worth. Surrounding yourself with people that you know don't mean you well but clinging to them to prevent loneliness. Taking an L is sitting here showcasing an ounce of compassion for the bully that made sure I buried my daughter before she reached 18." Sara blatantly explained.

"I get it." Allison managed to say.

"I don't think you do because taking an "L" is also battling depression but finding the strength to go to an academy with a bunch of rich snots that only wish to make your life a living hell. You're not sorry for Bailey, my daughter, your sister- you're sorry for you, & feeling sorry for yourself after everything you've done just makes you the spoiled little shit I always knew you were. I can be nice but to indulge in this is not healthy for me. You may be Bailey's sister & while that does sway me, it does not move me. You have a restraining order against me for defending my baby. I bullied you & your minions back when all I wanted to really do was put you in the ground! I took an L. Take your entitled energy & focus on growing up." Sara expressed while pacing the floor & grabbing her head. If baby girl didn't get the memo soon, she was going to be debuted in a homicide.

Allison had no words. She received everything Sara said & sat there in silence, sniffling with regret. Bailey's Girls put her on her ass & so did Sara. She cleaned herself up & made her way back to the front door. As promised, Sara gave her Riley's number. Allison thanked her & went back to the Four Seasons. When she entered her suite, she saw flowers had been delivered with a note attached from her dad. She grabbed it & sat on the loveseat. She held in one hand, her birth father's number & in the other, a note from the only father she's ever known. She contemplated heavily on who to address first. She threw the note & called Riley Hart.

While Allison fought to bring herself back down to Earth, Bailey's Girls were trailing a snitch in Miami, per Bennie's new request. The cold thing about this mission was that the potential snitch was from Bennie's inner circle. Although they wanted to help Bennie confirm his suspicions & get justice, they were fixated on the upcoming meeting for their company. This meeting was vital, as it would set the tone for the longevity of their brand, they were not happy; they wanted to be at home, closing the biggest deal thus far.

"If we miss this meeting, we'll never be taken seriously. It was hard to be recognized before, imagine bombing a meeting with these people- we'll be done for. I can't hack us into importance. Now, that I think about it, I know I could, but I want us to be legit. I don't want us tying Bailey or We Bitchin Fashion to anything shady." Trinity exclaimed while staring through a set of binoculars. They were staked out at this vintage bar in Miami, Florida, Lost Boy. Lost Boy was low-key; they had drinks, finger foods, & pool- which is what the girls needed to loosen up & get this show on the road.

"Like seriously, I love my padre (father), but these fashion partners are once-in-a-lifetime, if we miss this- I will take him out myself. It'll be the saddest kill shot I'll ever have to take unless I have to kill Jase one day." Scarlett shared.

"Yikes. Let's not get ahead of ourselves. What if we sped up this process so you won't have to do that?" Naree suggested.

"Yea, we could totally just snatch his ass & get the intel we need- voluntarily or involuntarily." Emma added, leveling each hand side by side. The girls all chuckled at her enthusiasm.

"Slow down, Killa!" Trinity laughed.

"She's on to something though." Scarlett agreed.

"I say we kick it real tough & stir the pot to get him to do what we need." Naree explained.

"Stir the pot?" Trinity questioned.

"Follow my lead." Naree reassured as she left their hideout to go into Lost Boy. She signaled for Trinity to keep watch & for Emma to follow her. Naree took her hair down & let it blow in the wind. She was feeling dangerous & it showed. They walked into the bar, fake IDs in hand, guns holstered in between their thighs, ready to drink & air out the place if need be.

"I'd like something sweet." Naree requested.

"I'll take anything strong." Emma smirked. As their drinks were being prepared, they zeroed in on Mr. Snitch- his name was Wade Herrera. He sat at a table fraternizing with Bennie's enemy, Rico DuBois. From the looks of it, he was running his mouth, but they weren't close enough to tell.

"Oh, screw it." Naree said, chugging her drink. Emma followed her lead, brows raised.

"I'm on whatever you on." Emma reassured. Naree looked around the dim bar & went for the pool table. She hopped up there & decided to scare the piss out of him. She started singing as though she were in a musical.

"Oh Mr. Herrera. Mr. Herrera. I hear you like to speak. Mr. Herrera. I hear that money makes you weak. Mr. Herrera. You've come so very far. Mr. Herrera. Tell me how you got that scar." She winked. Emma took her ponytail down & savagely shook her head. That drink was kicking in, so she joined along. She went right over to Wade & stared him in the eyes.

"Oh WADE! Tell me do you remember those days when your mother sat & prayed you'd make it HOME?! You don't want to be alone. But just maybe if you answered your phone, your Boss wouldn't think you rolled him in the ground." She said dramatically showcasing jazz hands, Broadway style. Wade's eyes began to bounce around.

"You shouldn't pillow talk with strangers. Your life could end up in danger." Naree sang again.

"I hope that you are taking heed. Because not even begging please- will save you from the wrath of Bennieee. Dun Dun Duuuun." Emma sang while she & Ree laughed hysterically. Trinity & Scarlett rushed to the back of the door as Wade took his leave. Everyone at the bar clapped & laughed, what a show. The girls bowed & bid Mr. DuBois a good night & exited as well.

Instead of following Bennie's orders, Trin & Scar decided to kidnap the infamous informer. Ree & Em caught up & witnessed his kidnapping. They hopped in their rental & trailed Trinity in Wade's car to Miamarina At Bayside. Boats were docked there, people were lurking; they had to be careful. Wade was losing his shit, but he kept his cool. Trinity hacked into Rico's connections out there & located his boat. If things went south- it'd be confirmed that he & Wade were last seen at Lost Boy, together. They held him at gunpoint & made him get onto the boat. Emma found a rope lying on the floor. She went to pick it up & immediately had flashbacks of the rope that snatched Bailey's life & the one that almost took hers. Scarlett noticed her discomfort & did the deed for her.

"This could've really been fun, but we can't afford to do this Bennie's way, long & excruciating. We've got shit to do, people to see, places to be. You know what I mean." Trinity enlightened as she strapped him to the chair.

"Short, painful, & sweet- it is!" Scarlett confirmed while opening a bag of tools she found inside of Rico's boat.

"No offense or anything. We just don't have time to wait & watch you screw up when we know you already have. It's wasteful, so, while we're young- please do tell us what you've been up to, Mr. Herrera." Naree led. Wade secretly took an oath of silence. He looked at them all & scoffed.

"You're just children." He laughed. "I hope you can take everything you dish out tonight."

"Alright, that's it. Let's go." Naree said, pinning her hair back up. She swung hard & quick, right hook to the left side of his face. She busted his nose; he bled a little. He smiled, unfazed. She hit him again & again. Trinity, Scarlett,

& Emma let her have at it until she began to lose control. Naree caught a glimpse of being shot while punching him; she saw her body lying on the floor at the Four Seasons, grappling for air. She saw the face of the man who shot her. She kept punching until she became winded. Wade began to beg for mercy. She took her knee & shoved it into his face with the quickness. The girls pulled her away from him. Ree panted & yelled, "You better tell us what you know. Trinity, now!"

Trinity pulled her phone out & began to record him, bleeding & shaking. "I don't know what you're talking about." He spoke. Scarlett took her gun from between her legs & cocked it.

"Are you sure that's what you're gonna go with?" She asked.

"No! Wait! Please don't kill me! I did it! I've been stealing drugs from Bennie! I've been using & selling them to Rico DuBois & the Russians so that I could come up too. I emptied his factory in Miami." He confessed.

"Did you get that?" Emma questioned.

"Sure did." Trinity confirmed.

Scarlett nodded & sent two shots into the heart of Wade Herrera. He died, instantly. The girls gathered around him, held hands, & shared their condolences. They cleaned up their mess & investigated Rico's boat for anything they could take to Bennie. They swiped some drugs & his plans for taking over Bennie's operation. This mission was finally complete. Bennie phoned Scarlett; she didn't answer. He phoned Trinity, Ree, & Emma; they didn't answer either. He began to worry. A few hours later, the girls finally responded & asked Bennie to meet them at Wake-Up Philly. Everyone arrived in the middle of the night, unsure of how this showdown would go. They deliberately disobeyed Bennie's orders. He sat there, frustrated.

"I asked you all to follow him. What happened?"

"He was stealing from you, Daddy. So, we killed him." Scarlett explained while handing him Trinity's phone. He watched his confession & even played it back. It saddened him to be betrayed by one of his own, but he understood their judgment call.

"Trinity put her hacking skills to great use. She covered our tracks, per usual, & she even left some bugs on Rico's boat, so that we can get a little more intel & some payback." Naree explained.

"Good job, girls. Where's the body?" He asked out of curiosity.

"Swimming with the fishies." Emma answered.

"If there's even fish in there at this point. You know how many bodies they probably dump out there?" Trinity laughed.

"We're really sorry, Daddy. We got carried away because we have an amazing opportunity in a few hours, we would've missed it, had we not done what we did." Scarlett further explained. Bennie nodded & went over the dirt they found on Rico. Rico was connected to the Russians. Naree remembered who shot her, but she hadn't said anything yet. Shit was about to get real.

The girls left Wake-Up Philly & went home to get ready. They got themselves together & then met up at a suite in Downtown, Philly. It was 7:30 am; they were tired as hell, but they were ready. "We've got this." Trinity reassured them all. They took a group photo in a body mirror nearby & shouted "We Bitchin Bitches!"

By 9 am, it was official. Bailey's Girls secured a 30-million-dollar deal for We Bitchin Fashion's entire line; they were now partnered with a fashion house that held locations in Paris & New York! Dreams really do come true!

During their meeting, the representatives were extremely impressed with Emma's idea to dedicate a denim jacket line to honor their best friend, Bailey Brooks. She shared that the hashtag for the line will be #GameOnForBailey. They were unequivocally sold. The talent from each of them solidified that they were the next big thing in the fashion world.

"Nothing can stop us now!" They shouted while raising their contract in the air.

~~Chapter 19:~~

<u>College Day</u>

Bailey's Girls were high from the joy of their final semester; they were only a kill shot & a catwalk away from becoming graduates of Ulysses Academy. They knew they'd come out on top, but never like this. Since closing their first major deal, life has been amazing. They learned that although time flies when you're hurting, it flies when you're having fun too. Being so invested in the cartel & We Bitchin Fashion took away their root existences. They pressed pause & spent a massive amount of time with their families; lots of dinners, amusement parks, museums, movie nights, & preparing for college. Each teen altered their family's lives for the better; new cars, new homes, & savings accounts with enough money to retire them all. Their parents were blown away at the success of their children, but they remained humble.

Trinity's mother & brother quit working their dead-end jobs & decided to go after their dreams too; they were preparing to launch a company making luxury gourmet meals, together. Trinity saved Trey's life, intentionally; she feared he'd end up falling into the stereotype of selling drugs & doing jail time. She couldn't let him go out like that- so, she blessed his game. The day he quit the diner was a pivotal moment, he fell to his knees crying & thanked God before handing the supervisor his apron. Reece was sad to walk away from helping the youth, but she decided it was time to help herself. Trinity was in a generous mood. Although she felt abandoned by her father, she loved him. She blessed his game too. He used the money to visit her more often & moved into a nicer condo.

Scarlett's mother continued to work as a paralegal, but she was inspired to continue her journey & obtain the proper training to become a licensed attorney. She found out that Scarlett had been repairing her relationship with Bennie, but she didn't pry because she didn't want to insinuate that he led a criminal life. She even found herself fawning over him when he came by the house for family dinners, but she managed to keep her cool. Scarlett was just happy to see them both in one room after all these years. The trauma of her parent's bullshit finally set in. She didn't know whether to be thankful or to let them both know how she was really feeling.

The Gem family basked in their daughter's win by taking a trip back home to see family they hadn't been able to visit in years due to lack of finances. They made lots of memories & planned for future visits. Ree's siblings became popular. Every student at Waterfall High wanted to be in their vicinity because they knew they were related to Naree Gem. Luckily, they didn't care about social climbing. They did however love the attention.

Although money could change a lot of things, it could not alter Ethan's disability. Emma wished there was more she could do to help her father. She paid for him to see the finest specialists & tried her best to encourage him to keep going but he already accepted defeat. To soften the blow, she upgraded his wheelchair to the nicest electric wheelchair she could find. Laura ended up closing on a suite to showcase art to *her* liking. The dream she envisioned for Seen & Unseen meant she needed to thrive on her own because her voice had not been heard.

The sun was shining bright in Philly. It was College Day at the UA; the girls were ready! When they arrived, there were college reps & tables decorated for every university you could think of. They were extremely thrilled. Allison was still a non-factor & so were her minions. Students bypassed those girls as though they never existed. The educators fell into routine & directed everyone to the gym. While attempting to structure proper lines for each table, various screams bolted throughout the school.

College Day turned deadly on campus when a group of unknown assailants raided the UA, armed & searching for Bailey's Girls. They were first in line, smiling & talking to the College Reps when the action occurred. Loud cries carried into the gym as students ran for their lives, warning everyone that 4 men with guns were headed their way. The attackers went door to door, aiming their guns at any & everyone. As they came up short, they moved it along because they hadn't identified who they came for. The girls overheard the commotion & automatically knew they had company. "Are you fucking kidding me?" Trinity asked as they ducked for cover behind the doors near the entrance of the gym.

"Shit! We don't carry our guns to school. What are we gonna do?" Emma questioned.

"We just have to kick their asses." Ree established.

"Agreed. Let's tap into everything from camp." Trinity added.

"But what about our identities? Wouldn't we be risking everything?" Scarlett asked.

"We can't let anyone die. Not on our watch!" Trinity replied. Scarlett nodded & pinned her hair up. She wasn't her usual spunky self but kicking some ass would certainly put her in the mood.

"I heard someone say there were 4 men. There's 4 of us, we got this!" Naree encouraged. More students ran into the gym. They were screaming, dialing 911, falling, crying, & shoving one another as they fought to make it to safety. The seemingly nerdy high school girls turned Thugs In Skirts- thrashed the 4 men unexpectedly when they came barging through the gym doors. Bailey's Girls gave those men everything they had. They stood off with each villain, one by one, & used the skills they learned in Cartel Camp- like how to subdue your target when they're armed & you're not.

"Whew, he's big as shit!" Emma grunted as she punched again & again.

"Don't give up!" Trinity yelled as she hit her target in his midsection, bringing him down to his knees.

"It's College Day, you assholes!" Scarlett yelled before taking her target's gun & knocking him out with it.

"The bigger they are." Trinity chuckled out of breath as her target hit the ground.

"The harder they fall." Naree laughed. She put her target on his ass with one spinning hook kick to the head, compliments to Taekwondo.

Emma got fed up & pounced on her target. She used her elbow to jolt him dead in the center of his face. He was out like a light & now, she had his gun. Bailey's Girls successfully overcame the attackers & had their guns to prove it.

"Who sent you?!" Trinity yelled. The men all stared at one another. She cocked the gun back & jabbed him in the chest with it. He coughed.

"You've got one second to answer me." She reiterated.

"Facts. If you don't, we'll just kill you. It'll still be warranted as self-defense." Scarlett educated.

"We weren't sent by anyone. We connected through one common goal." One of the assholes answered.

"& what was that?" Naree questioned, prepared to shoot.

"We saw you girls signed a deal for 30 million. Our goal was to abduct you all, hijack your operation, & see what we could get." Another one of the men answered.

"Are you fucking kidding me?!" Emma yelled before drop-kicking the nearest man in his stomach. They all took deep breaths, relieved to know they hadn't been sought out by any cartel affiliates. Trinity mentally noted to hack into the police's database to pull their records for confirmation after booking. They smiled & kept their thugging to a minimum because eyes were on them.

They continued to hold the assailants at gunpoint. Emma let it be known if they were to so much as breathe incorrectly, they'd be blown to bits. The police arrived right away. Students started coming from behind the bleachers, in between the bleachers, & from off top of one another. College Reps & educators came from hiding as well. The policemen expressed their gratitude for Bailey's Girls preventing a bloodbath.

During the commotion, some students recorded the attack & the takedown. They live-streamed it & sent links to various news stations. That's right! Bailey's Girls were exposed! When the bad guys were gone, everyone fixated on these smart, nerdy, teenage girls! The UA felt safe enough to continue College Day, it was extended to the evening. The girls enjoyed the festivities, as planned. Columbia University won their hearts as they conversed with the College Rep about their vision. It was official. They pulled up their offer letters together & accepted!

They were so happy; they couldn't stop screaming & shouting. They were going to New York, TOGETHER! Before it could even sink in, everyone crowded around them to talk about the 4 gunmen. In the same breath, their phones started ringing repeatedly, it was their parents. They knew they needed to get their asses home, neeeooowww! They hopped in their cars & got the hell off campus as quickly as they could. When they got home, they had to tap into Operation: *Fool Thy Parents*. Trinity told her mom she simply knows how to fight, it's in her blood. Scarlett explained to her mother that as a Hunter, her instinct to fight comes naturally- which made sense. Naree reminded her parents that she took Taekwondo lessons for many years, & Emma, Emma didn't know where to begin with her parents, so she pinned it on fear. "I got so scared, I just started mimicking what I've seen on TV." Their cartel entanglements remained a secret. A group Facetime was in order for Bailey's Girls.

"It'd be so much easier if we could just wipe their memory when we need to." Scarlett suggested, rolling her eyes.

"Naw, we just gone lie real good. It's the modern thing to do." Trinity laughed. Naree & Emma died laughing as well. They stayed on FT for hours, talking about their new journey. Trinity requested they bless Bailey's mom with 5 million dollars before leaving town soon, everyone agreed. Scarlett's energy was a little off, but neither of them read too much into it. Trinity hacked the database of Philly's police department. She gathered intel on the perps from earlier & saw they were no threat- just some small-time fish trying to become sharks. She kept copies of every file for future reference, in case they came back. She also sent a copy to Bennie so that his boys could pay them a visit when they were released. He also promised to have his incarcerated amigos deliver a message: *"Don't play with us."*

When Bailey's Girls returned to school, they were swarmed with attention. They were more popular than Allison had ever been; students made it rain with friend requests, follows, mentions, tags, & offers to exclusive events- they had it MADE. Reporters posted outside of the UA, Wake-Up Philly, & their homes every day, desperate to get an interview about their takedown. No matter how crazy things got, Bailey's Girls remained humble. As time moved forward, the media did not let up. Bennie encouraged them to speak. They approached the busy crowd united; Trinity spoke on behalf of them all.

"How does it feel to be Heroes?!" Reporter Newman questioned.

"I see how you think being a Hero is fighting off men who have already showcased themselves as *bad* to you. Realistically, heroes are the people who fight off those who are not already deemed or armored as bad. Bailey Brooks, for example, I didn't see you all here covering her story." Trinity led.

"Who's Bailey Brooks?" Reporter Springfield interjected.

"You mean, who *was* Bailey Brooks? Bailey Brooks was our best friend. She was gentle, kind, warm, & bright. She would've graduated this year had she not committed suicide in our auditorium after being bullied by Allison Parker, Maci Karr, & Kaylee Lopez. Before she committed suicide, her mother, Sara Brooks fought hard to hold this academy & those girls accountable for the way they tortured our sister- but because the ringleader, Allison Parker, is the daughter of infamous attorney, Frankie Parker & US Senator, Louise Parker, Bailey's claims were shut down immediately. Another thing that was shut down was an appeal for Todd Brooks. I find it interesting that only he was imprisoned for a property legally tied to Frankie Parker."

Reporters began to swarm furiously; they were about to eat this UP! Scarlett, Naree, & Emma stood firmly next to Trinity, nodding their head in agreeance. Trinity continued.

"Allison & her friends clothed themselves in scales that changed colors. Bailey wanted to believe they were not the bad guys, even when they proved themselves to be. She was the real Hero. We appreciate your generosity & while the attention is flattering, our only concern is to bring awareness to bullying & advocate for those silent Heroes. Please follow #GameOnForBailey on all major platforms to share your story today. Thank you." Trinity closed with a graceful smile. She turned to her sisters & instantly, the secret handshake was in effect & had been recorded for all to see. Bailey's Girls were famous! Everyone wanted to be them. Talk to them. Sit with them. Love them.

Allison sulked in regret & wallowed in pity as she replayed Trinity's speech in her hotel suite. She took it upon herself to visit Bailey's grave. She knelt beside it & finally uttered the words, "I'm sorry." She had been in communication with her birth father since her visit with Sara. He reached her, villain to villain, they spoke the same language. Riley explained to her that he lived his life making others pay for his pain, & that it only cost him his soul in the end.

Turns out, Alley Cat wants her soul after all. She decided to defer college for a year so that she could revamp herself from within & assist her birth mother with her drug addiction. Funny how shit change.

~~Chapter 20:~~

<u>The Headquarters</u>

Although Trinity dropped a bomb on the reporters, she & the girls agreed to avoid further media attention, they didn't need it. They liked being discreet, it was how they held the upper hand in light & darkness. It was almost time for them to say goodbye to Philly, but before they did, they had some loose ends to tie up, & just like any Bad Girl Club- they were going out with a BING BANG!

They arrived at their high school prom, dressed to kill- LITERALLY. Nah, just kidding, but they were about that life though. Ha, each of them sported their exclusive attire, launched in the name of their dear sister, Bailey Brooks. Their skirts were pop'n & their bling was bling'n- it was truly a party. Bailey's Girls had it going ON! They were a sight for sore eyes, that's for sure.

This event coagulated how much they blossomed, inside & out. Trinity was there with Josh & Scarlett was there with Jase. Ree & Em decided to fly solo, they weren't bringing any sand to the beach! They partied like animals, it was super litty! For once, the school wasn't divided. Kaylee couldn't keep her eyes off them, she was blown away & wanted to say so, but she chose to keep her distance- they still saw her gawking like a middle-aged man with his eyes on a PYT (Pretty Young Thing) though. The nerve- Allison came dressed to be crowned Prom Queen but to no surprise, she did not win... TRINITY DID! What a freaking play!

"Trinity, you led a rebellion. One that brought peace to Bailey & this academy. Come & get yo crown, Queen!" The committee announced as the crowd roared Bailey's name. Josh was crowned King & it was time to dance. Scarlett, Jase, Naree, & Emma shouted at the top of their lungs. A win for Trin was a win for them all!

They continued to party & burn a hole in the dance floor- it was UP! Allison took her L like a champ & sulked with Maci. Thank goodness she had her because if she didn't, she'd probably run into traffic, for real. She lost every part of herself that mattered for so long. Validation from everyone was like a drug, an addition she began having withdrawals from. Now, all she had was Maci. Maci was loyal but she was no fool. She knew that continuing to remain friends with Allison meant social suicide for her too, but she loved her enough to risk it all. She hoped that when Allison found herself again, she'd reciprocate that same energy. Friendship was important. Everybody had somebody but Kaylee. She was isolated, she decided she'd rather be alone than to ever be wrong again. It was as though she found a way to punish herself because she loved Allison & Maci, they're all she's ever known but growth was important to her, & so was her soul. Moving forward, she decided to save herself.

When Bailey's Girls left prom, they took the limo out on the town to turn up some more. They drank, smoked for the first time, & even twerked in the street, but one thing they were not doing tonight- was having sex. They prided themselves on valuing their minds & their hymens, so once the fun was over, they got rid of the boys & ended the night with each other. They decided to book the biggest suite they could find downtown- "Luxury is where it's at!" Trinity shouted as she swiped her debit card at The Rittenhouse Hotel. They stayed up all night & reflected on their lives leading to current. They weren't little girls anymore. Witnessing death right before them changed every part of who they were. They weren't sure where they'd be without working for the cartel, it embedded confidence they probably wouldn't have obtained until reaching the depths of adulthood. When they finished gossiping as much as they could, they fell asleep & slept in the next day. The sun was beaming brighter than a new set of pearly whites. The only thing on their to-do list was to gift Sara the 5 million they discussed & proceed with finalizing arrangements for NY. Life was good.

Bennie requested their presence at Wake-Up Philly. They arrived, ready for whatever. Unbeknownst to each of them, they weren't ready at all. When they walked through the back door, they found Jase lying on the floor. He had been shot, beaten, & carved like a holiday pumpkin. Scarlett couldn't control herself. She got down on her knees & tried to shake him awake. Perez sat in his chair like the King he

was, knocking back shots of vodka. Scarlett glanced at him &
saw his knuckles were bruised.

"Daddy, how could you?!" She cried out. "Por qué
(Why)?"

"Mi hija (My daughter), you have forsaken me."
Bennie informed.

"I have not." She responded.

"You continued to date this boy after I explicitly
forbid it." Bennie further explained.

"Daddy! This is not fair. I've done everything else
you've asked of me." Scarlett cried.

Trinity & the girls didn't understand their presence,
they stood there in shock. Was he going to make them kill
Jase?

"That's the thing about having parents. You don't get
to pick & choose when you listen to them, mi hija (my
daughter). You quickly learn that when you do, you suffer
the consequences." He explained.

"Mr. Perez. Please. Ever since we met Jase, he's been
nothing but a gentleman. He respects you so much & would
never defy you." Trinity vouched.

"I knew it would come to this." Naree spoke under her
breath. She was disappointed. She didn't think it was fair, but

she warned Scarlett, & Jase knew *firsthand* exactly who he was dealing with.

As a result, his body ended up on Bennie's floor, hanging in the balance. Scarlett began feeling for a pulse.

"Daddy his pulse is faint, you have to help him!" Scarlett pleaded some more. Perez didn't move one inch, he kept drinking. Scarlett went for her gun & aimed it at her father. Trinity, Naree, & Emma all gasped & tried to stop her until he went for his gun too.

"My gun is unmarked, recordar (remember)?" Scarlett cautioned.

"I gave it to you. You think mine isn't unmarked too?!" Bennie responded, raising his weapon at his only daughter. Trinity, Naree, & Emma snatched their guns from their garter belts. Perez's men busted into his office, on GO too. It was a showdown.

"Daddy, you have never given me anything. Regardless of how shit went between you & mom, YOU left ME, but I am *here*. You are here, & I have been working for you, playing by your rules. GIVE ME SOMETHING! I WANT HIM!" She said as her voice broke into ten million fireflies. Bennie lowered his gun & laid it on his desk. Although he found disappointment in himself, he still believed in respect.

"You tried to make a play for me & I gave fair warning, precisely, how that would end. I love you, mi hija (my daughter), but Jase must stand on his disrespect." Perez explained. He walked closer to Scarlett, both parties watched closely, gripping their weapon of choice. Scarlett looked her father in his eyes.

"Why did you tell us to come here?" She asked.

"I wanted to tell you cara a cara (face to face) that I knew you never stopped seeing Jase. I also wanted to grant you one goodbye to him." He answered.

"One goodbye?" She cried in confusion.

"We don't host funerals for rats or traitors." Bennie clarified.

"Padre (Father), please." She cried, hoping that he'd feel obliged to let her have her way, he did not. He stood firmly in front of the barrel of his daughter's gun. She was prepared to send his ass to the other side, but she caved.

"I have been praying you back into my life since I was 2 years old. I will not kill you. Tonight, you called me here to say goodbye to Jase, but I'm saying goodbye to you. You may be my boss but as my father- we are done." Scarlett snatched her gun from his head & pointed it into the air & let off a few rounds. Tears ran down the cheek of every face in the room- that was some kind of pain. Pain you could feel.

Bennie's men lowered their weapons after Bennie gave the signal. Bailey's Girls left the building. They got into Trinity's car & attempted to comfort Scarlett, but she was as solid as a rock. She pretended she wasn't boiling inside & told Trinity to proceed with going to Bailey's house, so they could gift her mom the 5 million.

It was an awkward ride. Trinity tried her best to see through Scarlett, but her dear sister ensured that she didn't. She put on her game face; they had things to do. They arrived at Bailey's home, uneasy, but very happy to bless her mother. They knew what came with the cartel, they had to shake death off like baby powder- it just is what it is at the end of the day. They knocked. So many emotions came rushing to the surface. When Sara opened the door, they felt so much love. It was as though Bailey said *hello* to them all through her mother's face. Sara invited them in, she didn't know why they were they were. Trinity led the show, per usual.

"Hi Mrs. B. I know it's late, but we have been working hard in the name of Bailey. We miss her so much." She began, smiling hard af.

"I know. I miss her every second of the day. You girls can come here, anytime." Sara responded, smiling too.

"We will always come to see you. No matter where our journey takes us. We wanted to gift you with something today. We know you've suffered tremendously since losing Bails. You're about to lose your home. Your car is gone & I know that Brent has been living with your parents for over a year. Things are not the same." Trinity continued.

"Things will never be the same. My husband is in jail & my daughter is gone. Brent will be okay. I miss him but he needs love that I can't give him because I miss Bails so much. My business is suffering, but it's life, ya know. I'll be okay." Sara unpacked.

"Mrs. Brooks. The love you have for Bailey should go right into Brent. He needs it. You don't want him to remember losing his sister & losing his mother, too. At least not forever." Naree shared. Sara nodded.

"We have 5 million dollars for you." Trinity announced. "You can get your son back, pay your mortgage, get a new car, anything you like."

Sara took a seat. She couldn't believe her ears. "I knew you girls made it, but never did I think you'd do something like this. 5 million is far too much. I really don't need anything at all. My life will turn out the way it should."

Scarlett pulled out her gun.

"Oh, you just trigger-happy tonight, huh?" Trinity questioned. "What the fuck?!" Trinity yelled before grabbing her gun. Naree panicked & called Scarlett's father, he wasn't answering.

"Wow. Scarlett. You'd really try to do me in?" Sara questioned. More shocked than afraid.

"Scar, I love you but so help me God, I will put a bullet right through that pretty face of yours if you take a shot at Bailey's mother. No cap!" Trinity warned.

"Scar! What are you doing?" Emma yelled.

"I am sick & tired of parents." She answered.

"Kill your own fucking parents then! Don't come for Bailey's mother!" Trinity snapped, cocking her gun. Bennie finally answered the phone. Naree put it on speaker.

"It's your fault that Bailey's dead. Parents." She scoffed. "They bring us into this world & bury us in their traumatic obsessions with power. They want us to play by their rules because their parents played games of *"because I said so" with* them, but I am done. Bailey would not have begun to spiral if she were not broken at home first. All those secrets. No father to call her own after all those years. A mother who lied to her. We didn't ask for your brokenness! We come into this world, butt naked & afraid. Screaming at the top of our lungs, gasping for purpose & all the while, here you go- mommy & daddy. Taking it away! We must survive your footsteps & pray we don't get stepped on in the process of finding out who the hell we are! I am DONE!" Scarlett yelled. He finally heard his daughter's core right before placing another bullet into Jase. He stopped.

"Mi hija (My daughter)." He spoke. Scarlett sniffled & looked toward Naree's hand.

"Mr. Perez. I love you. I love Scarlett. But if she shoots the mother of my first sister, my very first best friend, I will kill her, respectfully." Trinity explained with a tear racing down the side of her face. Sara sat, content. "Like I said. My life will turn out the way it should." She reiterated. Unafraid to die.

"YOU said we were fighting to avenge Bailey's death! YOU said you wanted to get justice! OUR way! How is this not it?! She started it, Trinity!" Scarlett cried, unsure of whether she was coming or going. Trinity clutched her gun like a bad habit & moved in on Scarlett.

"Mi hija (My daughter), you can't take your anger out on your friend's mother. Your beef is with me & Marcella. Put the gun down, ahora (now)!" Bennie yelled.

"Daddy. You know I love him, & you just- she cocked her gun. Trinity placed herself in front of Bailey's mother. "You'd just take him away from me. You never bought me flowers. Took me on a date. Showed me how men should love me. You just wanted me to do what you wanted me to do. Use me. The way I witnessed men use my mother all these years. Jase showed me real love." Scarlett wailed some more.

"I guess love changes things. I remember when I loved your mother. I still do." Trinity lowered her gun to her waist side & sighed in relief.

"Vengeance is mine said the Lord." Perez quoted. "I will allow Jase to live, but you will lower that gun & apologize to Sara for your behavior. We think rationally not recklessly." He continued.

Scarlett lowered her gun completely & fell to the floor, a sobbing mess. She suppressed so many emotions regarding her parents, it all came to a head tonight. She begged everyone to forgive her. "I would never hurt any of you. I love you all more than I love myself." She cried. Sara stood up & safely placed Scar's gun on the counter. She held that child as if she were her own. She knew what pain was, so she didn't judge Scar for her moment of insanity. What she did wonder was why the hell Trinity & Scarlett both had guns, Trinity hit her with four words- *"We live in Philly."*

The girls ordered some luxury cuisine & spent the night with Sara. They reminisced about their favorite moments with Bailey. Scarlett spent hours apologizing, she felt terrible, although her actions made sense. She was acting out & it showed. Luckily, Sara understood all too well.

Emma hid Scar's gun just in case she was feeling froggy again & Naree kept Perez in the loop on her mental state. They gifted Sara 5 milli as planned, which topped off their epic sleepover. Bailey was all up & through the living room, spreading joy, peace, & love. They left the next morning & bid Sara farewell. They hugged & cried as they set forth to embark on new adventures.

Scarlett confronted her parents- together & ironed out every way they made her feel. She told them she had been struggling for years, but she fought through it with hunting. Bennie knew if he didn't make things right, she'd go on a binge & start killing people, so his new mission was to do what was best for his daughter. He expressed his sincerest apologies to Marcella & asked if they could begin anew. She accepted his apology but told him they needed to be friends before exploring a relationship. She hadn't moved on, neither had he. They were crafted for each other.

The day before graduation, Bennie took it up a notch & requested that the girls come & see him at his high rise. They didn't know what to expect since the last time they saw him, he was flexing on Scarlett. When they arrived, he told them to take a seat. He presented a PowerPoint presentation. Showcased was the most beautiful high rise in New York City; brand new appliances, upscale, fully furnished, & it was all theirs. Bailey's Girls expressed he didn't need to gift something so expensive, but he insisted.

"I want you girls to run my cartel in New York." Bennie informed.

"Padre (Father). We've had quite the ride with the cartel. Could you please release us, so that we may live on our own accord? We signed a 30-million-dollar contract with one of the most sought-after fashion houses on the planet. We've got some serious work to do. Can we please focus on our own business now? I promise you; we will thrive!" Scarlett begged. The girls beamed with hope inside, but they didn't say anything. Bennie walked toward them & opened his arms, a group hug was in order. He squeezed them all &

responded. "I let you go" with a smile. They did not see that coming!

"You know what?! Columbia University can wait! WE ARE FREE! Let's do what we really want & RUN WE BITCHIN FASHION! ALL THE WAY! Trinity shouted.

"WE BITCHIN BITCHES!" Scarlett, Naree, & Emma shouted. Jase came walking through Perez's high rise, every organ in Scarlett's body stood still. He walked toward her & went in for the kill- a nice kiss that is. Bennie smiled & nodded his head in approval. Scarlett was elated & she was all in!

"Don't worry daddy. I believe in abstinence." She chuckled with the slightest tear making its way across her nose. Jase squeezed her tight, masking any physical pain he still had. Bennie was proud.

"I love you, Scarlett Perez." He said, forgetting any other souls occupied the room.

"I love you too, Jase Hernández." She responded. Everyone was happy & life was good again.

Trinity's statement to the media prompted Reporter Newman to do some digging into Bailey's story. Newman uncovered that Todd was framed for illegal activity because he questioned Mr. Parker about his connection to Riley Hart. Frankie wasn't sure what Todd was getting at, so he got rid of him. "I just wish I could've seen my Bails one more time."

Todd stated during his release. He also announced that he'd be suing the legal system for their failure to provide justice for him & Bailey. There were so many years to make up for, but before he began, there was one thing he could not miss.

The UA's auditorium flooded with music that lifted every student from their chairs. It was Graduation Day! Principal Ritton was so remorseful; he arranged for an empty seat to be reserved for Bailey next to her friends.

"If only Bails were here to see this." Trinity remarked, striking a tear from her eye as they stood, unchained & accomplished.

"I killed Vladimir Abakumov." Naree confessed aloud.

"Who the hell is Vladimir Abakumov & girl, you can't be saying that out loud?" Trinity responded. Scar & Em awaited an answer with their eyes bucked.

"The man that put me in a coma for nearly 3 months. I remembered his face during our mission in Miami, so I found him & I killed him." She further explained.

"Oh snap, didn't see that coming!" Emma teased.

"Damn, Ree. I knew you were a thug!" Scarlett added, amening her confession.

"My goodness. Who would've thunk it? A bunch of nerdy gangsters." Emma laughed.

"Correction. Thugs in Skirts, maim. Thugs in Skirts." Trinity laughed. They all laughed in unison.

"I'm glad you got him though." Trinity shared with Ree after telling her never to stray alone again. She let her know they'd always be down for whatever, especially regarding justice. Ree smiled. They held hands & soaked up that graduation energy.

Bailey's Girls shut it down when they blessed the stage with their presence. First & foremost, they walked-together. No introduction was needed. Students shouted their names & threw flowers. Standing onstage together, they peered into the audience at their parents, overwhelmed with joy. They stared even deeper into the crowd & saw three faces they weren't expecting to be there today- Sara, Brent, & Todd Brooks. They ran over after performing their secret handshake onstage. They hugged & squeezed Mr. & Mrs. Brooks while a slideshow played beautiful memories of Bailey. They kissed on Brent, pinched his cheeks, & then looked back at Sara & Todd.

"We will always keep her alive." Trinity shared as they hugged it out.

"Always!" Scarlett, Naree, & Emma cosigned in perfect harmony. Freedom sang. Although they couldn't bring Bailey back to life, she lived on through the memories they created together in her name.

Principal Ritton directed everyone to place their tassels on the left side. Hats soared into the air & Bailey's love came crashing down.

During the uproar, Bailey's Girls walked over to Kaylee. They were informed by Fernando Cruz that she confessed to stealing their designs for clout; the lawsuit was closed in their favor. Since she had a lot of experience from working in her mother's boutique, they invited her to work for them in New York. Kaylee couldn't believe her ears; she asked them to repeat themselves- she heard right. "OF COURSE!" She yelled with cheer. Allison & Maci stood from afar, watching her become what they struggled to be... a good person.

The girls threw a huge graduation party & lived in the moment with their families. They cried happy tears & sang tragically beautiful songs that carried them where they needed to be- adulthood.

College was on hold for now, but their dreams were not! New York was in for it. They purchased a mansion & walked in, lit! Ready to take on a new world the way they always had- TOGETHER!

#WeBitchinFashion #GameOnForBailey #WeBitchinBitches

THUGS IN SKIRTS

<u>PSA:</u>

"Being bullied will never equate to 'this world would be better off without you.' You belong in nice rooms with great people; know that your struggles are simply part of the climb. We want & need you here."

- Bailey Brooks

"Bullying doesn't make you top-tier, it makes you a coward."

– Trinity Woods

"Are *you* being bullied? Tell someone. If that doesn't work, tell someone else. You are worthy of being heard."

– Naree Gem

"Seek help if you seriously get a kick out of torturing others, your pleasure could become your pain one day."

- Scarlett Perez

"Bullying hurts everyone, including you. So don't do it."

- Emma Banks

"Come on. You read the book. The bullied seek revenge sometimes, don't make yourself a target!"

#ThugsInSkirts